R. GARLAND GRAY

WHITE FELLS

PRESS®

Jewel Imprint: Amethyst
Medallion Press, Inc.
Printed in USA

DEDICATION:

This book is dedicated to the wild horses,
may they run forevermore free —

And to Carmine and his beautiful jewel,
my uncle and aunt — with heartfelt
appreciation.

Published 2007 by Medallion Press, Inc.

The MEDALLION PRESS LOGO
is a registered tradmark of Medallion Press, Inc.

Copyright © 2006 by R. Garland Gray
Cover Illustration by Adam Mock

Printed in the United States of America
Typeset in Adobe Garamond Pro

10 9 8 7 6 5 4 3 2 1
First Edition

ACKNOWLEDGEMENTS:

To my husband Dov, thank you for the love and laughter.

To the ladies of CoLoNY, you know . . .

"Ms. Gray brings to vivid life the Celtic mythology, the Ireland of Fey, and the traditions that existed centuries ago. Her writing is evocative, her characters endearing, and the story completely captivating. A definite recommend for lovers of fantasy, Celtic history, paranormal, and gallant adventure."

–A Romance Review

"I definitely recommend PREDESTINED as a fantastic fantasy read!"

–The Best Reviews

"Magic is center to this book and it flows fast and swift to snare the reader within the first chapter. Ms. Gray's writing is a true joy to read as the reader gets a glimpse into her world and what she creates there left this reviewer awe-struck."

–Love Romances

FEY BORN

"This was a rich and well put together fantasy tale, full of magical creatures good and bad. This is a must read for all of those who wish to be transported to the magical and sometimes all too fierce and bloody land of the fey."

–Inez Daylong, Affaire de Coeur Magazine

"Romantic fantasy readers will enjoy this magical and enchanted tale of two-star crossed lovers who must fight against overwhelming odds to achieve their goal. Lana who always thought she was weak learns she has the strength to hold her own with her fairy man and love him with all her heart. R. Garland Gray has the magic touch when it comes to writing fantasy."

–Harriet Klausner

"This is one of the better fantasies coming forth from this interesting publishing house. Look out Tor and Baen, Medallion Press is here to compete and win. We rated this fantasy four hearts."

–Bob Spear, Heartland Reviews

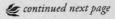 *continued next page*

R. GARLAND GRAY
WHITE FELLS

"One of the difficulties with which the Irish historian will always have to deal is to discriminate where the imaginary ends and the actual begins. It, in fact, ends and begins nowhere . . ."

—Dame Eleanor Hull

PROLOGUE

THERE WAS ALWAYS ONE BELONGING to the darkest unknown sister of the four winds.

One of reluctance and of strength.

Forced and forceful from the before time, the enchanted bloodline carried down through the distant ages, daughter to daughter, thinning in wait, becoming mere threads.

Always one.

Sovereign.

Servant.

Submissive.

Until the last and final blood inheritor.

Long forgotten threads, a tainting within *him* . . . a terrible vow soon reclaimed.

CHAPTER 1

Beltane Eve, May

IN THE DIMMING LIGHT OF a long hard day, Boyden examined the bloody gash on his thumb. Eyes narrowing to slits of pale gray, he glared silent retribution at the sharp ridge of the moss-dappled boulder. Better suited for a passage grave, he was trying to move it out of the blind druidess's ever-expanding garden without toppling the prolific growth of stunted hawthorns. To his right, the gaping ruins of a stone wall sloped down an emerald knoll and curved into oak trees. Horses stood quietly grazing on three separate hills in the distance, their tails swishing lazily in tranquillity. Bare from the waist up, every inch of him was covered in sweat and dirt, with the day nearly ending and the boulder not budging. He looked at his bloody palm and thought, *enough for today*.

Hiking himself out of the rocky ditch he had spent the day digging, he flipped a tawny plait back over his shoulder. Tomorrow he would borrow a horse from one of the farmers and pitch the animal's might against the rock. No task was unconquerable for a warrior of the

Tuatha Dé Danann.

Sucking his throbbing thumb, he walked into the cool shadows of the nearest oak and bent at the waist to avoid several low-hanging branches. He squatted over a black root. Moving his bronze dagger aside, he grabbed the leather pouch and brought the lip to his mouth. The water tasted cool, and he finished the remainder in two mouthfuls. Tossing the empty pouch aside, he looked down at his calloused hands. They were large, the fingers blunt, and the nails dirty with work from the day. He blew air out of his lungs, his hands fisting. At twenty-five summers, he could not shake the embrace of darkness and death clinging to him since birth. He detested it, detested the way it forced him to remain apart. Shifting around, he pressed his bare back against the tree trunk and found a comfortable position. For the moment, he was too exhausted to think or care, and with a heavy sigh he closed his eyes and slipped swiftly into a deep sleep.

Little by little, the nightmare crept once more upon him . . .

. . . gloaming gave way to night shadow and the feral winds of a rising moon, claiming him in the *gaoth* way, the wind way. He tried to flex his right arm, his fingers numbing from the tightness of the ropes restraining him. Behind him, the large fire circle crackled with flames and glowed against his bare back, an ominous warning of what would be endured this night. Boyden looked down upon himself in a blending of mixed curiosity and muted anger. He was on his knees in the black soil and trodden grass, dripping with sweat. Stripped of weapons, tunic, and menace, they tied his wrists with thick ropes. Those same fat ropes held his arms outstretched to the wooden stakes buried in the ground on either side of him.

He swallowed hard, the dryness within him a living thing. He shifted, trying to ease the strain of tendon and muscle in his shoulders and arms. A full mane of tawny hair plastered to the dampness of his nape and down the middle of his bare back. He felt dark and winded, his lungs taut.

He lifted his gaze to the moon goddess in supplication. Her luminosity seemed eerily bright and observant in the blue-black night of stars. He wished he were formed of feathers and wings so he could soar free of this nightmare and ancient blood binding.

"What a magnificent animal you make," his captor murmured with a silken voice of female possession.

Boyden lowered his gaze . . . to her, his breathing suddenly incomplete and hot.

A tall woman stood before him, slim and straight, a lethal warrior dressed in fitted clothing he did not recognize. He waited in stillness, meeting her concentrated gaze.

"Good eve," she remarked, fingers wrapped around the hilt of a short sword.

His brother's whore.

Darkness and threat engulfed him.

"Shall I tell you why you are here?" she prompted.

He exhaled in response, sharing nothing of himself. He could hear the whimpering of a child and felt the watchfulness of another, but they seemed mere echoes and shadows compared to the presence of the woman. Her hard eyes swept coolly over him, striving to find weakness.

His right hand clenched, the tingling sensation ongoing, blood dripping from his ravaged wrist. She stood just out of his reach. *A wise choice*, he thought vehemently.

The firelight caught her hair, reflecting the shiny darkness in it. An intoxicating creature of deception and familiarity, she attempted to prevail over a king's heart. Having failed miserably, she turned her charms and trickery upon his easily led brother.

"You were foolish to reject me," she said with hushed violence, regarding him from beneath a spray of black lashes. It was a seductive gaze meant to entice.

The numbness in his arm muted, and he tightened his fist. They stayed that way, locked in a test of wills, unmoving, except for breath and awareness.

Neither gave in.

"Must we battle like this? Do you not understand that you belong to me?" she said, a faint curve to her lips. "All is not lost, speak the wind vow to me."

He said nothing, breathing in the heat of the fire at his back, his nerves pulsing. The sounds of a child's anguish faded in and out.

The woman's head tilted and she lifted the sword, the tip grazing his shoulder in a threatening and fleeting caress, making his blood boil.

He answered her with mutinous silence, and fury leaped into her eyes. "Give me the wind vow!"

"You want the vow to have the power to rule my realm. Nay, I willna give it." Words formed in Boyden's mind, words not his own. "Only I control the lethal wind, a male blood vow of promise to the land."

"Your brother's blood be the same as yours." She pointed behind her to a white-faced man astride a mount shrouded in gray mist. That was the watchful presence he felt earlier.

"He be *rigdamnai*, of kingly material, the same as you."

Somehow, Boyden knew the younger brother possessed none of the noble qualities making the older brother a just ruler of the wind realm.

"The Elemental wishes freedom from your constant restraint. She came to us and pleaded for our help."

"The wind never pleads." He felt a snarling in his mind, rage and bitterness growing, his jaw clenching.

"Give your brother the vow, Conall. He willna be as forceful as you in his rule." She pointed her sword at a weeping girl. Swirls of mist receded in Boyden's mind and he saw the tear-stained face of a crumpled child as yellow-haired as himself.

"I promise to release you and your daughter. When I stand beside your brother, I will be Wind Queen and promise to offer pardon to you. You may live the remainder of your life far from here, but your line must end with her."

Caustic laughter echoed inside Boyden's head, hurtful and loud in rebelliousness. "Foolish female. You know little of what you speak. My brother and I have different mothers. The weakling standing behind you canna control the wind. He canna even control his own lust for a scraping whore."

"Wind bastard!" the woman screeched and lashed out with frustration.

Her sword arm rose in the blink of an eye.

Resolve settled deep within his chest and he took his last breath of free air.

The blade descended slowly, cast in the crawling pace of nightmares. Pain and fire sliced into his side, stealing his life . . .

. . . Boyden roared awake, heart pounding. He blinked to clear his mind from the clutches of the re-curring nightmare, pain and dimness gradually releasing him. His lungs expanded unhindered, dragging life-sustaining air into his tense body. He shifted sideways and vomited up his supper. Breathing heavily, he did not hear the approach of soft footfalls.

"Wind Herald?"

Wiping the back of his hand across his mouth, Boyden turned to the sightless druidess. "Derina, what are you doing here?" Moonlight turned her waterfall of white hair into shades of gold.

"Ships come from the sea," she said low, pointing with her hazel walking stick.

"What ships?" He looked over his shoulder. Amongst the sounds of the night, he could hear only distant waves crashing against the shore, a soothing resonance.

"The ships carry kin to the traveller, Íth," she explained almost trancelike. "He be wrongly killed last season. Remember, Wind Herald?"

He remembered and turned back to her. "How do you know who walks those ships?" Empty eye sockets stared at him in a long silence. "Derina, what are you trying to tell me?"

"They come seeking vengeance, Wind Herald."

"How do you know?"

"I know."

Instinct told him to trust her. Reaching behind him, Boyden grabbed his purple tunic. He climbed to his feet and shrugged into it. "Where waits our chieftain, Derina?"

"He stands with the elders by the goddess boulders."

He nodded, sheathing the dagger at his waist. "I know that stretch of land by the shore."

"He asked me to fetch you, Wind Herald."

Boyden knew why his chieftain chose the sightless village druidess to find him. As a loner, he tended to stay away from the village. Yet, Derina had a way of always finding him. She was one born of the fey realm, though most knew little about her. He glanced at her smooth face and pale, empty eye sockets.

"I see and sense," she murmured as if reading his thoughts.

Discomfited, he grunted in response. With her fey sight, she saw more than simple shapes and movement, he suspected. "Go back to the village, Derina. Have all make ready for the battle coming."

Lost in the black shimmering behind the trees, the *Gaoth Shee* watched the sightless druidess and the lean warrior go their separate ways. She was an ancient being and watching him created a great hunger and need within her. A creature of shade without form, she was one of the lost magical, a bringer of endings across the lands and waters. The olden ways had faded into forgotten memories. The blood threads of possession were gone, except for this one warrior.

The blood vow of the Servant King flowed deeply hidden within him.

This last one.

Sovereign.

Servant.

Submissive.

She glittered into vapor, leaving strings of silent whispers amongst the boughs of the ancient trees and followed him.

No longer did she wish him free.

CHAPTER 2

A SENNIGHT HAD PASSED SINCE the invasion, leaving behind seven days of blood spill and battle.

In the lee of night winds, Boyden moved silently along the shore edge of the invaders' camp. Pausing near the looming protection of a gray pillar stone embedded among the trees, he crouched low, becoming shade in waning twilight. A few horse lengths beyond, the trees gave way to sand and a foamy sea littered with anchored ships. Tilting his head, he focused on the argument going on between a black-haired female and an older man.

"Princess Scota, I want you to remain here with the warriors guarding my ships."

"Amergin," she protested firmly, holding windblown hair off her face.

The druidic bard leader of the Milesians, Boyden thought, recognizing the name from what he heard. He did not know the warrior princess.

The man held up his hand. "You may look like a

submissive maiden, but I am once more reminded of your outspokenness and stubbornness. You will do as I say."

"Amergin, although I accompanied you in payment for my father's land taxes, I believe in avenging the wrongful death of your uncle Íth. He was always kind to me."

"That may be. Yet here you will remain. You will act as my emissary to Captain Rigoberto until I return, and that is the end of it."

Without further comment, the leader of the Milesian invasion walked up a rocky path from shore to a camp of fire circles, mounted his horse, and rode away with a group of twelve.

Boyden looked back at the princess. Pulling the dagger from his waist, he thought she would make a fine captive.

She remained where she was, windblown and angry, giving the front laces of her white woolen shirt a frustrated tug, unaware of his presence. A brown leather armguard protected her left forearm from the snap of a bowstring, marking her weapon of choice.

He took a step forward and stopped. Glancing over his shoulder at the sound of approaching footfalls, he backed up into the shadows once again.

A short man walked down the rocky sand path to the shore where she stood bathed in spray and moonlight.

"Where is Lord Amergin, Princess Scota? I was told he was here."

"He left, Captain Rigoberto." The princess adjusted her armguard, her manner one of distinct coolness and obvious dislike. "I was told to remain here with you and act as Lord Amergin's emissary while he is away."

"I know," the captain grumbled with displeasure.

"May I be of assistance to you, Captain?"

The captain studied her, openly showing his interest. "You could come to my bed this eve."

"I gave you my answer, it remains the same as before, no."

"You will regret denying me."

She nodded, showing no fear of him. "That may be. Why did you come looking for Lord Amergin?"

"We captured some of the *Tuatha Dé Danann* tribe."

Boyden muttered a silent oath at the captain's statement. Returning the dagger to his waist, he slipped back into the newborn night, intent on rescue.

Princess Scota faced the pig-nosed captain.

At thirty summers, Captain Rigoberto was a short man, the top of his head barely rising to the bridge of her nose. His features, considered broad and thick among the camp whores, reminded her of a pig, although she maintained that a pig's countenance was far more pleasing to the eye. He was a man of dark coloring and still darker disposition. She had developed an instant dislike of him upon their first meeting, but his ferocity was not to be questioned. Lord Amergin seemed to favor him, giving him the task to protect the ships.

"Take me to them, Captain."

He waved a hand in dismissal. "They are worthless, Princess, a blind crone and two children. I would not bother you."

"Yet, you found them important enough to seek out Lord Amergin. Show me, Captain. I wish to see them."

Captain Rigoberto's eyes narrowed. "Come, then, if you wish."

Scota accompanied the officer back up the curved path into their fire-lit camp.

Men lounged among themselves, twenty in all, eating and drinking. Whores walked around them, showing their wares to those interested, but looking away when the captain passed by.

Penned in a paddock of hastily erected wood fences, the warhorses grazed quietly, tolerating the stray wolfhounds.

A large bonfire warmed the camp, flames crackling in response to the light sea breeze, shooting heat and sparks of blue into the night. Near a single oak at the left, two children clung to an old bent woman who stood in ankle-length brown robes. The two men posted to guard them looked bored by their duty.

As she came closer, Scota stopped in her tracks. "The crone has no eyes."

"I told you they were worthless."

She agreed about the crone and quickly dismissed her as useless. The children, however, were another matter. Dirt-smudged, a boy of about ten summers and a girl of about seven summers would make good slaves, once cleaned up.

Along the perimeter of the camp, one of their guards bellowed in surprise and sounds of a scuffle erupted.

"What now?" the captain growled and ran over to investigate, leaving her alone with their prisoners.

Scota felt the hairs on the back of her neck rise. Remaining where she stood, she glanced at the crone. Twigs of dried rosemary stuck out of white plaits. She heard the herb symbolized knowledge and protection from the crone goddess. *Hag of the night, bless me with wisdom's sight.* The first phrase of the old blessing lingered in her thoughts. The blessing was performed outdoors when the hazel moon of the harvest month, *Lughnasa*, August, began to wane, but *Lughnasa* was far away.

Scota dropped her gaze to a lined face set in masked stillness. The ancient continued to watch her, if one considered a sightless being capable of watching anything. She seemed haggard and weighed down, but there was an eerie quality to her, a seeping of threat and understanding unsettling Scota's nerves.

Her study dipped to the children. They were indistinct, with brown hair and very pale skin. They stood in quietness next to the crone, faces downcast in submission. From what she could see of their features, they looked to be brother and sister.

"What are their names?" she inquired with authority.

"Cavan and Nora," the crone answered with a voice surprisingly smooth and youthful for one so exceedingly old.

"Are you their mother?" she asked.

"Nay. I am the village druidess. They became separated from their parents in the disorder you wrought."

Scota ignored the crone's accusation. "They are brother and sister?"

"Aye, they be thirsty and hungry, too."

Scota motioned to the closest guard. "Bring them water, bread, and meat to eat."

"For the crone, too?" the man asked with displeasure.

"For the crone, too. Let them sit and take ease. It has been a long day for us all."

The guard walked back into camp to do her bidding. The crackle of flames filled the silence. She could feel the crone's focus on her back.

"What do you want, crone?" she prompted.

"Beyond the fire, your destiny comes."

Scota glanced over her shoulder. "What did you say?"

The ancient woman pointed her finger in response.

Scota turned back and stilled.

Three of the captain's men were dragging a half-naked warrior by the heels toward the fire circle. A wild mane of tawny plaits flew about hard features. Covered in the blue dye of the woad plant, his upper body strained against the ropes binding his wrists. He was big, and she quickly reasoned him to be one of the warriors of the *Tuatha Dé Danann* tribe.

Four guards attempted to contain him. He fought them, but it seemed to Scota that his efforts were crafted to create disturbance, rather than to gain release and freedom.

"He be your destiny," the crone repeated behind her

and Scota walked over for a closer look, dismissing the sightless ancient from her mind.

Boyden caught sight of Derina and two of the village children, Cavan and Nora. They were all dirt-smudged and unharmed, *thank the winds*. Over the past few days his tribe had been too few in number to battle the new enemy and so retreated to their fey brethren. Some made it, and some did not.

Being fey born, he knew Derina could easily evade capture. There was another reason for her delay and now he understood. In the chaos of retreat, the children had become separated from their family and the druidess stayed behind to help them. The children were *idir*, like him, caught in the between.

Although he did not plan on being captured, he was exactly where he wished to be, near them. He kicked out, clipping one of his captors on the side of the leg and bringing the thin man down.

"Hold him," someone of authority bellowed and Boyden thought the whiny voice came from the short man with the pig nose.

He allowed himself to be flipped onto his stomach and his face pushed into the dirt. Knees followed, pressing weight into his back. He ceased struggling and waited, feeling a strange whisper of presence, a delicate fragrance of wildflowers in the air . . .

"Captain, I did not realize four of your men are needed to bring down only one of our enemy," a female taunted with a voice low and soft.

"Get off him," the one called the captain snarled.

The three guards digging their knees into his back moved off and Boyden rolled to his side, breathing heavily and taking a moment to regain his perspective. He sat up, looking for the owner of the seductive voice and his heart stilled.

By the winds!

It was . . .

. . . not her.

He forced himself to remain motionless, to not show emotion.

Not her, his mind reasoned, *but one fashioned by the goddesses in similarity.*

This black-haired beauty with delicate winged brows appeared more a maiden than a hard-edged warrior. It was as if the gods and goddesses blended her features and added or forgotten a missing ingredient of his nightmare.

The woman in his nightmare did not make him subservient.

This princess with the dimpled chin would not succeed, either.

"He looks at you with lust, Princess," the pig nose said slyly.

Scota looked from the captain to the bound captive. The warrior watched her, the wind blowing a wavy mane over a strong shoulder. She could not help but stare back. The touch of the warrior's angry gaze sent a swirling heat through her blood. In the light of the fire, his eyes reflected the peculiar color of silvery gray storm clouds on a windy day. He had a strong chin and angular features, his nose streamlined and perfect, but his lips were what caught her attention. They were humorless and extremely sensual. They parted, an enticement just for her it seemed, and she heard his inward breath, her own trembling in response. He appeared physically perfect, muscular and lean in the way of wild animals, and she guessed him to be around twenty-five summers. She was twenty summers; a five-season difference set between them. Her gaze moved to the bronze neck ring resting on his collarbone. She heard the adornment referred to as a torc. Most of the Tuatha tribe wore them, along with bracelets and cuffs on their wrists. The torc was the only adornment he wore, except for the blue paint on his sweaty flesh.

Her gaze lifted to his face once again and collided with stormy gray. The smell of fire-laced air burned in her lungs and she took another deep breath. The captain was watching her and the bound warrior with a strong attentiveness.

She took a step back, putting distance between herself and the warrior. His eyes did not blink once since settling upon her. This rough-hewn captive would never submit, would never be a slave. His only use would be the information he could provide about the *Tuatha Dé Danann* tribe.

"I wish to question him, Captain."

"Why? Do you fancy him?"

"Captain, your lineage is showing. I want the

information he can give me about his tribe, not the bulge between his legs."

"I will question him about his tribe and tell you what he says. There is no need for you to remain and not seek your rest." A slight smile of anticipation played about the man's mouth, giving her a feeling of disquiet.

"I prefer to remain," she countered.

"I prefer you did not, Princess. In the presence of a female, males fight harder to preserve their pride."

She nodded reluctantly. "As you wish. Lord Amergin will no doubt want him alive."

"Understood." The captain fingered a jeweled dagger at his waist.

Turning on a heel, Scota strode away, her heart heavy for reasons she did not comprehend.

Captain Rigoberto studied his captive with a critical eye toward gaining what he most wanted, wealth and power.

He hated large muscular males almost as much as he hated females. From early on, he liked to hurt the girls from his village. It started out as tripping them when they walked by and moved on from there. The first girl took a season's worth of planning. He followed her into the woods when no others were around, came up from behind, and hit her on the head. He grew hard thinking about it, and about the other five girls he took in the months that came after. He brought them into the moonlit fields beyond the village, stealing their precious innocence while they were barely conscious. He relished defiling them. Before long, suspicion fell on him and he ran away to seek his fortune elsewhere. He tried satisfying his needs with the local whores he came across. It was not the same. As he considered the whores already ruined, he turned to other means of gratification. No one cared how a whore died, no one listened to her cries.

Upon being introduced to the highly spirited princess, a deep craving took hold, keeping him up at night. He wiped his sweaty forehead. He thought about what he would do to her when he got her alone. How he would force himself into her while tightening his hands around her throat. He would anchor her wrists above her head. Tie her ankles, spreading her long white legs wide while he ground himself, hard and fast, into her.

He licked dry lips.

The only thing staying his lust was the thought of Amergin's wrath. It prevented him from acting out his intentions with the haughty princess, for now. A new plan took form in his mind. With wealth, he could buy worthless village girls who looked like the princess, defile them as he wanted, then sell them to the whorehouses.

He met the hooded glare of the bound warrior.

He needed only capture one of this land's mysterious fey creatures.

One who could lead him to the great faery treasure he had heard of.

One formed of perfection.

His hand rested on the hilt of the dark magical dagger at his waist.

CHAPTER 3

BOYDEN DISMISSED THE WARRIOR PRINCESS from his mind and focused on the shorter man called the captain.

The round black eyes above the pig nose were full of menace and excitement. He wished he could see into that one's depraved mind.

"Take him to the sea and clean him up." The captain motioned to the four guards who stood aside, waiting. "I want to see what he looks like beneath the blue paint."

Boyden's gaze narrowed. *What possible difference do my looks make?* he wondered. The guards swooped in, akin to birds of prey. Their hands clamped around his body, fingerlike talons lifting him.

The pig-nosed man stepped forward and grabbed a chunk of hair.

Pain sliced through his scalp.

Sour breath scorched his face.

"The way you look at the crone and children leads me to believe you tried to rescue them. Be warned, warrior. If you struggle, I will order the crone killed."

Boyden bared his teeth at the coward. Hiding behind an old woman, this enemy captain played at being a leader of men. The pig nose released him and gestured toward the sea. "I want him clean and unharmed. Make sure of it."

The guards carried him through the fire-lit camp, a piece of meat ready to be butchered. He fought the urge to struggle, fought the urge to take them all down, and decided to make it as difficult as possible for them. Arching his back, he tossed his head and managed to rake his teeth over a guard's exposed flesh, drawing blood.

Scota stood in a small ditch near the abandoned circular house of stone and wood, examining broken pottery and gathering her thoughts. The Tuatha warrior unnerved her in a way she had never experienced before.

In the camp, a man squealed in pain. She looked up at the disturbance, the sound of the sea no longer a gentle lull in her ears. Through a small grouping of moonlit trees, beyond the penned horses, she saw four guards carrying the Tuatha warrior toward the sea.

Her hands tightened about the clay pottery as she watched the procession. She had retreated to this broken-down home of thatched roof, plank, and willow supports to clear her mind of the enigmatic warrior. Never did she allow a male to affect her so.

She tried to refocus on the broken piece of clay pottery in her hands. Since coming to this land of mist and stone, rest eluded her. She did not know why, only that she could not sleep. Across her feet lay a tree's tall moon shadow. The illumination provided enough light to easily see and walk by. She looked at her surroundings. The round house was buried among the oaks as if the builder sought protection from the sea. Located a hundred paces from the camp, it smelled of age and mold. Branches of thorny bushes invaded the doorway behind her, climbing inward and seeking shelter. She heard said thorns belonged to the faery creatures. Scota dismissed it. Thorns were thorns as trees were trees. Yet, she could not shake the strange feeling of presence lingering among the dark shadows. Brought in by the breezes of the night, the shade felt warm with another's breath, whispers urging her to . . .

One of the guards carrying the warrior yelped loudly in pain. Scota dropped the broken shard of pottery. She turned toward the sound and instead found a peculiar shimmering in the trees. It felt almost alive with magical threat.

A gust of wind nearly toppled her and she braced herself, reaching for her dagger.

Green leaves shivered softly, undersides upturned in silvery gray.

She swung around, dagger drawn, searching for the menace.

In the pens, a large black warhorse snorted and pawed the ground, sensing the disturbance.

The horse senses the strangeness of the air, too, she thought, scanning the land and finding nothing. She resheathed her dagger with annoyance.

"Foolishness," she muttered to herself.

"Your destiny comes." The echo of the crone's words entered a sudden beat in her heart.

She shook her head. She was a Milesian warrior princess who made her own destiny, a destiny claimed with bow and arrow and her own resourcefulness.

"Your destiny comes." She rubbed her temple. The crone's voice would not leave her mind. She wondered if the other distant and forgotten relatives of their great King Mil had such difficulty in trying to forget what another said.

"Your destiny comes."

She refused to acknowledge it.

"Your destiny comes."

She muttered an oath. There was no help for it. Her hand wrapped around the hilt of the dagger at her waist while her legs carried her toward the sea.

She rounded the pen of horses and headed down the uneven path toward the rocky shore. A few horse lengths down to the sea, she skittered to a halt in a foamy puddle of retreating waves.

In the shallows, four guards struggled with the captive warrior, as if trying to tame a wild stallion. The light winds suddenly kicked up, creating long pronounced sea waves and spraying her with cool water.

"Captain, what are you doing?" she demanded, holding the hair out of her eyes.

The captain stood in the shallow waves, hands on his hips, feet spread apart in authority. "None of your concern, Princess."

"Be this a new form of torture? Drowning a male for information?"

"As I said before, this is none of your concern."

"It is my concern," she said forcefully.

He looked over his shoulder, his face set with contempt. "Your concern?"

"I speak for Lord Amergin."

"How do you speak for Lord Amergin?" His tone indicated his strong irritation. "By walking away from a prisoner?"

Her eyes narrowed. "You said males tend to fight harder when in the presence of a female and asked me to leave. I agreed."

She could feel his eyes roaming her face, seeking flaw and something she could not define.

"I am not finished with him," he said.

"You are now. Bring the warrior ashore, Captain."

The captain turned away.

"I said now, Captain. I wish to question him."

"About what?"

"Lord Amergin wishes to know more about the noble tribe."

"Noble tribe," he repeated sarcastically.

"Yes, the *Tuatha Dé Danann*."

"How do you know that warrior belongs to the tribe?"

She huffed with exasperation. "Warriors who enter battle painted in blue plant dye belong to the Tuatha. I was there, when Lord Amergin told you this."

"I forgot," he said after a pause.

Self-indulgent and witless man, she thought and rested her fingers around the hilt of her dagger. "Bring him ashore, Captain."

His gaze turned to ice.

"Now."

"As you wish." Raising a reluctant hand, he called out to his men. "Bring the warrior to shore. We gave him enough taste of the sea."

She was not going to admit it, but she was furious. The four guards, struggling with their coughing captive, made their way back. Battling the outgoing currents, they carried him facedown, each holding an arm or a leg.

As they approached, she noticed he wore only the bronze torc. The guards had relieved him of all else.

Ropes.

Paint.

Clothes.

Not that he wore much initially, only a bronze neck ring, low-hung brown breeches, and scuffed boots.

The warrior lifted his head and looked at her from beneath wet lashes.

Heat leaped into her while she held his gaze.

Her body went quiet.

Silence and yearning welled up inside her and she looked away.

"Where do you want him, Princess?" the captain growled with barely contained rage.

"Bring him to the fire circle," she replied viciously in turn and walked away.

"As you wish."

A confrontation was brewing between her and the pig-nosed officer.

She must keep her wits about her. Spying the warrior's discarded breeches and boots near a grouping of rocks, she picked them up and continued walking up the path. Why did she feel compelled to help this enemy? She was not some young maiden taken in by muscle and brawn. She was a female full grown. Looking over her shoulder, she made sure the guards followed with their shivering burden. Being nearly drowned could steal one's strength, but when healthy, recovery came soon after and this warrior definitely appeared healthy. She headed for the far side of the fire circle, away from the smug and curious interest of both warriors and camp whores.

"Bind his wrists and stake them to the ground over there." She pointed where she wanted him placed.

"His legs?" one of the guards prompted, holding onto a strong ankle.

"No need, the water robbed him of strength, just his wrists for now."

They forced him to kneel and tied his wrists.

When they finished their task, Scota motioned for them to leave. "Go rest and dry yourselves off. Extra mead all around."

The men nodded their thanks and left, leaving her alone with the naked Tuatha warrior. It was disconcerting to see him this way, an untamable male, tied and bound. She dropped the warrior's clothes near him and waited.

Out of the corner of his eye, Boyden saw his boots and breeches tumble to the grass. He lowered his head in exhaustion and took a moment of reprieve to recover some of his strength. He felt weak as a babe and his lungs hurt. One of the guards had taken great pleasure in holding his head under water. He vowed to take great pleasure in removing the man's head from his neck.

The heat of the fire god performed magic, removing the raking chills consuming him. He took full note that the druidess and the children were unharmed. Derina sat with her back against the tree, the children clinging to her lap in sleep. She nodded once to him, her head tilting slightly and he turned to see a pair of small booted feet.

He looked up at the slender, black-haired woman who rescued him from drowning and ordered him staked to the land.

"So, you still can breathe," she said indifferently with the smooth tones of night and danger.

Pushing back aching shoulders, he readied himself for the next battle. Waiting for her next move, he studied her as he would any other enemy.

Scota studied him in turn, as well. He was beautiful and dangerous in the ways of a captured predator, kneeling before her in feigned submission.

Shivers raked over him, though he fought hard not

to show it.

Tiny bumps of chill from the night sea dunking and the insistence of the sea breeze covered his pale skin.

Wet hair, freed from its plaits, clung to his shoulders, back, and chest. Her gaze lowered to a slightly furred chest and followed the gold stream down his lean belly, to a darker nest between muscular thighs.

She considered him large, having seen many naked male slaves among her father's holdings. If his proud will could be made to submit, he would be worth much—after she achieved what she needed for Amergin.

Her turquoise gaze met silvery gray fury.

"Good eve," she said with a purr of seduction. "Shall I tell you why you are here?" *Shall I tell you why I rescued you when I cannot explain it even to myself?* she thought.

The warrior said not a word, his lips drawn in a thin line.

"What are you named?" She expected him to offer up his name with gratitude but instead he stared defiantly back at her, his right hand clenching and unclenching.

Scota looked down at the knots digging into the flesh of his wrist. "Would you like me to loosen those knots for you?"

His gaze lowered to his wrist and she saw him stiffen as if remembering a terrible dream.

"There will be no loosening of bindings on him," a voice ordered from behind her. Scota turned to the captain and the guard accompanying him. The captain rarely traveled without the protection of men loyal to greed.

"Do you not think I know how to handle prisoners?"

"I do not know what you know, Princess," the captain sneered. "All I know is that this warrior is dangerous and your actions place us in peril if he escapes. You may choose to endanger your life because of your lust for him, but as long as I make the military decisions in this camp there will be no loosening of the bindings."

"I had no intention of loosening his bindings," she said, battling her temper.

"Ah, then I must have misunderstood when you asked, 'Would you like me to loosen those knots for you?'" He locked his hands behind him. "Look, Princess, the night grows late and I am weary. The prisoner will be here in the morning, and we can discuss this matter then."

Scota was reluctant to leave the Tuatha warrior alone with the captain's men. "I want him unharmed, Captain."

The captain gave a curt nod. "So do I, Princess."

"Then why did you nearly drown him?"

He smiled gently. "I found the blue paint offensive and merely wished him cleaned up. I disciplined the men. There will be no further attempt to do him harm. He is safe, I can assure you. We both serve Lord Amergin, do we not? Perhaps this warrior has information to help us find the murderers of Lord Íth. I want the bloodshed of innocents to end as much as you do."

His sudden charm raised the hairs on the back of her neck. Not only did he not care about the bloodshed of innocents, it seemed to her that he actually enjoyed it. Scota did not move, distrust and weariness warring inside her.

"I have your word he will not be harmed?" she asked, battling indecision.

"You have my word as a captain." He turned to his guard. "Secure the prisoner's bindings and post a two-man guard here for the night."

He motioned her to accompany him around the fire circle. "It has been a long day, Princess."

"Yes," she agreed, walking beside him.

Her small tent was on the other side of the fire and he brought her to the entrance.

"Do you want company?" he asked.

She glared at him.

He held up his hands and chuckled, stepping back. "You can not blame me for continuing to try."

"Captain, I gave you my answer."

"So you did, but I am a patient man."

She had the impression he sought to get her off guard.

"My answers remains no." With one last look at the offensive officer, Scota retreated to the inside of her tent. Maybe tomorrow she could think more clearly.

Boyden was not fooled by the falsity spilling out of the captain's mouth and suspected he would return sometime in the night.

When footfalls sounded, he was ready.

The captain motioned away the two guarding him and kept his own man close.

"You like the princess, do you not?" the captain taunted, coming to stand in front of him. "A fine and highly spirited mare, she is. Give a warrior like you a superior ride. If you tell me what I need to know, maybe I will give her to you."

Boyden remained mute, his gaze narrowing at the captain's promise of reward. He doubted the princess even knew she was a prize.

"Get me some mead," the captain ordered, motioning his man away. "It is going to be a long night."

Boyden allowed his gaze to sweep over the camp. With the children sleeping in her lap, Derina continued to remain alert, several paces to his left. The fire circle was at his back, turning wet chill to heat and sweat. The ropes were tight on his wrists and the light winds from the sea ruffled his hair. He could feel the invisible presence of the *Gaoth Shee,* the blood threads of her flowing in his body. She waited his summons to do death.

With one mind call, he knew the lethal wind would blow into the camp, paralyze and kill indiscriminately, the druidess and children, the men, whores, horses, dogs, and one enemy princess.

His fists clenched.

He would not summon her.

It was the same as before.

The same as seven days past when he refused to summon the wind, refused when his tribe first spotted the enemy ships heading toward their shores.

He had no control over the deadly, land-born wind. Anything the *Gaoth Shee* touched became paralyzed and often died. He would not risk his people, would not risk the deadly wind sweeping across the land on her way to destroying the ships at sea. Instead, the tribal druids called up a thick fog to stay the enemy ships, hoping they would turn back. The attempt proved worthless.

At the camp's edge, a strong wind picked up in response to his disquiet. Small tree branches began to sway in motion, leaves whistling in dread.

The druidess's head lifted toward the trees, noting the disturbance in the air, and he forced calmness upon himself. Only in anger did the winds of the land respond to the turbulence inside him. *Only in anger.*

His hands clenched.

The leaves shimmered into silence.

"You are one of them, the faery creatures," the captain said with flushed excitement, noting the abrupt arrival and departure of the winds. "I knew it." He took the silver cup of mead from the returning guard and motioned the man to give him privacy with the captive. The captain emptied the cup with several loud gulps, tossed it away, and wiped the back of his hand across his lips. "You want the princess? I give her to you. You want the crone and children? I give them to you." The man's black eyes gleamed with a kind of red fever. "Tell me where I can find the faery treasures."

What treasures? Boyden mused darkly. The only

treasures the faeries guarded were the magical talismans, and those they would never part with.

The first talisman was the *Stone of Fal*, which would scream whenever a true king placed his foot upon it. The next talisman was known as the *Answerer*, the magical sword of the dead faery king Nuada. When drawn, it would inflict only mortal wounds. There were also hushed whispers of a spirit sword of dark enchantment, but he did not know if those whispers were true and so discarded it from his tally. The third talisman was the *Spear* of the faeries' new High King Lugh. It was said that it never missed its target. The final talisman was the *Cauldron of Dagda,* from which an inexhaustible supply of food came forth. Those were the only treasures he knew of, and he would never betray their location at Tara.

"Tell me right now and I will have the princess brought here for you. I know you want her. Your eyes burn with lust for her."

Boyden did not move.

"Tell me what I need to know." He watched the captain pace with a bouncing gait, becoming more agitated with his wants. "Or I will hurt the crone and children."

"You hurt them and I will kill you," Boyden snarled in warning.

The captain stopped in mid-stride, eyebrows shooting up. "So, you can speak."

"I can speak."

"Tell me where to find the faery treasures." His captor came closer. "In a bog? Among the trees? Near a rowan? I heard those trees are magical. In a thornbush? Where?"

Boyden said not a word.

"I must know."

"Know what?"

His captor's fist shot out, clipping him on the jaw.

Boyden's head flew back, blood spilling into his mouth. He glared his hatred and spat on the ground. His bottom lip cracked in seeping crimson, and his jaw ached, but these were minor inconveniences compared to what he planned to inflict on the captain once he got his hands on him. Like the faeries, never did he forget or forgive.

"I can see this is going to take all night with you. Maybe we can move things along with my dagger. It is an extraordinary weapon. Are you familiar with it?"

The captain pulled a small glittering dagger from his tunic and Boyden grew very still inside. *One of the mystical blades. Where did this enemy get his hands on one of the ancient Darkshade daggers?* he wondered. The faeries held two of them, the few remaining were buried in places not known. Crafted in the long-ago time, the daggers varied in form, yet each could kill a powerful fey born guardian by infesting them with fever and madness. They were the only weapons that could. A nip to the flesh was all that was needed.

"I see from your expression you know this dagger. An old villager gave it to me while begging for his life. He told me the inscription names it Darkshade, feller of faeries and guardians."

The pig nose got some of the legend right, Boyden thought. *The dagger works on guardians alone, and aye, I recognize it well enough.* The threads of ancient winds and primordial guardians diluted his mortal heritage, fashioning him of a varied bloodline. It was a taint he fought hard against. Yet it was those guardian blood threads pulsing within him now, a warning of threat.

Because of his unusual bloodline, Derina told him he might be susceptible to the black enchantment of the ancient Darkshade. He guessed he was going to find out if that were true.

The captain turned the dagger over and wrapped stubby fingers around the hilt. "Shall I cut the crone and children?" he taunted.

With a snarl of rage, Boyden lunged forward and nearly pulled the wooden stakes out of the ground. He felt the left one give more than the right and concentrated his efforts there.

The captain jumped backward, caught off guard by his ferocity, and gestured impatiently for his man's help. "Come and hold him! I want to cut him and see what I have here."

The guard came up behind him and locked a thick arm around Boyden's neck, blocking his air.

The captain came in close. "Show me your wings and purple-tinted eyes, faery."

Boyden fought, trying to get his legs out from under him, but he was off balance.

He saw the gleam of the dagger from the corner of

his eye, and his blood began to boil.

"Where is the faery treasure? If you remain stubborn, I will cut you, then I will cut the crone."

"You cut her and you are dead."

"Let's see how defiant you are."

The dagger cut into his left temple like a blazing spear of white fire and moved toward his eye, blinding him with blood.

"*Captain!* Stop this at once!" The princess spoke with cold authority and outrage from somewhere to his left.

He thought she had gone. His torturers jumped back with a hiss of surprise, and Boyden's head sagged between his shoulders. Wetness spilled down his face, dripping onto his chest. His fists tightened convulsively. It hurt. Unseen darkness slithered into his mind. Shadows shifted in his vision. He gulped in air, his muscles turning to water. He forced himself to remain alert and not splinter into night and nothingness.

He drew in a deep ragged breath and peered up at his rescuer.

Princess.

The pig nose and she were talking in low angry voices.

CHAPTER 4

Scota was furious. A strange wind had blown inside her tent of animal skins, waking her from an uneasy sleep. She did not question how wind blew inside her tent or why she smelled blood. She had remained clothed in a white woolen shirt, brown breeches, and boots. Quickly grabbing her short sword, she flipped the tent's entrance cloth up, and bolted out of the tent.

"Captain Rigoberto, what do you think you are doing?" she demanded.

"The captive refuses to answer my questions," the captain said with a quick explanation of his actions.

"You lied to me."

"I did not lie. I only changed my mind and decided to question him."

Scota could not see how badly the warrior was hurt. "You question him by cutting his face?" she asked tensely. An odd glimmer from the captain's dagger reflected the light of the fire and nearly blinded her. "What is that?" she demanded.

"A Darkshade dagger."

Darkshade? It was double-edged, and she saw runic symbols etched into the strange metal on both sides. It did not look bronze- or iron-worked to her.

"No matter how you choose to explain your actions, you lied to me."

The man remained uncharacteristically silent, and Scota regained control of her temper. She took a deep breath. "You said the warrior would be here in the morning." She pointed with her sword. "From the looks of him, I doubt he would be alive by then."

"I had no intention of killing him. I consider him too valuable."

"Valuable?" she burst out with anger. "This is how you demonstrate value?"

"Look at him," the captain said. "What do you see?"

"Blood."

"I see perfection." He smiled, turning Scota's heart cold. Eyes of evil regarded her from a being untouched by suffering, one who thoroughly lacked empathy. Besides his tendency to humiliate the camp whores, she suspected his loyalty was to greed and self-indulgences rather than to Amergin. It terrified her to think he led men.

"What does perfection have to do with anything?" she asked cautiously.

"This dagger is a teller of faeries and mystical creatures called guardians."

"You know I do not believe in faeries."

"Well, I do, Princess. If you cut one of these beings

with this magical dagger, it forces them to show their true form."

"Which is?"

"Purple eyes and wings."

"Then what?" she asked.

"The faeries hoard great treasures and I mean to have them." He pointed at the bleeding warrior. "This is one of those fey creatures."

"Since you cut him and he appears not to have sprouted glittery wings, I believe your mystical dagger is but an idiotic notion cast on a bard's tongue."

His lips thinned. "He will turn."

"I doubt it. You cut him. He bleeds. I see no wings and therefore claim him as mine."

Scota knew she pushed the captain too far. He took a step toward her, his face blotted with berry spots.

"You dare question my authority, Amergin whore?" he snarled with fury.

She wielded her sword in warning. "Do you challenge me, Captain Rigoberto?"

It would make her life easier if she could kill him with a swift thrust of a sword and be rid of him once and for all.

"The warrior belongs to me," he said in a fury.

"The warrior belongs to Lord Amergin," she countered and decided to placate him. "When I am finished questioning him, you may have him for your little treasure hunt," she soothed, with no intention of following through. She would not hand the warrior or the crone and children over to Rigoberto.

The captain's eyes darted between her and the silent and bloody warrior, giving her statement some thought. He nodded reluctantly, his eyes shiny with undisguised hatred of her authority.

"You should have shared my bed, Princess. I might be more lenient with you then." It was a warning and she took it as such. Signaling the other man to follow, he walked stiffly away, heading for the whore tent.

Scota exhaled a sigh of relief.

These little battles with the captain were growing wearisome. The man's sickly fixation on her was unreasonable, and his obsession for riches would lead them all to ruin instead of conquest. She forced the greedy captain from her mind and turned her attention to the bleeding warrior.

The crone and children were on their feet behind her with the single guard keeping them in place. The strain on their faces showed their concern for the injured warrior. She hoped she had not been too late to save his left eye, and she knelt in front of him without thinking. Wet crimson stained the left side of his face, and she laid the sword on the ground between them.

Heat radiated from his body into hers. "I will not hurt you," she said gently. Pushing silky-smooth hair aside, she examined the wound. It was not deep, but looked hurtful. Features drawn with pain, nostrils flaring, his eyes were fiercely shut, keeping the world out. The cut traveled in length from his temple to the center hairs of his light brown brow. Scota felt thankful that the cut did not reach the eye.

He exhaled, a murmur of breath leaving parted lips.

Compassion fought against the cold warrior inside her. She should not be seething with rage for what he suffered. She should not feel, not for him.

Long lashes lifted, one brown laced, one red stained.

Her stomach somersaulted into oblivion.

A new violent heat licked over her face . . .

Hooded eyes no longer the silvery gray of a windstorm swirled with irritated shades of amethyst twilight. Magnificent with intensity, they were sprinkled with flecks of sun-kissed gold, markers of a faery kin. Before embarking with his men inland, Amergin spoke of the faeries. He believed some of the tales real and spoke of a strange fey marker in the eyes, an amethyst hue with shards of gold.

Scota stared at a hard angular face, stared at a— male faery.

Immediately, she reached down for her sword and found a large hand gripping the hilt.

In the next instant, the tip of the blade pressed into the tender flesh under her chin. She was captor no longer. The way they knelt facing each other, Scota knew the guard did not see the swift change of authority.

"Doona move." His voice was low and darkly caressing, yet no less commanding.

Spreading muscular thighs wider, he shifted closer to her, shielding the weapon between their bodies, hers clothed, his most definitely not. A knuckle brushed the tip of her breast sending awareness through her. Level with her eyes was his bronze torc, the rounded tips ending in tiny loops. The sharp blade pricked her skin, and she struggled to remain calm and in control.

"I said doona move."

Up close, his features were merciless, perfect in shape and form. She sensed great power in him and waited while his eyes drifted over her face again, stealing her air, her breath, as if he claimed it for his own.

Boyden stared into a pair of contemplative greenish-blue eyes surrounded by long black lashes. He expected fear from her, certainly shock, but not curiosity. In fascination, he watched as she gathered her courage to combat him, the scent of wildflowers drifting in the air he breathed.

"Where are your wings?" she asked softly.

His head tilted with puzzlement. *What wings?* He was not faery bred.

"What is your name? Can you tell me your name?"

He stared at her with sullen silence, reluctantly admiring her boldness, especially with a blade pressed to her neck. Out of the corner of his eye, the druidess and children watched, waited. He nodded ever so slightly. The ancient pulled the children to her and they settled back down against the trunk of the tree, pretending a return to sleep. His gaze slid to the red-haired guard, a man with bushy eyebrows and a scarred face. It was obvious to Boyden the man was bored by his duty. He settled back down, as well, no doubt thinking the princess planned to enjoy herself with the naked and bound captive, and he took another slug of mead from his leather pouch, settling in for a nap.

"I asked you your name," she said with a hushed tone of false impatience.

He gave her his full attention.

"Your name, golden one," she prompted with an arched brow.

He felt no desire to share his name and continued his examination of her face. "Why would you want to know my name?"

She gave an exasperated sigh. "I would like to know who bleeds on me."

For a moment, she shimmered in front of him, a vague outline of dim light, a falsity of reckoning from the Darkshade enchantment flowing in his blood. Queasiness settled in the pit of his stomach.

He looked into the fiery depths of her eyes, concentrating on her, and only on her, and dropped his voice in answer. "I am Boyden."

"Well, Boyden, I am Princess Scota, and I suggest you release me or I will call for help."

"You willna call," he replied, feeling a small break in the mounting shadows crawling within. Though mortal, it seemed he was not immune to the enchantment of the Darkshade dagger after all. The threads of his guardian ancestry were making it so.

She arched a delicate black brow at him, one of decided scorn. "You are mistaken."

"Nay, I doona think so. You would have called out by now. Besides, you plan to subdue me on your own, do you not?"

He saw the truth of it in her eyes. A strange thrill of excitement pushed through the dimness within him at the thought of her attempting it.

"Release my right hand, Scota."

"Release it yourself," she hissed decisively. "You freed your left hand. Free your right."

They were practically nose to nose, he looking down and she looking up, breathing each other's air. Her breath was sweetened with mead and his, no doubt, smelled of coppery blood and bitter sweat. The violent pain in his head receded to pounding and a new, cruel heat stirred in his blood. He felt it burrowing into his bones and shifted uncomfortably.

"You do not look so good to me, golden one. Give me the sword and allow me to tend to your wound. I promise I will not hurt you." A soft hand rested on his arm. "Let me help you, Boyden."

He looked down at her hand, coolness seeping into his flesh from long, white, delicately shaped fingers. He was going to regret this and lifted his gaze to hers.

"Free my right hand, Princess," he demanded with quiet authority, "and I will consider your offer."

"Give me the sword, Boyden," she countered, fingertips grazing the inside of his forearm. "Let me help you."

He gave her a sour grimace. "Scota, doona make

me hurt you."

"Would you?"

He looked at her. "Aye, I would."

Her eyes widened slightly with surprise.

"Free me," he said.

"I must lean down to reach your hand."

He nodded, keeping the tip of the blade touching her throat. Black hair fell away from her shoulder, exposing a slender white nape and delicate jaw. Blood pounded in his temples while white fingers went to work on the knots digging into his right wrist.

"This is too tight." She gave a weighty sigh. "I do not think I can loosen it."

"Try."

She straightened and looked him squarely in the eye. "I said, I can not loosen it."

"Try again."

"You must cut it with the sword."

Testing the ropes binding his right hand to the stake, he found it as tight as before. He stared at her, anger and attraction brewing below the surface.

"Untie me," he growled.

"Untie yourself."

Threads of his magical heritage swirled inside him, ones of menace and intolerance. He could feel the dark amending him from within; feel the fey marker of his blooded kin staying the amethyst hue in his once-gray eyes.

"You are one of them," she said.

He did not bother to deny her assumption, but took

advantage of it. "Do you see the amethyst twilight in my eyes, Scota? Know that I am nothing like you have ever encountered before. Untie the rope."

"Or what?" Scota heard herself say in rebellion. Although he appeared young, she felt as if she stared into the long-ago past, into mesmerizing twilight and into dangerous enchantment. He was a warrior of hard arrogance and secrets, and, indeed, nothing like she had ever encountered before in her life. To her profound puzzlement, she found herself intrigued.

He tilted his head, a sinister presence watching her. It was as if the world gave pause and all the creatures waited in watchful terror for something terrible to be unleashed.

"Untie me," he commanded with a voice of smooth darkness.

Her left hand reached out of its own accord, feeling the straining muscle and flesh of his arm. She could not read the intentions of this one; his emotions were kept carefully hidden.

"I need both my hands," she said.

He nodded, leaning down with her. Strands of gold mingled with her black tresses. A droplet of blood splattered on her hand.

"I need more room," she whispered breathlessly.

"I doona think so."

A peculiar sensation settled in the pit of her stomach. Warm breath caressed her neck and ear, sending shivers down her spine despite the warmth shedding from the fire circle. Angered at her response to his closeness, she purposely elbowed him in the stomach and found it rock hard.

Air left his lungs with a hiss. "Doona do that again. I doona like being poked."

"Neither do I," said Scota, indicating where the man part of him prodded her thigh.

"It canna be helped. Being a warrior, you must know this happens to males in battle."

"Are we in battle?" She jerked at the knots.

"A different kind of battle, methinks, and I wish you to loosen the loops, not tighten them."

"I am attempting to do so," she said through her teeth.

"Do it faster."

She turned to respond, her temper getting the better of her, and her nose collided with his.

He did not pull back.

Up close, his unblinking eyes appeared even more startling . . . and mysterious, a gateway into the twilight flames and ancient wisdom within him. His fist and the sword's hilt pressed low between her breasts, creating heat and awareness.

"If you continue to give me your air, Princess, I am going to have to claim you here and now."

She faced away from him and yanked at the confounded ropes.

"Pull the left loop," he suggested.

"I know which loop to pull."

"Then do it; you are stopping the blood flow in my

arm."

With jerky movements, she managed to free his wrist and straightened abruptly. He was right there with her, the tip of the sword a constant source of irritation against the underside of her chin.

Scota could hear her own breath loud in her ears.

It felt like they were all alone in the camp, despite the sleeping men and numerous warhorses. On the other side of the fire, probably at some distance, one of the soldiers grunted loudly while finding his pleasure in the sheath of a willing whore.

The blond warrior heard the sound, too, unmistakable and richly animal in the night air.

She locked gazes with those fey eyes.

His brow arched.

All around the camp, the winds rose in ominous voices calling in clouds, mist, and storm.

He was linked to the land somehow, she surmised.

"Are you one of the fey creatures of this land?" she voiced her question aloud, not knowing what to expect. She had never seen a faery, and until moments before did not believe in them, but this tawny-maned warrior seemed to embody the magical. He must be.

"Do you believe in the fey of this land, Scota?" he countered softly.

Unconsciously wetting her lips, she answered honestly. "I do not know."

His lashes lowered slightly.

She had him, she thought triumphantly.

Hardness jabbed her in the stomach, instantly recognizable.

Without looking, and with a single fingertip, she traced the veins pulsing beneath hard flesh, the bulbous tip large.

His eyes darkened in storm.

Maybe she could use his lust to an advantage, she reasoned. Looking at him coyly, she moistened her lips with her tongue again, a smooth slow glide of wetness meant to entice, a whore's tease.

A muscle jumped in his jaw.

The thumb of his sword hand brushed her taut nipple and she sucked in a shaky breath.

" 'Tis dangerous to tease me in this state, Princess."

Her jaw set, refusing to acknowledge the attraction heating between them. "Do not presume . . ."

He smiled darkly with understanding and her body went queer inside.

Head tilting with a predator's scrutiny, he murmured, "Forgive me."

"Do you plan to kill me?" She was surprised to see a flicker of regret pass over his features. "Be done with it then," she said boldly. "I grow weary of the wait." The air stirred around her in threat and chill, his hard gaze the last thing she saw.

Boyden clipped her in the jaw with his fist, knocking her unconscious. He did not want to do it, but she gave him little choice with her teasing. He did not need grinding lust joining with the Darkscape enchantment spreading in his blood.

In the next instant, he bolted toward the sleeping guard and took him out, laying the still body down in silence. The druidess and children were on their feet, silent and immediately alert.

"Stay here," he commanded with a hush.

Derina nodded, holding the children to her.

Boyden doubled back and quickly donned his torn breeches and boots. Hefting the unconscious warrior temptress over his shoulder, he grabbed the short sword and hurried back to where they waited.

"Follow me," he commanded.

He led them back into the cover of night, their welfare his responsibility. His second stealing of the night, besides a teasing enemy princess, would be among their warhorses. Even burdened with her light weight on his shoulder, the children and the druidess would be unable to keep up with him . . . at least for the time being. Soon, he would drop in fever and madness. He had little time left.

CHAPTER 5

SLOW, ACHING SENSATIONS RETURNED.

Thump, thump, thump . . . her stomach went.

Lush green woodlands came into hard focus, rising about her like an army.

Her mind registered the feel and sound of hooves encountering moist soil. She lay across a black horse's powerful shoulders. The confounded warrior had bound her wrists together with thick rope. Soreness spread through her stomach from the rocky movement of a horse's gallop, now slowing to a jostling trot. She gritted her teeth, about to complain, when the animal slowed to a walk.

She stared at a brown-booted foot—a large one. She wondered what he would do if she leaned over and took a bite out of his shin. Probably toss her on her head, she mused, trying to shift into a more comfortable position, a hopeless proposition when lying across a horse.

Below her, light and shadow spilled over a rock-strewn ground with clumpy green-gray moss. She looked at his shin again. How dare he kidnap her! The steaming scent of horse sweat assailed her senses. Painfully, she lifted her head higher as the horse came to a stop. The warrior put a hand on her lower back and slid off the horse, narrowly avoiding her head. *Clumsy goat.* She looked over her shoulder, wrinkling her nose at a foul smell. The horse's long black tail lifted high, fragrancing the air as the animal . . .

Beside her cheek, a large hand stroked the animal's neck. "Good boy, Shade."

She turned.

Her captor said not a word to her. Long, blunt fingers slid through the hairs of the animal's night-black coat with calming. In the back of her mind, she thought he cleaned up well enough. Beneath the strands of blond hair, the wound arrowed from his temple to his brow, congealing in a red line. It only added to the dangerous quality of his rugged features.

He leaned into her unexpectedly and inhaled, as if taking the scent of her deep in his lungs for memory and recall.

Scota pulled back as far as she could, given her position on a horse's shoulders. "What are you doing?" she said with outrage. As far as she was concerned, between the horse's sweat and dumping, the air reeked.

He said not a word, but continued his sniffing perusal without regard for her comfiture. Nostrils flaring, he then shifted back having found whatever scent he wanted.

She glared at him. The whispers among the whores

in the camp said the men of the *Tuatha Dé Danann* tribe scented their women. If true, his actions made little sense to her. She smelled of sweaty horse, not the water of lavender she put on her skin to repel insects, nor the aromatic wildflowers she sometimes crushed on her wrists and behind her knees. The whores' eager commentary also included something about a mating bite ritual where the Tuatha male bit a large chunk out of the female's jaw before mating her. The whores found it thrilling, fanning themselves with their hands. She thought it would be extremely painful. No one was going to take a bite out of her jaw. Intolerable! The women of the Tuatha tribe probably all had scarred faces. *Stupid whores.*

"Are you going to get me off this horse?" she demanded.

He continued his leisurely petting of the animal, his eyes unreadable.

"Take her down, Boyden," the crone said from somewhere nearby.

He seized her arm and pulled forward.

"Stop!" Scota protested, imagining her face hitting the ground before her feet. "Let me slide off the other way."

He ignored her.

A hand snagged her hip, flipping her into his arms.

Scota instinctively kicked out, grabbing for a hold to stay her fall, hands bunching in soft blond hair.

With a muttered oath, he set her firmly on her feet, but did not step back.

Scota stared into amethyst fire, her will and rebellion melting with each jagged breath.

He waited, silent and predatory, as the shadows in this place closed around them.

A brown brow slowly arched in question.

She released his hair and stepped back, taking a few strands of dark gold with her.

His eyes narrowed.

"Methinks she be awake, Boyden," the crone cackled to her right.

"Aye," he muttered and rubbed his scalp.

"Bring her here and let me have a closer look at her."

"Nay, Derina. She is too rebellious for the moment."

Rebellious? *More like enraged!* Scota thought and looked fiercely at him. He stood like one of the ancient gods, feet planted wide. Torn brown breeches clung to long muscular legs, offering glimpses of blond, dusted skin. Scuffed boots protected his feet. At the waistband of his low riding pants, the hilt of a silver dagger glittered menacingly.

Two leather straps crossed a muscular chest anchoring a stolen scabbard at his back. It was there that her short sword resided, the hilt peeking over the slope of a shoulder.

Scota's gaze lifted to his, her body responding to the dark magical calling of him. It was inescapable, this confounded awareness, and she took off at a run.

He must have expected her to bolt for he had her in three steps. Fingers wrapping in her own dark tresses, he yanked with just enough force to pull her up short.

Her scalp smarting, Scota pivoted and kicked out, trying to unman him.

He caught her ankle with one hand and flipped her onto her back in the dirt. She landed with a loud "ooomph."

Breathing raggedly, she stared defiantly at him.

"Are we done?" he asked sharply.

In the empty silence that followed, she swallowed audibly.

"Doona hurt her," a girl child's voice pleaded from the other side of the black horse.

"I willna hurt her, Nora. She needs a wee bit of discipline to understand her place."

He stepped forward, reaching for her, and she kicked at him again.

Easily swatting her foot aside, he grabbed her bound wrists and yanked her to her feet.

Hands grasping her upper arms, he turned her so fast she did not know what happened until a hard chest pressed into her back.

Scota squirmed in rebellion, trying to stomp on his foot.

Muscular arms locked around her with a sweeping possession. Teeth clamped down on her ear.

She froze at the unexpected action, breathing rapidly.

Warm breath pummeled her cheek and temple, adding to the heat and frustration within her. His body threatened.

A low growl vibrated in his throat, a warning she should heed.

They were deep in the woodlands. The air was thick with dawn, and a gloomy white mist swirled at their ankles like a living thing. She felt caught in another realm, an outsider who must learn patience in order to escape.

She nodded.

He released her ear, pushing her around the front of the big black horse who stood obediently still during their scuffle.

Under low-hanging branches, the two children sat astride a lathered chestnut mare with a white fetlock. The crone stood nearby, watchful and alert, a bent hand slowly caressing the arching neck of her sun-red roan. She nodded once in greeting, and Scota glowered at her too, thinking it peculiar for a blind woman to be permitted to ride a horse alone. And how did she know to nod at her? She rubbed her tingling ear.

The black horse stomped his hoof several times with impatience.

"Easy, Shade," her warrior captor soothed, petting the animal's shoulder while his other hand held her in front of him.

"His name is Blacksword," she muttered under her breath.

The animal blew air out of its nostrils, its sides expanding in and out from a long run, no doubt carrying both her and the warrior. Blacksword was one of the captain's prized warhorses, standing at least eighteen hands, with great power and stamina. All of these horses were prime bred, of good temperament and fast speed. What amazed her was that they were unbridled, yet were easily controlled by their riders.

"You steal well," she observed.

"I did what was needed." Soft lips grazed the tingling

spot where he had held her with his teeth. Scota swatted at her ear as if he were an annoying insect and vowed to ignore the fluttering in her stomach.

A male's chuckle infuriated her before he propelled her forward. "Free the horses, boy. They can take us no farther."

"His name is Cavan," she corrected with sweetly contained antagonism, "and his name is Blacksword." She pointed to the black warhorse with a sweep of her bound wrists.

"I know the boy's name, Scota, and Blacksword prefers to be called Shade."

"Prefers?" she choked.

"Do you not listen to your animals?" he asked with all seriousness. "They have preferences, as we do."

"Listen? What, you can speak to animals?"

"Nay, only listen when they wish it," he answered simply. His belief unnerved her.

"Cavan, the mare caught a rock in her hoof. Remove it."

The boy helped his sister off the horse.

"Right front," the warrior directed.

With firm gentle hands, the boy lifted the mare's hoof and expertly removed the small rock.

"Is he your son?" Scota heard herself ask.

"Nay, he is one of the children from the village you burned."

Her insides turned. Though she greatly disagreed with Amergin's command to burn the villages, there was nothing she could do to prevent the needless waste.

"Done, Wind Herald," Cavan said, straightening. "Her hoof is not injured."

Scota agreed with the boy's observation. The chestnut mare shifted her full weight back onto the leg.

"Good, release them," her golden captor commanded.

Taking his sister's hand, Cavan tapped the chestnut on the rump. The crone did the same to her roan and Shade trotted after them with a soft whinny. The horses disappeared into the dark woodlands for well-deserved rest and freedom.

"You are freeing the horses?" she remarked with astonishment.

"Aye, they have traveled far and fast this night and canna go where we are going. They earned their freedom."

"Where are we going that they can not go, and why do you need me?"

He gave her a sardonic look edged with anger.

" 'Twas a Darkscape dagger the pig-nosed man cut you with, Boyden?" the crone interrupted, coming up to them as if she could see. It unsettled Scota, this seeing without eyes.

"Aye, 'twas Darkshade, Derina."

"Did the blade carry the runic marks?"

"Aye, from what I can remember. He came at me from the side, and I only caught a glimpse of it."

The crone turned to her for confirmation, and Scota looked into those pink, empty eye sockets.

"Did it?" the old woman asked.

She gave a curt nod, not understanding why symbols on a dagger were of any importance.

The crone scratched her head. "Methinks it be one of the older blades of the long-ago times, Boyden, verra bad, for a guardian born."

"I am not guardian born."

"The wound willna heal," she argued against him, her tone laced with irritation.

The girl child started weeping and buried her face in her brother's side.

Her tears unnerved Scota, and she sought to ease the child's worries. "It is a minor wound, nothing to worry about."

"It be more than a flesh wound," the crone explained, "much more than you be ever imagining."

Scota studied the old woman. Beside her, the tension of the warrior was undeniable, thickening the air she breathed.

"Derina, she of all people has no need to know this," he said coldly.

"Nay, she needs to know. Needs to know for what comes after."

"Nothing comes after."

There was a short silence before the crone retorted, "You need her, Boyden."

"You speak stupidity," he said with annoyance.

Scota stood in silence, watching the white-haired crone argue forcefully with the tall, powerful warrior. She almost pitied him, but it was a breach she intended to widen in order to hasten her escape.

"Tell me, crone," she interrupted them, wanting to know, needing to know all weaknesses pertaining to the enemy. And, she reminded herself, this tawny-maned warrior is the enemy.

"There be nothing to tell." His fingers tightened on her upper arm with threat.

Ignoring him, she focused fully on the druidess. "Tell me."

The ancient woman looked up at the warrior with her empty eye sockets, a faint curl of satisfaction to her lips. "He be born with the blood threads of the wind guardians and an ancient king."

"Derina," came the warning, and Scota missed the mention of the word *king*. "Blood threads?" she prompted, hoping to get as much information as she could before another argument ensued. She pushed hair out of her eyes. "I do not understand your words."

"The blood threads in his veins be belonging to the long-ago times. He be one born of the air."

"Derina, she has no need to know this."

The crone waved away his protest. "She needs to know, Boyden."

"She is the enemy," he said impatiently.

"Is she?"

Scota looked up at him and had the most curious impression of a godlike being about to crush an annoying insect—*her*.

She focused back on the crone. "What are wind

guardians?"

"They steal your breath," Boyden said edgily with a firm shake.

Scota felt her shoulder wrench and turned to him. Amethyst eyes burned with golden shards of dark light. "Would you care for me to steal your breath?" he asked barely above a whisper, a sensual threat for her ears alone.

All around them the branches of trees started swaying in response to the rising of a suddenly cold wind. They stood at the edge of a steep slope, a small dell of trees and rocks ahead. Out of the corner of her eye and behind him, she thought she saw a reflection of herself standing beside a gray boulder spotted with green moss.

The girl child's weeping grew louder, more frightened . . .

"Hush, Nora," the crone said with soft reprimand, not turning to look at the child. "The Wind Herald willna harm us."

Gold light flashed in the warrior's eyes with a terrible realization, and he looked away, nostrils flaring, his hand slipping away from her arm.

Scota took an unsteady breath herself as the eerie winds dwindled, the trees quiet once again . . . and the strange reflection of herself gone.

The old woman pushed a tumbled mass of white hair off her forehead, and the child gave a small pitiful gulp, thawing some of the ice locked around Scota's heart. She did not want to feel compassion for a child.

"What was that strange wind?" She lifted her gaze

to the warrior for an explanation.

Boyden had no intention of explaining anything to this princess. He went and knelt in front of Nora, seeking to calm the child's fears. Never would he bring the deadly wind down upon them. "Nora, you are always safe around me."

She sniffed, eyes glassy with tears and uncertainty.

"Do you believe me?" he asked.

She nodded with another loud sniff.

He touched her hand. "This be no time for tears and weakness, Nora. We must be strong and swift this day."

"I am swift, Boyden," Nora swiped her nose with the back of her hand and smiled valiantly.

His heart went out to her. "I know you are, Nora. This day we must be extra swift and extra silent. Can you do this for me?"

The child nodded and stiffened her shoulders.

He smiled reassuringly. "Methinks I need a hug, Nora."

A small body slammed into him, arms locking tightly around his neck. "I am not afraid."

He held her close, for he was. "I know."

"Will you be sick soon?" she whispered in a small voice and pulled back to look into his eyes.

"Aye, but not for a long while yet," he lied, and she understood that he did.

He gave her a reassuring smile and looked up at the boy. "Cavan?"

"I do what we need to do, Wind Herald."

Boyden nodded and climbed to his feet. He gripped

the boy's shoulder, one warrior to another. "Keep your sister close to you, Cavan. She is your responsibility."

"Aye, Wind Herald."

Boyden released him, admiring bravery in one so young. This day called for it, and all the children of his tribe answered to it. He scanned the tall trees, their would-be protectors. He had chosen this area of the woodlands specifically because there were no clear paths to follow. The enemy's superior numbers had beaten the *Tuatha Dé Danann*. Those remaining of his tribe scattered to the hills, some retreating to the sanctuary of their fey brethren, others unable to. At least he had played a small part in saving these three.

He glanced over his shoulder at the pushy princess. She stood straight as a stick, confident and watchful of his every move, his every weakness. Taking her was a mistake, he realized, but the alternative did not suit him. The captain did not respect her. She was merely a prize to the pig-nosed man, to be done with as he pleased, whether she was willing or not.

A shiver of painful heat sliced through him, and he stumbled back, holding his head, teeth clenching.

"Boyden?" The crone touched his arm in concern.

He held up his hand to stay her. The power of the Darkshade flowed in his blood, attacking the magical within him. He clung to his humanness, hoping it would be enough to see his purpose done.

"It passes, Derina."

"It doona pass."

"It passes," he said firmly.

"What passes?" the princess prompted, wanting to know all. "Are you sick?"

"I have been cut with a dagger," he replied, "and my head aches."

"The Darkshade simmers your blood in the olden ways. It will only get worse."

He glared at the druidess. "Be silent, Derina."

"The princess needs to know so she may help."

It was hopeless, he realized.

"Know what?" asked the princess, looking between him and the meddling one.

"I speak of an evil enchantment from the long-ago times, affecting the guardian born," the druidess said.

"I am not guardian born," he argued uselessly.

They ignored him.

"You speak of the dagger?" the princess asked, a deeper understanding lighting her lovely eyes.

He had no desire for her to know anything more about him. "Derina, enough of the dagger. We have other things of importance this day." He turned to the north, to the great expanse of ancient woodlands and mist. Sanctuary waited for them.

"Derina, listen to me. If I can get you to the *nematon*, can you lead the children to our fey kin?"

The holy well resided in the *nematon*, a circular clearing of divine and earthly union. Surrounded by a thorn thicket and boulders, the stone well was located in the woodlands, not far from where they were. The sacred place resided deep in the well providing an entranceway to the Otherworld. All waters, from a trickle in a stone crevice to a sacred loch, were entranceways, if one were born of the fey.

"Boyden, you must listen to me. We must find the herbs to heal you."

He shook his head. "Nay, Derina, there be little time. Our enemy pursues us still. We must make haste and get the children to safety."

"You should have kept the horses then," the princess complained. "The captain will."

He attempted to pull her forward but she planted her feet, refusing to go anywhere.

"Scota, doona make me carry you."

"I do not mean to be carried but simply heard."

"I doona have time to argue with you," he said.

"Make it then."

He showed his annoyance with a tick in his jaw.

She showed her annoyance with a loud sigh, but continued with what she intended to say. "The captain pursues you and the children so keenly because he wants me. Release me, Boyden. I vow I will not speak of the direction you take."

"You expect me to trust you?" he muttered incredulously.

"I give you my word."

He gestured for the druidess and children to walk down the steep hill leading into a denser pocket of trees. "What worth is an enemy's word?" he propelled her forward.

"My word is my oath," she said, trying to wrench free.

He gave her a warning shake, and held firm to her arm. "That may be, Scota, but I willna risk the lives of the druidess and the children. The captain pursues us so intently because he wants me, not you."

"Nonsense," she remarked.

"You think so?"

"I know so," she said, almost too vehemently.

He managed a wry smile and suspected she did not fully believe her own words.

The druidess and children were already several horse lengths ahead, climbing between black roots the size of men, and creating their own path. The ancient one appeared surprisingly agile beside the children, and he once again reminded himself of her fey born heritage. Her aging years were not the same as a mortal's, no matter how old she looked or pretended to be.

The princess tugged at her arm, seeking release. "Let me go, Boyden. If you release me, I will lead the captain and his men in another direction."

"Why did you not escape when I went to comfort Nora?"

Fury flashed in her eyes.

"No answer?" he smiled smugly. "You like me."

"You are mad."

"Eventually."

"Let go of me!"

"The captain has only one need grinding a hole inside him, Scota. It is greed and lust for power. He believes I am one of the fey born and can take him to a great treasure."

"I know that. I can dissuade him."

"Methinks not, Scota. He offered you to me as a reward if I would speak of the treasure's location. He shows no respect for you."

She showed her shock. "That greedy bastard would not dare."

"I see you doona call me a liar. You believe me then."

"Of course, I believe you. That useless . . ." Her mouth snapped shut and she stared at him with a creased frown.

He regarded her back just as steadily. "It says something when you believe the word of an enemy over that of one of your own."

Her lips thinned, but she did not voice an objection to his observation.

"It seems we are in agreement."

"We will never be in agreement," she spat.

"Step over that root and watch your head, the branch is low."

He climbed over the root with her and avoided the gray vines.

"Where are we going?" she demanded.

"Into the woods."

"I do not wish to go."

"Your wishes are of little concern to me."

She gave another tug. "Why have your eyes not changed back to the color of gray?"

"Why have you noticed the color of my eyes?"

"Answer me," she commanded, a princess showing her true form.

"What color are they now?" he asked, half-afraid to hear.

She looked into his eyes, her gaze pausing, and Boyden felt caught in the allure of her.

"They are the color of twilight, purple with flecks of gold," she grumbled, but he could detect a small awe in her voice.

He nodded, looking away. The fey marker of his birth now showed constant in his eyes, permanence he did not need or understand.

"Are you going to answer my question?"

Beneath the woolen sleeve of her shirt, the muscles in her arm tensed.

"Step over the roots." He gestured for her to watch where she walked and guided her around a thick-trunked yew, yellow flowers peeking out from among the ground moss.

"Are you going to answer my question, Boyden?"

"Nay."

"Are you one of those fey born creatures?"

He looked sideways at her.

"Well, are you?" she prompted.

"If I answer, will you be quiet?"

She nodded.

"I am not fey born."

"What are you, then? Never have I seen eyes this color."

Taking her had definitely been a mistake, he decided. "The amethyst shade be a fey hue of what resides in my blood," he replied, unwilling to share more.

"The blood threads of the wind guardians . . ." she murmured, ". . . that is why your eyes changed to twilight gold."

She was too quick. "Leave it be, Scota."

But he knew she would not. This one was too inquisitive, too full of life.

He watched her study the children walking in front of them, the boy holding his sister's hand in guidance and support.

"The children are fey born," she murmured.

"Nay," he replied.

"Nay?" she mimicked his inflection. "Not the sightless crone?" she said with hushed skepticism, looking at him with wide eyes.

He did not think Derina would like being called a sightless crone. "Derina is a druidess, one of our wise women."

"Is she?"

He pretended not to hear her, and she exhaled loudly.

"Is she fey born, Boyden?"

"Aye, she is fey born."

She continued to watch him, and he knew he would have no peace unless he explained what he wished not to explain.

"The children and I are one of the *idir*, the between."

"What does between mean?"

"We have the blood threads of the fey in our blood. We stand between the worlds of both mortal and fey . . ."

". . . as you soon will be," the druidess said from up ahead.

Boyden looked toward the druidess, brown robes held high over skinny white legs. "Derina hears in the ways of our fey brethren, exceedingly well."

"She heard everything we said?" the princess lowered her voice.

"Aye," the ancient replied, not even looking back at them. Her voice was soft, but it carried clearly in the cool silence of the woodlands.

"I am Milesian," Scota said tersely.

"It matters not," the old woman replied. "You walk this land now and the wind accepts you."

"Enough, Derina. Keep walking."

Lovely turquoise eyes turned to him for answers. "What does she mean by that?"

He shrugged, not understanding or liking Derina's words, either.

In the archaic tree shadows and the multifaceted reality of her existence, the *Gaoth Shee* followed, silvery whispers touching branches and fluttery leaves—waiting.

CHAPTER 6

THEY WALKED THE REMAINDER OF the long day into night shadow and isolation, a constant progression into thick mist. The trunks and branches of the large trees about them were covered in creeping moss.

Blackness flanked them. Sounds were muffled and strangely close. Scota could not see a thing, not even her hands in front of her face.

"We rest here," the warrior said, a moving shade beside her. He left her alone, giving aid and direction to Derina and the children. She dropped wearily to her knees in the soft muck. Even if she wished to escape, which she did, she could not muster the strength or risk running headlong into a tree or a ditch. Hungry and chilled, she felt lost in a strange land of seeping night.

"Get up."

He grabbed her bound wrists, pulled her to her feet, and guided her forward.

"I can not see." She balked.

"I can. Sit here." He pushed her down, her thigh

resting against a tree root. A cool breeze rustled the leaves, and Scota shivered.

"Cold?" he asked.

"No."

"Liar." He settled down behind her, and she stiffened.

A powerful arm wrapped around her waist and yanked her back.

She elbowed him in the stomach. "Let go of me."

Her back hit the ground, and a heavy weight settled atop her.

She could not see his face, only the glint of angry shards of gold. He held her arms above her head, warm breath puffing alongside her cheek and temple.

She tried to butt him with her forehead, but he sensed her intent and grabbed a handful of hair, staying her.

Breathing furiously, she waited.

Boyden held her under him, determined not to hurt her. His impulse was to kiss her into submission, but the pain raking his blood stole all purpose.

"Scota, listen to me well. I am tired, ill-tempered, and wish to seek my rest. The children and druidess sleep close together, sharing their heat as I am offering to share my heat with you."

She shifted under him, and he moved his hips away, conscious of her every curve.

"Why would you offer to share your body's heat with me?" she asked.

"You are shivering." A simple answer, he gave her.

"I am enemy."

True. "You are my responsibility."

"A strange captor you are," she whispered.

"Or I can tie you to a tree while I sleep. Your choice."

"I do not sleep well when tied to a tree."

"Neither would I. Do I have your word that you willna elbow me in the stomach or escape?"

"I give you my word I will not escape *this* night. I can not control what I do in my sleep."

"Fair enough." With a hand remaining on her arm, he easily moved around her. "We can fit between the roots if you press back into me."

She scooted back, the curve of her bottom fitting snugly against his hips.

"A strange captive you make," he said softly. "Put your head down."

She did as he requested, and his arm came to rest in the curve of her waist. He pushed several of her hairs off his chin.

"You tremble." He pulled her back into him and in a few moments, her shaking stopped.

"My thanks for sharing your heat," she murmured tiredly.

He said not a word and closed his eyes. His mind and body were worn out from the Darkshade and hard travel. Moments later, he slipped into a light sleep.

Scota remained awake long after, listening to his breathing and wondering at the unexpected offering of warmth from her enemy.

In the late afternoon of the next day, Scota continued to ponder the actions of her brooding captor. She lay on her back listening to the hum of the oak-woods, the children and druidess resting near. She stared up at the summer-solstice trees. They were sacred to her people, as well, representing strength, fortitude, and loyalty.

The oaks were entranceways between the light and the dark halves of the year. She scratched her eyebrow, staring up at the thick branches. The trees also tended to draw lightning. *A most uncomfortable propensity when hiding under one in a storm*, she mused and exhaled loudly. The air felt unusually warm, and moisture dampened her skin, making her hair flatter and straighter than usual. She could hear the sound of rain on the green canopy above, tiny drumbeats echoing constantly, but not a trickle of water landed on the ground where they rested. It was difficult to tell the time of day in the veiled light and shadow of these woods when one was unable to see the sun.

They had traveled a good deal of the day and though exhausted, she felt too agitated to close her eyes and seek rest.

To her right, the children nestled together in a cradle of black roots and green moss, sharing their small horde of berries. She had learned that both of them loved horses and that Cavan considered himself an excellent rider. Behind them, the crone curled in feigned sleep under a low hanging limb dangling with green clumps.

"How feels your stomach?" Scota asked, since the druidess complained constantly.

"Better if I had food to fill it."

Scota had the impression of the sightless woman blinking. The druidess complained often about her empty stomach, except when speaking about the garden of woman herbs in her backyard, which, no doubt, was burned and gone like the village.

She thought Amergin's orders to burn the village a waste of resources and men, but there was no arguing with a vengeful bard.

A silent sigh escaped her lips as she continued to study the children, now homeless and alone. She did not expect to like them, but she did. She liked the inquisitiveness of the girl, the silent strength of the boy, and the unending patience of the druidess. The brooding warrior was another matter entirely. She did not like the way he looked at her, all silence and mystery, as if he saw into her very being and knew her intimate pain and isolation.

"Why did he kidnap me?" she asked the crone.

"He wants you."

She snorted with disagreement. "I am enemy."

"Are you?"

"What do you mean by that?" she asked suspiciously.

"Your eyes follow him."

"How do you . . ." Scota frowned, looking into those sunken eye sockets a bit longer.

"Think I canna see, Princess?"

Scota turned away with harsh dismissal of the crone, a peculiar feeling seeping into her stomach.

She always achieved whatever she set her mind to, and she set her mind on escape. Whether it be through seduction or battle, her captor would not win over her.

She shifted to a more comfortable position and breathed in the woodsy scent, a subtle and magical life fragrance in this land of unfamiliarity. They were taking an hour of stolen rest before they must move again.

All around them, black and brown tree trunks rose like massive pillars, leaving behind orangey shadows spilling over enormous twisted roots. The oak-woods felt primordial to her. Besides representing strength and endurance, the oaks also symbolized male potency. Even in winter's dormancy, mistletoe sprouted with white berries, semen of the woodland lord.

Speaking of the lord . . . resting her hand under her cheek, she peered at him.

He sat far apart from them all, near a holly, his profile to her. She smiled in thought. The qualities of the holly were warring instinct and courage, a male dominion of energy. He definitely fit the description of a dominant male, all leanness and muscular quickness. One powerful arm rested on a raised knee while he scanned the shadows for threat, a guardian of the children and crone. Her gaze dipped to the bare span of ribs and the easy breath. Liquid quivering touched the low reaches of her woman's place. He may be enemy, but her annoying body wanted him submitting to her ride. Her gaze dipped to the scabbard resting on the ground beside his brown-clad leg, easily reached if needed.

"Would you like some of my berries, Princess?"

Scota looked up at the girl child in surprise. Clear blue eyes marked with shards of gold regarded her from an oval face smudged with dirt. The girl plaited her hair with horsehair taken from her chestnut mount.

"I found them myself," Nora said proudly.

Pushing up to a sitting position, Scota tucked a leg under her. Her mouth watering, she cupped her hands and a small pile of dark berries tumbled into her palms.

"We did not find many, but these taste good." The girl clasped her berry-stained hands in front of her. "I like mutton for supper and pudding, too, but we doona have any."

She understood immediately. This was all the food there was. She should eat the berries to keep her strength and return none to the child. "Would you share the berries with me, Nora? There are so many here, I do not think I can eat all of them."

"Nora," her brother called in hushed command.

"I canna stay." The girl leaned forward and held out her hand.

Scota cupped the girl's hand, which proved difficult, given her bound wrists. "Here, take them. I only need a wee bit." She poured the majority of the berries back into the purple-stained palm.

"My brother says you are the enemy, but you gave

us food and water in the camp. I doona think you are the enemy."

"Your brother speaks rightly, Nora."

The girl looked at her in open disagreement, delicate brows drawn together. "I doona think so or the Wind Herald would not have rescued you."

"Rescued me?" she echoed, bewildered by a child's interpretation of what had happened.

"Aye, from the bad man." The girl leaned forward again. "Here, take some of these back." Half the mound of berries tumbled back into her hands.

"You should share the berries with the Wind Herald and thank him for saving you. He is one of our warriors."

"Nora, I can not . . ." she protested.

"He likes you. I can tell."

Was she the only one in disagreement here?

"Nora," the brother called more firmly.

"I have to go." The precocious child returned to her scowling brother, and Scota shifted her gaze toward the large holly, unable to help herself.

The warrior regarded her coolly, his gaze, like the man himself, distant and unreadable. She felt herself separating from the real world, becoming part of the unity of the prenatal land all around her and . . . of him. Dropping her gaze, she ate three succulent berries and stared at the rest. She could handle anything but kindness and gentleness and decided seduction might be the best way to gain her freedom.

Sitting next to the holly, Boyden dragged his gaze away from the princess and watched the druidess approach in sullen silence. The old woman used a curved tree branch as a walking stick.

"Derina," he greeted.

"We must speak."

He nodded and adjusted the bronze torc resting around his neck. His thumb traced the tiny scar under his chin. She gave it to him with a quick jab of her walking stick many months ago when he was not paying attention. He scratched his chest, his focus once more settling on the princess. He felt decidedly grimy and wondered what the princess . . .

Poke.

"Ouch," he yelped, rubbing his shoulder.

"I wish your notice, Boyden. You may look at the princess after."

He exhaled loudly. "You have my notice."

"Boyden."

"That is my name." He stared up at her nose. It was rather easier than staring into empty eye sockets.

She settled both hands on the knob of the walking stick. "We will talk of the princess, but first we must speak of the winds."

"I was afraid of that," he grumbled.

"You have the dark blond coloring of the wind guardians, and the marker of the bloodline lives in your eyes. Command what you should command."

He stiffened. "Derina, I am born of the between, a mere distant cousin to the four winds." He held on to his patience. "I canna command them, you know this."

"Aye, but you can command the darkest sister, Boyden."

His eyes narrowed.

"No retort this time? Mayhap the wind guardians ignore you, but the darkest sister, the *Gaoth Shee* listens well enough."

"I doona wish to argue with you about this again."

She jabbed the stick into the ground. "I be not arguing, I be telling."

He grunted. "Arguing . . . telling . . . it sounds the same to me."

"Horse dung." *Poke.*

He gave her a menacing look, rubbing the sore spot. "Sit down and stop jabbing me in the chest."

She huffed with exasperation and settled down, knowing not to block his view of their captive.

"I see the battle weariness in you, Boyden. No longer can you deny your nightmares."

How does she know about my nightmares? Uncomfortable, he sought to redirect her. "I am battling the Darkshade, not nightmares, and I have much that calls my thoughts."

She sighed deeply. "Boyden, I am fey born and verra old."

When she wanted something of him, she always

lowered her voice and mentioned being "verra old."

He looked at her sidewise. "I know the pace is fast, but we must move quickly."

She nodded in agreement.

"Derina, you know I have been devoted to you ever since I pulled you out of that rocky ditch in your garden, two summers ago."

"Doona remind me of that. I tripped on a piglet."

"I know." He grinned.

She gripped the walking stick, her knuckles white. "My thanks for that, as well as for this rescue. You know, I went back for the children."

"Doona thank me, Derina. I knew it must be important. They are our future, if we are to survive."

"It needed saying." She sighed heavily. "We must speak, Boyden."

"Have we not been speaking?"

"This be different."

"All right, Derina. Say your words. You willna leave me in peace until they are shared openly between us."

"Boyden, do you resent being born of the between?"

He frowned. "Why do we talk of this now?"

"Because of her." The ancient gestured to the princess, who pretended not to watch them.

"Why does she matter?" he asked.

"Your heart chose your Wind Queen, Boyden, and I think, mayhap, you will listen to me now."

He studied her face, curious, and decided not to question her words or continue arguing his denial. She was willing to tell him, but in her way, not his. "All right, Derina. I have no notion of your Wind Queen, but let us talk bluntly. Aye, I resent being born of the between. One in my female line mated with a wind guardian long, long ago, but it matters no longer. I am a simple warrior and follow the laws of my chieftain."

She tilted her head. "Those born of the between must walk the twisting paths between the worlds of the mortal and our fey brethren. It be not easy."

"I know this well."

"I know you do, Wind Herald. Though you wish to deny it, you be belonging more to the magical than the mortal."

"You wish to add more enchantment to my mortal blood?"

"Aye, I do. You are distant cousin to the four primordial guardians of the winds, of this you reluctantly admit. But your blood be distant still further to a Wind Servant King."

She was maddened.

"Do I look like a king? I lived at the edge of our village in a round house with a leaky roof. I own neither horse nor goat to show my kingly wealth."

"None of the wind guardians can command the *Gaoth Shee*. The lethal wind chose you, Boyden. She recognizes you as her Servant King. The black thread of her essence flows in your bloodline, a resurgence from an olden time long lost in memory."

He shook his head, rejecting her claim. She was

simply an ancient druidess with ancient beliefs and a penchant for mead-laced goat's milk in the morning. "No one commands the *Gaoth Shee*, Derina. The Elemental steals a body's air indiscriminately. I canna command her. Even if I wished to," he hesitated, "even if I wished to bring a single enemy down who stands among many, the wind kills all living things around her, trees, horses, birds, grass, and us."

"You have not tried to command her, Boyden."

"Never will I try. The risk is too great."

"It be true the blast kills, but that be also the reason you must learn to command her."

"Command her," he laughed cynically. "I command my sword and shield. That is all I need."

She jabbed the tip of her walking stick into the ground. "Foolishness. You have such force and power in you."

"I doona wish to talk any more about this."

"Well, I do. The blood memory of your ancestor haunts your dreams."

He stilled. "Never have I spoken of those dreams, Derina. How do you know what visits me alone at night?"

"It be time, Boyden. You have reached your twenty-fifth summer. It be the same age as the death of her servant."

"I am servant to no one." He glanced around the ancient to the princess.

The druidess looked at him with bewilderment. "*She* be not your enemy, Boyden. Command the wind, Boyden. Submit to her."

A muscle ticked in his jaw.

"I am done speaking my thoughts for today." She climbed to her feet and looked down at him. "Did you hear anything I said?"

He nodded.

"I will leave you then."

CHAPTER 7

BOYDEN SET HIS JAW. THE princess, his supposed Wind Queen, smelled of the wildflowers found in the meadows beside his village and of the sweet, dark-purple lavender growing in the hills. He should not have taken her, but the vulnerability he glimpsed below the brittle surface ensnared him. With a flick of the wrist, he tossed the small dead branch aside and climbed to his feet. Grabbing the scabbard, he fitted the straps over his shoulders and secured it once more to his back. Walking around the holly, he unlaced his breeches and took care of his body's needs.

Upon finishing, he retied his laces. Wiping his hands clean on moist leaves, he paused at the sound of footfalls.

A twig snapped.

Pivoting, he locked his hand around a slender neck and shoved the princess back against a black-barked tree.

"You are choking me," she gasped, her eyes bright with indignant anger.

"What are you doing here?" he snarled.

"Bringing you berries. I must have lost my wits."

Looking down, he saw squashed berries in her right fist.

"Derina," he called quickly over his shoulder, unable to see his charges through the thick branches of the holly.

"We be fine, Wind Herald. Enjoy your delicious berries."

Mischief quivered in the druidess's light tone and his gaze slid back to his lovely, self-assured captive. Even with her hands bound, she was cold and proud in the warrior way. Fires of outrage burned in the depths of her turquoise eyes igniting his dominant nature. He watched her in unblinking silence, listening to her increased breathing and admiring her spirit.

To their right, a free-ranging pig crossed behind a leafy green bush in its unhurried path back into shadows.

"The pig has better manners than you. Unhand me." Scota stared into glittering eyes, a male face set in the studied quiet of sensual ruthlessness. Why the female inside her found him attractive, she would never know.

His grip loosened only slightly. Long, calloused fingers lingered over her heated skin, holding her. He leaned in and sniffed at her jaw.

"What are you doing here, Scota?" His voice pitched low with a strange raw intensity making her stomach flip flop.

She turned into him, refusing to cower, her nose nearly grazing his cheek. "I already told you. I brought you berries."

"Why would you do that?"

"Nora wished it."

He searched her face and pulled slightly back, no longer invading her space. She saw him thinking, deciphering her strength, spirit, and secrets.

"Why would she wish it, Scota?" he asked with a smooth, husky voice and relinquished his hold on her neck.

"The child seems to feel I should be thanking you for rescuing me, *Wind Herald*," she emphasized the name Nora gave him and rubbed a tender spot on her neck, leaving a trail of midnight blue berry juice. "Why does Nora call you Wind Herald, Boyden?"

"Among my people, my name means 'herald.'"

"What about the wind? Why does she call you Wind Herald?"

"Open your hands."

He loomed over her once more, effectively pinning her against the tree.

"What?"

He arched a brow. "You wished to feed me."

"I said no such thing."

He looked pointedly at the berries in her hand. "Then why are you here?" His breath mingled with hers.

To seduce you, she thought, unable to make her body move.

"Open your hand for me, Scota."

Her hand opened of its own accord.

"My thanks for your offering."

She watched with astonishment as he cupped her

hand in his own larger one, leaned down, and licked the squashed berries and juice from her stained flesh. His tongue, feather-light, stroked her flesh. She stared down, mesmerized by the tawny strands entwined with brightness and darkness. He smelled of the feral woods and of a powerful male's desire. She felt her resolve seeping away, becoming the seduced and not the seducer. His tongue caressed her wrist, sending sparks of fire into her womb. She could barely breathe. When he suckled her right thumb, wet desire spilled into her woman's place and her legs went wobbly. Pleasure spread through her blood in a female's primitive need. His mouth seared her, teeth scraping against the fleshy pad of her thumb, and she shuddered uncontrollably.

"Stop," she croaked.

He released her thumb with a soft, wet pop, and straightened.

His eyes were dark, watchful, waiting.

His chest gleamed in the obscure light, the primitive scabbard straps rising and falling with his increased breathing.

"Boyden," she protested breathlessly.

"Aye." His head lowered again, mouth brushing her cheek, pausing at her jaw line, then moving to sample her throat. "I still hunger, Scota," he murmured against her sensitive flesh, his mouth settling possessively against her pulse, creating desperation and need.

Her head tilted back, her body achingly alive under his gentle hands.

Her heartbeat increased.

The enemy.

Seducer.

Him.

Not her!

In the next instant, Scota realized what was happening and shoved him roughly away. Bolting into the dark trees, she did not know if she ran from him or herself.

Caught off balance, Boyden had her in forty steps this time. Swooping down, he grabbed a hip and dragged her under as they went down. Rolling, he took the brunt of the fall, keeping his weight off her and hitting his heel against a solid root.

Breathing hard, they stared at each other. Despite the darkness eating away at him, his body reacted to the slender feminine curves beneath. Fingernails dug into his chest, and he looked down at the small hands bound by ropes.

"Get off me, you beast."

"If you truly wish it."

She shifted and he settled more intimately in her feminine cradle, effectively stopping her struggles. Pain and desire spun a burning heat in his blood. His body hurt, unable to distinguish between passion and the enchantment of the Darkshade. Craving the sweet taste of female, the oblivion of her womb, he wanted respite, wanted to disappear into the flames . . .

"Do you wish it, Scota?"

Did she? His strength was incredible. Scota could

not look away from the smoldering gaze bathing her in hunger. His breathing was quick and uneven, a tempest beating at him. He frightened her as she had never been frightened before . . . because she wanted him, a forbidden attraction that both infuriated her and made her womanly soft.

He tilted his head, a lethal warrior curious of his prey, his gaze unblinking. "Tell me to go and I will."

She could not answer him, her breath caught in her throat.

"You did not come to share your food, Scota. You came to share your body, to bend my will to yours and ride me. Shall we see who submits?" His head bent, waves of hair falling over one powerful shoulder.

Feminine desire rose sharply in a hot storm of yearning.

The bastard.

She had come to seduce him. Instead, her craving for intimacy, the weakness she kept carefully hidden, was aiding him in becoming the seducer.

"You came for this, Scota."

Warm lips lowered . . . paused in harsh breath and misery above hers . . . then touched, a gentle caress, a simple asking.

He was inviting her to taste him.

Not forcing.

Not demanding.

Asking.

Something terrible slackened within her, a loosening of self, and to her utter horror, her lips parted beneath his pressure. He tasted of sweet berries and male mysteries, and she wanted more.

His hunger dissolved into her, made her part of him, all madness, ache, and unknowing. Her bound palms flattened against a sweaty chest of crisp golden hair, hands clenching and unclenching. For the first time in her life, she felt a strong connection with another being, but why did it have to be him?

Powerful muscles tightened under her hands, and she kissed him back, an animal sound rising up in her throat and spilling into his mouth. She burned hotly, a frantic longing to be fulfilled, to be one with him, this enemy, this male warrior of sun-kissed temptation.

Breathing raggedly, Boyden drank of her, fitting his hands on her perfect white throat, holding her in firm quietness. She opened her mouth to him in unexpected willingness, and he was losing himself in her, losing his ability to think clearly. He wanted her begging and convulsing as his root invaded her cave. He wanted his seed to find fertile ground and knew he was going to mark her with the mating bite of claim.

Scota's breath caught at the hard press of his body upon hers. He lingered over her throat, and she closed her eyes in pleasure while his decadent mouth settled over her jaw. He found that most sensitive spot on her right side and licked. White teeth scraped against her skin, causing a profound shivering in her limbs, and she tilted her head back, giving him better access.

Boyden suckled the side of her jaw in preparation.

The mating bite of the *Tuatha Dé Danann* was a confirmation of life, freely given by a male and freely accepted by a female. He shuddered, fighting the dark enchantment corrupting his mind, his body. The mating bite was a binding promise to mate, which he intended to do with her. He felt himself dying, and he wanted to leave a piece of himself with her, mayhap a son or a daughter if the gods or goddesses deemed it so.

He lifted his head. "Scota, I wish to mate with you."

Her eyes were bright, cheeks flushed with passion.

He did not wait for her response and kissed her, coaxing her with his tongue and the mating tension in his body. He moved to her cheek, trailing wetness to her jaw. Slipping a hand over her mouth to stifle a possible scream, he nipped her jaw without breaking the skin, initiating the mating bite of claim.

She jolted under him and he suckled the slight bruise, using his saliva to heal as was the way of the males of his tribe in claiming a female. His scent would remain upon her forevermore, warning other males away.

"To you am I bound," he breathed the words of his tribe's Claim of Binding in her ear. "To honor. To twilight. To land."

He took her mouth fiercely, relighting the passion within her. He felt her momentary confusion and anger, palms pressing in protest against his chest. With a quick reach for his dagger at the waist, he sliced the ropes binding her hands and freed her.

"I have claimed you, Scota," he said huskily against her

lips, dropping the dagger behind him. "Now take me."

His hunger and urgency mingled with her own. Her jaw throbbed, an exquisite and delicious sensation adding to the yearning growing in her body. The momentary surprise and hurt from his claiming, or whatever that tribal custom was, slipped away. He was kissing her throat, his hands making quick work of removing her woolen shirt. She arched into him, fingers tangling in his thick silken mane, urging him downward.

Lips sipped at her neck and shoulder, his tongue marking her with ownership. He cupped and kneaded her breasts with calloused palms, and she moaned in desperation, pushing his head down. She wanted his mouth on her. For a moment, she blinked at the hilt of her sword, rising from the scabbard at his back, an ending for both of them should she reach for it . . . but then he suckled her and she fell into the delicious sensations of him.

Boyden lathered each breast with infinite care, tracing the creamy roundness and salty curves with his tongue before descending upon each brown nipple. The taste and feel of her entered his ailing blood, momentarily blocking the pain. Fingers burrowed into his scalp, turning his insides out. Hunger welled and she reached for the loose laces of his breeches. He shifted to make it easier for her, and cool fingers slipped into his nest.

Scota wrapped her hands around the throbbing length of him, and a guttural moan vibrated in his throat. He was hard, his body trembling, a male wildness ready for her taming. She spread her legs in invitation and he released her nipple, taking her mouth in a fierce control. She suckled his tongue, holding on to him, his man root pulsing aggressively in her hands. With gentle fingertips, she measured him, stroking his responsive flesh, cupping the place of his seed. He turned turbulent like a windstorm and removed her boots and breeches. Rising between her thighs, he breathed raggedly, a warrior of dark magical ferocity.

Boyden grabbed her wrist, forcing her to release his man root. He was close to spewing his seed all over her white stomach. Anchoring her hands above her head, he pinned her, hips settling between pale thighs, his root pulsing intimately at the apex of her damp, silky cave.

She was breathing hard against him, soft breasts crushed against his chest, her body rigid with desire. From her responses, he knew she was no frightened virgin maiden. It mattered not. This was his one last chance for pleasure, one last chance to sire a child, and leave something of himself behind.

"Give me your air, Scota," he commanded roughly.

Capturing her mouth, he thrust forward into her, drinking greedily of her gasp of pleasure. She was slick and wet, able to accommodate his length and he took advantage.

Scota thrilled at his invasion. Pleasure stormed over her with ripples of shock and heat. He was moving between her thighs in a slow rhythm, meant to entice. She could barely breathe with his mouth taking hers. Her fingernails dug into the powerful arms that supported his weight above her.

In.

Out.

His hips moved.

Tortuous pleasure bloomed.

She spread her thighs farther apart, and he drove deeper in response. Longer, harder strokes sparked fires through her womb. She felt like screaming, the pressure building until it hurt, and still, he would not release her mouth.

A dull roar consumed Boyden. He could not get enough of her; he would never survive this scorching mating of body and air. Nails scored his arms, a pleading for release, and he thrust harder, crushing her under him, taking her with him to that pulsating realm of lost breath and ecstasy.

She screamed her release in his mouth, her body clenching around his root and . . . he exploded in a rage of thunder, a male climax rippling through his blood with both life and ending. He gave her all she claimed, burying himself deep into the mystical reaches of her womanhood. He gave her his seed, for she claimed him, as was her right.

Scota dragged her mouth free, struggling for air, convulsing in pleasure and liquid flames. His large body rose above hers in steam and sweat. Arms quaking, head bowed, he slipped free of her. With eyes closed, he settled next to her left side, the strength of him momentarily sapped. She glanced at the shell shape of his ear peeking between damp strands and thought distantly that now was the time to kill him and end it. *Reach for the sword and impale his heart. Reach for it.* Instead, she listened to him breathing, the sound going slow and deep, lost in exhaustion.

Scota swallowed. Out of the corner of her eye, she thought she saw a reflection of herself once more and lifted her head to see over the clean slope of his back. Standing by a tree, unmoving and dull in a light breeze, the reflection stood in a white dress with wings woven of crystals. Blinking to clear her vision, she looked again, but the likeness was gone. Dropping her head back down, she attributed the white image to the swirls of mist and moving shadows of the oak-woods.

Eyes fluttering closed, she found herself cradling him close. She recalled the memory of when she first saw him and thought herself right in her assessment. Once his spirit was tamed, he would prove useful. Peace settled in around her, a constant hum of life renewing.

"You are mine, now," she whispered, expecting to feel a sense of triumph and not this slow, dawning dread. Pushing the unsettling feelings aside, Scota succumbed to the requests of her weary body and slept.

CHAPTER 8

SHE AWOKE DROWSILY TO THE tasting and teasing of honey-sweetened lips on her own. For an agonized moment, she kissed him back, thrusting her tongue into his hot mouth. It was a luscious moment, an indulgence that she allowed herself before pulling forcibly away and staring back at him with accusation and grievance.

His lips turned into a mocking smile. "Get dressed, my woman warrior."

She looked down. Her nakedness made her fully aware of what had occurred before. All around them leaves rustled with nightfall breezes. They had slept . . . just barely. Beyond the trees and holly, she could hear the children asking the druidess questions about her. She shoved him away from her. Scrambling to her feet, she made a grab for her scattered clothes and bolted behind a thick tree.

"Doona think to escape, Scota."

In her hurried flight, she had to step carefully among the old acorn shells littering the ground, but her mouth did not cease cursing him.

He chuckled loudly at her anger, antagonizing her even more.

"Stay away from the prickly bush, 'tis hurtful to the softer parts of . . ."

"Be quiet," she said with annoyance. After taking care of her pressing needs, she reached for her brown breeches and quickly dressed. Shoving her feet through the legs, she silently fumed over her weakness for dominant, muscle-bound males.

"Scota."

She lifted her head. He sounded closer.

Taking a fortifying breath, she turned around and faced him, clad only in boots and unlaced breeches.

Her enemy lover leaned a shoulder against a near tree, studying her with a hooded intensity. Arms folded across a bare chest, she felt the kindling of him return in her body.

"We must talk," he said quietly.

Her gaze dipped to the bronze torc resting on his collarbone. It seemed almost a part of him.

"There is nothing to talk about," she replied, reaching for her woolen shirt.

"There is."

She did not see him push away from the tree as she was giving her shirt a firm shaking out. "We both took our animal pleasures, Boyden."

In the next instant, a large hand locked around her wrist, staying her efforts.

"Is that what you call it?" Warning rippled in his tone.

"Yes," she replied, feeling both desperate and angry. "What would you call it?"

He said not a word. A sudden grimace of pain tightened his features, and he released her wrist.

"Boyden?"

"Aye," he mumbled. He reached out and braced a hand on the trunk behind her and lowered his head.

"Is it the Darkshade bothering you?" she asked, peering at him.

He smiled faintly, his body covered with a fine sheen of sweat.

After a long moment, he looked up.

"Are you all right?

His head tilted. "I claimed you in the way of my tribe, a sacred vow," he declared softly. There was a strange paleness to his features, an early marker of the battle weary. "You belong to me."

"I belong to no one."

He reclaimed her wrist and squeezed firmly, forcing her to drop her shirt.

"I claimed you, Scota."

"We mated, nothing more," she argued, forcing herself to deem it so.

He regarded her with defiance. "You doona believe your own words."

"You are arrogant."

"Aye, I am," he easily agreed.

She stared back at him, a curious wrenching within

her heart. "I am a warrior, Boyden."

"You are my chosen mate." A smug smile curved his lips.

"I am not your mate, not now, not ever," she protested with a hushed denial. "We are enemies."

Heat returned in his eyes, the mark of a fiery passion. "Was I your enemy when you fed me berries from your hand?" His voice lowered to raw sexuality, caressing her right down to her toes. "Was I your enemy when you took my body into yours? You dinna feel like an enemy to me." He cupped her face possessively. "We both know the truth of what we felt."

"I felt nothing."

"Did you not?" Amusement crept into his tone. "Shall I show you again?"

His mouth found her jaw, where he marked and claimed her in the ways of his people. Jolts of lightning darted through her blood. "Your body wants me, Scota. You want me."

Her eyes fluttered closed even as she sought to deny him. "You are my enemy."

"I am your mate," he countered softly, sipping at her throat, turning her into a liar. "Want me, Scota?" A hand cupped her breast. "Want to ride me?" he asked.

She was helpless under his spell. Her breasts ached, and her womb shuddered with moist anticipation. He knew her preference, the bastard. She was drawn to dominant males, drawn to thoughts of a final taming when they lay on their backs and submitted to her.

"I will submit to you," he murmured against her ear, breath and heat and want almost as if he understood.

She hugged her thighs together.

"I will allow you to teach me, Scota, to thrust under your rein."

Her hands clenched against his chest.

"I will do what you want," he murmured with a voice laced with open desire. His mouth lowered to hers in a deepening kiss, a denial of male submission.

She bit him.

He pulled back, his bottom lip bloody.

Immediately, she regretted it and snapped, "I do not like teasing."

He lifted his hand to his mouth. "I doona tease."

Thoughts of him thrusting under her hips made her heart pound, igniting a fire within her blood. "What do you want of me?" she breathed, battling her body.

"Help me," he whispered.

She stilled at the need in his voice and the return of darkness in his gaze.

"Help you? How?"

"I know you are confused. I know you have feelings for the children and the druidess. I know you feel for me."

She wanted to rebuff him, wanted to ignore the uncertainty giving her heartache. She was a Milesian princess, emissary to Amergin, but she was not a killer of children and old women.

"Scota, there be little time left, and I need your help."

He pulled back and she saw the Darkshade fever

growing in him.

"You are a warrior, and I trust your word as one warrior to another. Will you give it to me?"

"You trust me?" she said with amazement.

"I trust your word as a warrior."

But not as a woman, she thought and gave him a nod of acceptance. He kissed her, the sugary taste of honey lingering on his tongue. Her aching breasts pressed into his naked chest and she dropped her shirt, burying her hands in the raw silk of his hair. She wanted him and was unable to help it. She wanted to feel the strength of him between her thighs; the closeness and compulsion were undeniable. She savored his mouth, pressing up against him, and he stepped back with a muttered oath, running a hand through his hair. Leaning down, he scooped up her shirt. "Cover yourself, warrior, before I am forced to submit to you again."

She drew in an unsteady breath and took her shirt from his hand. Shrugging into it, she regarded him and waited for him to speak.

"The druidess has found honey and more berries to eat."

That was not what he intended to say, she thought. "You said you needed my help, Boyden."

He nodded, looking away. "If I should falter . . ." He seemed to gather his strength. "If I should falter, I need your promise to see the druidess and children to the safety of the *nematon* and to keep my tribe's secrets."

"The Darkshade is that bad?"

He hesitated in answering, and the past seemed to glimmer in his eyes and the world shifted out from under her. The simple life she knew as a warrior was ending, and she felt strangely vulnerable. If they were to save the children and druidess, she needed him to look forward not backward. She blinked in realization. She wanted to save them, wanted to save him. "Boyden, I must ask you one question."

He nodded.

"Did you or Derina have anything to do with the killing of Lord Íth?"

He shook his head. "Neither of us or our tribe had anything to do with that."

"Do you know who did?" she asked.

"Aye," he answered slowly.

"Will you give me their names?"

He shook his head. "I was not there, Scota. I doona know the truth of the words that trickled down to my tribe in the days following the death."

"Can you tell me what you do know?"

"Nay, Scota. I willna do this. I willna spread untruths that could hurt innocents."

"Will you help me discover the truth then? I do not want my people to extract vengeance upon more innocents."

He nodded before answering. "I will help you with the time I have left after the children and druidess are safe."

She let a breath out slowly, her heart going curious inside. *Time left . . .* "Agreed."

He stood waiting.

"Share your secrets with me, Boyden. I vow to keep them."

"Your vow as a warrior?" he prompted, softly.

"Yes," she answered. "My vow as a warrior. Is this about the Darkshade dagger?"

He looked away. "I am of the between, Scota, but unlike Cavan and Nora. Their ancestry belongs to both mortal and fey. Part of my ancestry harkens back to the olden time of the primordial guardians. The Darkshade daggers were conjoined in the great battle of the before-time to quell guardians."

"What are guardians?"

"Protectors," he answered simply, offering nothing more, and she willingly accepted it.

"The captain's dagger is one of these Darkshade daggers?" she asked, beginning to understand.

"Aye, according to Derina, it is one of the olden ones."

"You are not guardian born?" she asked slowly, feeling her way.

He nodded. "A female of my line bore a guardian babe long ago. I carry the threads of that mating in my blood."

It unnerved her to think of him as magical because she did not comprehend it, refused to comprehend something so unknown.

"Blood that is susceptible to the Darkshade's enchantment?" she inquired slowly.

He nodded.

"What does being susceptible mean to you?" she asked.

He shrugged. "Madness and death."

Time I have left . . . It became all too clear. She stared at him with disbelief, struggling with her feelings. *He was going to die?* Terror and loss nearly overwhelmed her, and she pushed it deep inside. Very carefully, she said, "I give you my vow, Boyden, one warrior to another, that I will guide the children and druidess to safety." There was no greater promise to her way of thinking than a pledge from warrior to warrior, even among enemies. "Tell me where is this *nematon?*"

"Derina knows," he answered wearily. "It is not far from here."

"Will you be able to make it?" she inquired, but he was walking away.

Boyden paced Scota as they entered a patchwork field of purple and green ferns. He stopped to regain his breath, while the children and druidess moved forward along a hidden path. Chills and sweat raked his body, a lightness coming to his mind, stealing both his balance and surety.

"Boyden?" his warrior mate whispered, no doubt seeing the creeping shadows under his eyes.

He shook his head, keeping his expression unchanged, while the inside of him burned with flames and unreason. He felt strange and calm, a dreadful dwindling of his life force. " 'Tis what is expected, Scota," he replied shakily and gestured her forward. "We are near."

She walked ahead of him, her stride confident and

alert. In weakening moments, he wondered if trusting her would be the ending of them all. He adjusted the scabbard ropes across his chest. Staring at the rich night darkness of her long hair, he decided his decision was true. She was a warrior woman of spirit, strength, and freedom, and she excited his nature as no other ever had, despite the illness of the dark enchantment. In the past, he had chosen to remain alone in life because of his link with the deadly wind. He mated whenever one of the older widowed females wanted him, but had never issued a mating bite of claim, except for now.

"Is this it?" she inquired, pausing to wait for him.

Boyden nodded. In the center of a clearing, a square stone well rose before a thicket of silver thorns from a hilly backdrop of granite boulders. Four familiar stone columns grew out of the enchanted well at each end, rising toward the blue cloudless sky, tips blunted.

Around the base of the well, a small red squirrel sat among the twisting brown vines and white roses, black eyes watchful while munching on a nut.

"It is beautiful," she murmured, and the squirrel darted away.

"Beauty must be with all things faery, Scota. This is one of our primal places."

"The clearing feels alive to me, almost like it is breathing."

He heard the awe in her voice and was pleased by it. "It is a place of forces and magic. No matter the weather beyond the woodlands, warmth always seeps from the soil here, a fey gift from our brethren."

He moved closer to her, and she unconsciously moistened her lips, refusing to meet his gaze. He could feel himself nearing the end of his endurance.

"Scota."

Scota met his gaze, feeling miserable and hot. Here in the ending twilight of the most unusual time of her life, she felt the unfolding of a terrible awakening. It was a sensitivity she had always been able to beat down before, but not now.

His eyes shone with dark fever, a pulsing fervor stealing her resolve and she willingly let him. He said her womb would bloom with his seed; she had not known her heart would bloom with his trust.

"I am sorry there could not be more between us," he whispered and smiled. "I would have enjoyed being ridden by you."

"Would you?" she rasped.

"Aye, Scota." His hand reached for her cheek, a gentle caress heralding a final parting.

She hated him for making her care and hurt.

Whoosh . . .

A child screamed, "Boyden!"

They turned in unison to the clearing.

An arrow embedded itself in the ground at Cavan's feet, a near miss.

"Cavan, get down," Boyden roared, charging forward to protect the children. Nora screamed in terror as another arrow zoomed past her and then another. The child, paralyzed with fear, did not move.

"Nora, you silly nit, get down!" Cavan yelled, trying to pull her with him.

"Stop!" Scota cried into the unseen dark woods and charged after Boyden. "I am unharmed. Do not hurt the children."

"Derina, with me." Boyden scooped up the crying girl in one hand and grabbed the boy's arm with the other. Another arrow whizzed past their faces, and he checked his stride, narrowly avoiding an arrow that would have sliced his cheek.

"Derina!" he commanded.

"I come," Derina grunted, lifting her brown robes, half-limping, half-running.

"Now!" he bellowed.

Gulping in air, Scota locked her hands around the crone's thin arm and dragged her after Boyden and the children. They needed to get behind the stone well for protection; only then could she reason with the captain. Reason or kill him, she thought, preferring the later.

Another arrow flew by, and Scota yanked the druidess down, protecting the frail body with her own.

"I doona care for this," Derina mumbled, her nose smashed into the soil.

"Then move, Derina." Jumping to her feet, Scota pulled the crone with her and raced after Boyden.

What she saw next put dread in her heart. "Boyden, stop!"

He was holding Nora above the opening of the well,

about to drop the child to her death. "Stop, Boyden!" she cried out with disbelief. He was going to kill the children rather than allow them to be captured!

"Boyden!" she screamed in horror. Releasing the druidess, she slammed into him, but his balance held and it was she who hit the ground instead of him.

He looked at her briefly, turning back to the boy.

Climbing to her feet, Scota grabbed his right arm. "Stop this, Boyden. Put her down."

"Cavan," Boyden called, glancing at her sharply.

"Here." The boy climbed up the gray stones and crouched near the well's opening.

Changing tactics, Scota yanked her sword from the scabbard at his back. If reason did not work, force would. In the next instant, she held the tip of the blade pressed to the strong pulse at his neck.

"Put Nora down, Boyden."

He ignored her. "Cavan, take your sister and go into the well."

"Is it safe, Wind Herald?" the boy asked, trusting.

"It is safe, Cavan. Our brethren willna allow anything to happen to one of their own. You and Nora are *idir,* of the between. Hold your sister close to you and jump."

The boy wrapped his arms around his sniffling sister.

"No, Cavan," Scota countered loudly. "Do not listen to him! He is ill."

The boy held on to his sister, taking no notice of her protest and worry, and jumped.

"STOP!" Scota made a grab at them, but it was too

late. She leaned over the edge and looked down into the well . . . hoping frantically . . . but both children had disappeared into the long darkness.

"How could you?" she rounded on Boyden. "You killed them needlessly!"

In response, he calmly held a hand out to the druidess. "Derina."

The ancient came into his arms willingly, and he scooped her up as if she weighed no more than an oak leaf.

"Her, too, Wind Herald," the druidess said pointedly.

He froze. "Derina. The princess is not of the between and would die."

"Her, too. She willna fall. Trust me."

Whoosh . . .

A barrage of arrows whizzed by them, imbedding in stone and soil. He dropped Derina into the safety of the sacred well and reached for her.

Scota shoved his hands away. "Have you lost your mind? What have you done?"

Without answering, he knocked the sword out of her hand. "Trust me, Scota. Derina says you willna fall, then you willna fall."

She did not fight him.

He scooped her up, strong arms swift and sure.

A kind of shock set in, turning her body cold. The ending had come. It was too soon.

"Boyden." She clung to his neck.

He held her close, arms tightening for the last time.

Pivoting he dropped her, feet first, into the dark abyss.

CHAPTER 9

SCOTA DID NOT FALL INTO water-filled darkness or a cold drowning death. She landed lightly on her feet, drifting downward through air and gleam onto solid ground.

She could not believe it. Her body frozen with astonishment and wonder, she stood motionless in a cave of crystal reflections, the echoing resonance of dripping water thunderous in her ears.

"Derina?" she said hoarsely. "Nora? Cavan? Are you here?"

No answer but the sounds of the dripping water.

She fell into the mysterious below of the land with no passageway of escape other than the dark ominous opening of the well above her head. A shiver raked through her. She disliked closed-in places like ship holds and land caves. She looked up, eyes widening in realization, and quickly stepped out from under the opening to make way for Boyden.

Given his heavier weight, he would probably fall faster than her.

She waited, a frown creasing her brow at his continued absence.

"Boyden?" she called, searching the upper darkness.

Again, no answer.

She felt indescribably alone.

"You could have told me I would not drown," she muttered, looking around, then up into the opening once more.

Maybe an arrow brought him down? *No*, she thought with quick disagreement. It would not be so simple a thing as that. He did not come by choice, she reasoned and felt discarded, tossed down a well to wither and die in air instead of water. Her fists clenched in anger and she took a moment to regain her perspective. When she saw him again, she would tie him to a tree and . . . what? *He is dying.* The thought came unbidden. *Never will I see him again.* Grief welled up in her breast, choking her with misery at the mere thought of him forever gone. She would not think of it. Looking around, seeking freedom, she vented vows of retribution.

A mysterious light floated over stone walls embedded with clear azure jewels and rock gems. A tiny stream of water trickled from a crack near her left shoulder. Stepping closer, she placed her lips against the crack and drank, the cold water hurting her teeth. Pulling back, she wiped the back of her hand across her mouth.

Warm moist air flowed over her skin and over the cold rock walls, creating moving columns of vapor. About a horse length to her left, water seeped from tiny cracks in the ceiling and wall, forming a strange prism in the shape of a shield. It was the color of flickering flames. Below the man-sized shield and around the perimeter of the cottage-sized cave, bluish crystal and pink fibrous flower petals radiated upward. Portions of the wall's silvery slab pulled away as the sparkler petals reached for a never-seen sun. She took a step closer to the shield, curious of its intent, and experienced a sudden lowering of temperature, a warning of the magical.

Straightening, Scota felt caught in a void of air-filled enchantment, surrounded by exquisite crystal scenery and fragile wildness. In the dim reaches of her mind, she wondered if she were dead, a body floating in a well. Perhaps all this belonged to a place of endings. Was she being punished or rewarded? she wondered. Lifting her gaze, she again searched for Boyden in the dark, round opening of the ceiling. "Where is he?" she murmured to no one but herself.

"He willna come."

Scota spun around in surprise and faced the blind druidess. The old woman looked different. She was clean. A spotless white robe draped her bent frame where there should have been a soiled brown one. Clean white plaits fell about her shoulders, woven with twigs of fresh rosemary. She looked behind the ancient for the children, but they were nowhere among the protrusions of rock and water vapor.

"W-what?" she stammered. "How?"

"Boyden willna come," the druidess repeated. "He

knows your captain wants him and he willna jeopardize us or one of our sacred places. He leads the enemy away from us, following the path of a blooded protector."

"Captain Rigoberto is not *my* anything," Scota snapped, glaring at the druidess's empty eye sockets.

"Be the Wind Herald your anything then?"

"I do not understand you. Where are the children? Where is this place? Why are you dressed like that? I gave my word as a warrior to Boyden to bring you safely to your brethren."

"I know. The children be safe with our kin. Doona worry." The ancient gestured toward the shield as if it were a secret opening to a passageway. "This place be of the well. Only those belonging to the fey may enter."

"I am not of your tribe or of your land," she protested sharply.

"True, but your womb carries one of the between, a wind child, methinks."

Scota pressed her hands to her stomach, shocked. "How do you know? I only just mated with him. How do you know I am with child?"

"I sense the magical. Through the babe in your womb, you be sensing the magical verra soon, as well."

"You speak nonsense." She protested, yet felt strangely pleased.

"Do I?" The ancient woman smiled. "Boyden be like none other you have ever met. His bloodline be belonging to the wind guardians but also to the threads of a most ancient line, though he refuses to accept it. He be of the *rigdamnai*."

"I do not understand you."

The ancient nodded. "Listen well then, warrior princess of the invader. Boyden be *rigdamnai*, of kingly material. He be a wind descendent from a royal line of the long-ago times, a time of gods and goddesses and fury and storm."

"He is a lost king?"

"Not lost. Destined so."

"What does that mean?" Scota was confused.

"Wait and see."

"You make no sense."

"I have been told this before. Ending comes soon, princess. Do you have the courage to face it? I wonder."

A quiver of forewarning raced down her spine. "Whose ending? Do you speak of Boyden? How can he be a destined king and die?"

The druidess did not answer, and Scota looked once more at the prism shield, a magical doorway into the unfathomable.

"I can not help Boyden here," she stated carefully, concern for his safety gnawing away at her.

"Aye," the old woman agreed.

"How do I get out of here, Derina? Through the shield?" She moved closer to the prism shield. "Does it slide open?"

"Nay, the fey willna allow you entrance into their realm. You may carry a magical babe in your womb, but they consider you still the enemy."

"So be it." She would find another way. She thought of Boyden and how the captain would take advantage of his illness. "Can I climb back up?" she asked as she positioned herself under the opening in the stone ceiling.

"Aye, but first you must take this."

Scota looked over her shoulder. The druidess held up two brown sacks, one larger than the other.

"The larger one be food for you and Boyden," the druidess indicated the one in her right hand. "This other be for his healing."

The bitter scent of herbs wafted into the air.

"What is in it?" she asked, drawn in by curiosity.

"It be an olden remedy with traces of garlic and comfrey root for wound healing and other plants like purple bit for pestilent fevers and poisons. The rest of it, you would not know."

Scota knew a little bit about healing. Purple bit was a plant used by her people, too, one with dark leaves with rounded heads of purple flowers.

"Smear the green healing paste on the Darkshade wound at his temple. He will be feverish and may fight you. Doona let him. Keep the wound always covered with the paste. You must do this soon, Scota. Though his mortal blood remains strong, the magical part of him dwindles and he canna live without it."

As if able to see, the blind druidess placed the healing sack in her hands. It pulsed with warmth and life, a fey destroyer of dark enchantment. "Where did this come from, Derina?"

"Time moves differently in the fey realm. I gathered and prepared what I needed before your arrival."

Scota's brows arched with skepticism. "Boyden dropped me in the well right after you. There was no delay between us."

"Aye," the old woman replied knowingly and Scota shook her head, deciding not to question it further. She determined early on that extraordinary happenings in this land escaped reason and explanation, let alone understanding. Looping the healing sack's brown cord of horsehair over her head, she tucked it safely under her dirty woolen shirt next to her heart. It rested securely between her breasts, a promise of fey born healing. The heavier food sack she swung over her left shoulder. Catching the scent of bread, her stomach grumbled.

"You should eat to keep your strength up," the druidess urged.

"I will, Derina, but not now."

Moving back under the opening of the well, she could not detect any light above.

"Do you have any weapons, Derina?"

"The fey doona give weapons to the enemy."

"Do you still consider me the enemy?" she asked.

"Do you still consider us the enemy?"

Scota kept her attention on the ominous opening in the ceiling once more. "No longer."

"Good. You be finding what you need up there."

"All right." If time moved differently down here in the fey ways, what time was it up there? Morn? Eve?

Another twilight?

"Do you sense Boyden, Derina?" she asked, her heart heavy with concern.

"He remains strong yet."

"Are you sure?"

Out of the corner of her eye, Scota saw the druidess's perceptive smile and decided not to question this knowing either. Derina was one of them, one of those magical fey born creatures that the captain so wanted and so insisted were perfection formed. She considered Boyden physically perfect. The sightless, fey born druidess, however . . .

"Perfection be seen through preference."

Scota pulled back. "How did you know what I was thinking?"

"Your expression."

"My expression?" She shook her head. The well looked to be a long climb up, and she experienced a sudden doubt of her ability to make it. She turned back to the druidess, standing there in solid mystery and certainty.

"How am I to get up there? There are no footholds, nothing but an open shaft of smooth rock."

"Use the rope."

"What rope?" Scota blinked at the sudden appearance of a shiny black rope. It dangled in front of her face, reaching upward into the darkness of the well. Orange light glowed in the threads of the weave, and shaky laughter burst out of her. "This rope was not here before."

"So you say. Mayhap you failed to notice it."

Scota slowly reached for it.

"Princess Scota."

Her hand stayed a finger's length from grasping the enchanted rope.

"Doona fear the wind."

"Why would I fear the wind?" Grabbing the rope with her right hand, a chill climbed into her limbs, a feeling of displacement. In the next breath, she lay on her side in the open air beside the well of stone. Prickly vines curled near her hip and a white flower brushed fragrance onto her cheek.

She had returned to the outside world of mortal men. The sun appeared high in the cloudy blue sky, indicating middle afternoon. But which day?

Holding the food bag against her hip, she climbed quickly to her feet.

At the top of a grassy, elongated ridge, near the loop of the river, Boyden stumbled to his knees against the horizontal entrance stone to the tomb. He had made it to *Brú na Boinne*, the Womb of the Moon, the sacred passage tomb of the before-time. Wiping sweat from his brow, he took a moment to regain his breath.

Known by the local villagers as the Grange, the great barrow was built only of local stone and not wood. Under a cloudy blue sky, thirty-five stone pillars formed a great circle around the sacred mound, sentinels from the forgotten past.

About thirty-five horse lengths in diameter and six horse lengths in height, surrounded by decorative and weathered stones, the Grange always felt female to him, defiant of all things male. It gave him an uncomfortable feeling, and so he had not visited this place in many a long year. It was here his ending would come. *A fitting place*, he thought. Lifting his head to embrace the light winds, he squinted at the bright afternoon light, his body awash in the illness of Darkshade. In his fever, hallucinations of angry slashing winds and wailing gray-cloaked banshees slid in and out of shade. He fought it, hanging on by a mere thread.

Three days had passed since he dropped his charges into the safety of the well, three days of clouds and afternoon rain showers. *'Tis the season*, he thought.

Resting his arm on the cool surface of the entrance stone, he blinked at the five large spirals carved into it. There were additional carvings on the face of the stone, nested arcs and smaller circles, representing the female womb. Adjusting the dagger at his waist, he looked over his bloody shoulder and scanned the flowing field of wildflowers and trees.

The captain was too zealous in his wish to capture him alive. He had escaped the pig-nosed man's grasp with only a minor shoulder injury from a sword. He had taken five of his enemies down before leading the rest on a merry chase, far away from the well.

Passing through empty farmland surrounding the

local village, he headed for the *stray sod*, the enchanted faery ground that caused many to lose their way, although, for some reason, it never misdirected him. Marked by a magical talisman, like a triple-trunked hawthorn, the *stray sod* most often appeared as a small field of the bluest green. He knew his pursuers would be unable to track him through it, unable to find the hallowed passage tomb beyond.

He glanced aside at the entrance of the tomb and pulled himself up, his body heavy and slow. Forcing his legs to move, he half-walked, half-lurched under the roof stone into cool darkness, the passage sloping upward.

Swept with sickly waves of weakness, he flung his arm out too late to catch his balance. He slammed hard into one of the standing stones along the wall and slid unceremoniously to his knees. He knew he would not make it to the cruciform chamber at the end of the shadowed path, and he shut his eyes, mildly curious at his ending. Scota, Derina, and the children were safe, he reminded himself yet again through the burning and sickly heat ravaging his body. If he had been born a true guardian, he would have died within hours of the Darkshade cut, instead of days. His mortal blood gave him the time he needed to see his will done.

It was enough. His tribe was losing to the invaders. There would be other days to fight, he thought in a swirl of gray mist, or mayhap, their true destiny lay with their fey brethren in the Otherworld below. He experienced a twinge of regret that he would not be around to find out.

He believed in living in the present. The past was gone and the future uncontrollable.

His head lowered, cheek scraping against hard stone.

A whisper of cold breath touched his cheek.

He shut his eyes.

It was her, the *Gaoth Shee*.

She came to claim him in death.

Slowly, his body crumpled, the back of his head hitting the floor with a dull thud of pain, the empty scabbard at his back jamming into his flesh. Arms flung wide, he felt a sense of sorrow sweep over his sweaty flesh. Cracking red-rimmed eyes open, he saw a reflection of Scota, a shimmering of bright light, and blinked to clear his vision.

A black-haired creature of transparency and gems knelt beside him. It was her, the Elemental, the one who chose a form resembling his mate. *Now, in this ending time, the deadly wind reveals herself,* he mused in detached gloom. He heard one of the villagers call her the *Sí Gaoith*, the faery whirlwind, swirling and twisting, carrying a bale of hay up into the sky. He knew what the villager saw had not been her, not his deadly blast of feral air. His wind came of true darkness.

"What do you want?" he rasped, hearing only the winnowing wind, hollow and scraping in his ears.

The edge of his vision grayed. His eyes fluttered closed, casting him into the churning sea of nightmares and ancient realms once again.

As before, it came . . .

Darkness swirling.

Fading into slithering black mist.

Glittering firelight climbed up his sweating body.

Naked and hurting, he tugged at his bindings in throaty rebellion. He was staked to the ground again, wrists bleeding, a constant weight refusing to release him.

He flung his head back and roared in rage, feeling her within, knowing her in every pore of his being. The blood threads of his ancient ancestry throbbed mercilessly in his blood, mating with the Darkshade enchantment, leaving him open and vulnerable . . . to her claiming.

The winds picked up, and he felt her presence, felt the terrible emptiness and aloneness of her.

The *Gaoth Shee.*

Dropping his head, he stared into eyes dark with unworldly passion and frightening need. Alarm spread through him. She knelt before him, her face sculpted in the perfection of his mate, Scota. Rose-hued lips parted with soft breath, glistening with temptation.

Torn between craving her and hating her, he attempted to turn away, but found he could not move.

She smiled knowingly, a queen tolerant of her servant's revolt.

A soft white hand moved over his shoulder and slid around his nape, fingers digging into flesh, holding, dominating. Her touch sent curling warmth into his loins, a physical remembrance of a before-time when his blood flowed in a reigning king.

She rose on her knees, a graceful creature dressed

in veils of translucency, her small breasts pressing into his chest.

He struggled against her supremacy, fought her will and endless power.

Warm lips slid wetness along his jaw, and his heart slammed inside his chest. Fingers buried in his hair hurtfully, purposeful and directing. The other hand grasped his jaw, tilting his head. He felt like an animal, hungry for her.

He tasted her breath before she took his mouth vigorously in fey possession. She drank of his air and his life, a forcing of submission and servicing.

His body tightened, hardened . . . and he refused her, denied her, falsity and fear rising in him.

Laboring for breath, he tore his mouth free, the ancient craving inside coiling back in pain; he slipped once more into the desolation of the Darkshade.

She could not save him. The *Gaoth Shee* slipped away and became a cyclostrophic wind, rapidly rotating over the sacred passage-tomb, round and round, the cold outflow of anger and grief spilling into the air, adding pressure to an approaching thunderstorm. Never had she the power to save life, only the bursting of it, the becoming and forced ending of it. She was olden in the before-time. Newborn, when the land and waters formed, shaping her. Powerless now.

Powerless.

Enraged.

The will and breath in her stilled . . .

Listened.

. . . to his struggling heart.

. . . to the other's straining heart.

The one he claimed as mate had returned to the world of mortal men and was running.

She flowed down the ridge to meet her.

CHAPTER 10

SOAKED TO THE BONE FROM the fast-moving rainstorm, Scota stood beside a whitethorn tree, wringing out her wet hair.

"I should have plaited it," she mumbled and flung the wet mass over her shoulder and out of the way. At the moment, her main concern rested with the food and healing sacks. Seeing the sudden gathering of clouds, she had ducked under a nearby tree and wrapped the sacks with bunches of green leaves for protection. She inspected them and found the contents of both dry. She blew out a relieved breath. Tucking the healing sack back under her shirt, she looked up at the sky. Above her head, the booming sounds of thunder dissipated as quickly as the storm had roared in. It had been a sudden drenching and departing without even a crack of lightning. *A strange storm*, she thought.

Lavender afterglows seeped across the rolling hills now, a new foreboding in the day's ending light. She rubbed her arms and studied the radiant blades of blue-green grass dipping their heads to the breezes. The scent of the whitethorn tree behind her was rich and fragrant in her lungs.

She stood before an open field and glanced back at the triple-trunk tree. Long, sharp thorns, the size of a man's finger, sprouted between snow-white petals and green leaves. She sighed deeply. This was her third time passing it.

The sound of men carried in the air, too, and she scanned the land.

The voices were angry at being as misdirected on this enchanted patch of grassy sod as she. Scota moved behind the thorny tree. A high-pitched bellow of rage followed. She recognized that voice. It was the captain, wayward, too. The narrow-minded man had no idea of the truth of what he sought. She did, however. Having seen a mere glimpse of it, she wanted more. The unexplained fascinated her, as Boyden fascinated her. He was like the wind to her, elusive, indefinable, and compelling.

When he regarded her in those moments of stillness, she felt spellbound, a mass of quivering flesh with womanly desires. Now his seed rooted within her womb, an unexpected joy. Foolish tears welled in her eyes, and she brushed them impatiently away.

While greed continued to dictate the captain's wants, her life's path veered toward another journey. This beautiful land of blowing winds, rugged hills, and crystal lochs called to her spirit. Boyden called to her spirit. Deep down inside, she knew not all the people in this land could have been responsible for the death of

Lord Íth. She vowed to find the murderers and end the bloodletting of innocents.

She took a step forward.

All of a sudden a nipping breeze tugged harshly on her wet hair, pinching her scalp.

Scota yanked the tresses back, her gaze probing a shimmering of empty air.

She felt a wintry presence of something magical.

"FOLLOW ME," a voice sounded within her mind, the hushed tones of urgency ringing in her ears.

"Who are you?" she demanded with a rush of breath, poised for attack. Yet, no enemy showed.

The chilly wind grew slashing, gusts pushing her toward the grove of oak and yew trees at her left. It blew around her only, a singular purpose. The slender branches of the whitethorn tree were unmoving in response.

Planting her feet, she pressed her lips together, feeling a twinge of apprehension. The magical had found her once again.

"You know where Boyden is?" she cautiously guessed aloud, her voice carried away in the blasts of air. Hair whipped hurtfully across her cheeks and nose. Whatever this windy enchantment, it insisted she follow it.

"Show me," she whispered, "my unseen companion."

Pulling the wet hair out of her eyes, Scota followed the cold wind into the grove of tall trees. Urgency beat at her, and she picked up the pace.

"Doona fear the wind," the druidess had warned and so she chose not to. Legs pumping under her, she ran at a steady pace with the howling wind, a strong propelling force at her back. Storm clouds grayed overhead, casting shadows upon the large circle of pillar stones she intruded upon. She felt a momentary panic, her eyes stinging from the insistence of the chilly wind. The loud roaring of a river sounded near and she ran onward. Up a green ridge she climbed, her lungs near bursting, to the sweeping presence of a stone dwelling of white quartz. She entered a forecourt of dirt and stone. Here there was nothing but the feeling of long-ago death and sacrifice, a tomb of the unidentified. Scrambling around an entrance stone carved with spirals, she entered the tomb. "Boyden?" she called, intruding into unfamiliar darkness. She stumbled over a prone leg and landed atop him.

"Boyden," she rasped, untangling herself and pushing up from an expansive chest. Her left hand slid into caked blood on his right shoulder. "Boyden." She grew frightened at his lack of response.

His handsome face was turned away, his breathing sounding labored. He mumbled incoherently about banshees, those wailing, red-eyed creatures who presage a coming death.

She retreated off him. "I will not allow banshees here," she reassured, knowing all about those creatures of myth. Some of her people believed in them, too.

Laying the food sack near her hip, she bent over him. Pushing strands of tawny hair aside, she inspected the Darkshade wound. He felt hot.

"It festers," she whispered and pulled the healing

sack out from around her neck. Placing it in her lap, she carefully opened it . . . and froze.

White mist curled in circles near Boyden's head, and a banshee suddenly emerged in a glimmer of air. The creature appeared nearly transparent. Scota gazed calmly into a face etched in grief. Long, flowing hair swirled in a tempest around the waif form.

She did not ponder how she could see this fey born creature. Did not ponder the magic of the unborn babe altering her blood to the knowing of magical beings. Instead, she narrowed her eyes with warning. "You can not have him. Go away."

The female wraith tossed her head back and wailed loudly.

"Screaming will not change my mind. Go away, I said."

She leaned over Boyden, a destined and dying king. "This is special healing from the druidess," she explained, just in case he understood. Cupping her fingers, she scooped out some of the cool green paste, nearly gagging at the bitter stink.

She thought to clean the wound before smearing the healing mixture on his heated flesh, but this was an illness of enchantment and she did not think cleaning would make much of a difference.

The banshee continued to wail loudly, and Scota thought about punching the wraith in the jaw to shut her up.

"Boyden, you must hold still for me."

Fists clenched at his sides, he arched his back, tossing his head from side to side.

Grabbing his chin, she held him immobile and smeared the paste over the thin, ugly wound slicing his temple to his brow.

He hissed with pain, teeth bared, and tried to push her hand away.

"Boyden," she commanded, holding his chin tightly. "It must be done. Stop fighting me." She smeared the paste liberally while cursing the captain under her breath. Boyden continued to toss, his body arching and fighting some unseen force.

Still holding him by the chin, she closed the sack of healing mixture with her free hand.

"All right, Boyden. I am here now and will take care of you." She kept talking. "Derina's healing will draw the Darkshade out of you. You are not alone."

Carefully laying the sack aside, she lifted his head to her lap and forced the banshee to step back. That seemed to ease his turmoil.

"You can rest. Take ease, my brooding one. I am here and will protect you." Burying her hands in silken hair, she held him, her hands gently massaging. Shadows lived under his eyes, and his lips were cracked. The bronze torc gleamed dully on his collarbone, and she watched the shaky rise and fall of his chest. "That is better," she said to him. "Ignore the banshee and breathe for me."

Behind her, the wailing abruptly ended, and Scota glanced over her shoulder.

The banshee shimmered and was gone, a good sign. She returned her attention to Boyden.

If he had only blood threads to the magical guardians, maybe the enchanted healing would be faster. She hoped so and sat thinking about what else she needed to do to aid his recovery. She dared not think about the other path, the path of death. Reaching for the silver dagger at his waist, she sliced the hem of her woolen shirt and quietly wrapped his head, protecting the wound and covering one eye. Next, she removed the scabbard from his back and examined his injured shoulder. It appeared to have been a slashing flesh wound, not deep, not infected, and she reached for the healing sack. Smearing the stinky paste on the shoulder wound, as well, she once again closed the sack and placed it carefully aside.

"Boyden, can you hear me?"

She caressed his bristled cheek, and he groaned, his right hand clenching.

"You need to fight this. Can you wake up and talk to me? The banshee is gone, and your guardian wind nearly battered me into finding you. Wake up for me."

He did not respond, caught with unconscious agitation once again.

Scota looked outside the passageway. The storm had returned with a fierce torrent of rain and thunder. Whatever tracks existed were being washed away, and she was thankful for it. When the captain eventually found a way out of the stray sod, there would be no trail to follow. Shifting with Boyden's head in her lap, she rested her back against the stone wall and closed her eyes "Do not die on me, you oaf."

Suddenly a hand gripped her wrist so hard, it hurt. Her eyes flung open.

"I willna submit to you," he slurred, eyes fiercely shut.

She gulped in a relieved breath. "Boyden."

His eyes fluttered open, and he tilted his head back to look at her.

She looked into eyes glazed with fever.

"What—are you doing—here?" his voice broke.

"Saving you." He was trembling under her hands.

"Why? I be nothing like you," he snarled. "Leave me be."

"Boyden."

"I willna submit to you ever," he said with anger. "Do you hear me?"

Submit? She had no idea what he was talking about. "Boyden, you are hurting me."

He released her wrist and clutched at his head, trying to roll off her lap. "Her mouth eternal licks at mine."

Whose mouth? She felt a wave of jealousy for the woman in his dreams. "Derina's healing paste should help you. I smeared it on the Darkshade wound."

"It stinks," he moaned in objection, eyes closing.

"It does," she agreed, the pungent stench of garlic staining her lungs. She pushed his hands down. "Lie still. Boyden, stay on your back."

"I doona want you near me anymore," he said with a low voice.

She held tightly to his shoulders, hurt by his words, and relieved at his strong showing of spirit. "I do not want you near me, either. Now fight this Darkshade poison," she commanded firmly. "You are a warrior of the *Tuatha Dé Danann*. They be strong and courageous and a stubborn, brooding, baffling people."

"It is not her," he rasped, trapped in the agony and misery of ill dreams, "not her. I can tell." Rising to his elbow, his eyes opened and fastened on her.

"Not who?" she said, staring into raging fever.

He watched her, eyes never once wavering.

"Same face and yet not," he muttered.

"Boyden, you confuse me."

His eyelids fluttered closed, lashes dull against paleness. "Hurts."

"I know." She reached for him. "Lie down."

He placed his head in her lap once again. "Scota, not you," he mumbled, starting to toss this way and that. "Belonging to me."

"Boyden, if you do not stop moving, I am going to stake you to the ground." She adjusted his head bandage, the green paste already discoloring the creamy color of the wool.

In his delirium, he must have comprehended the warning in her tone for he quieted, slipping back into the deep slumber of illness.

Scota waited a few more moments, listening to his breathing. He gleamed with sweat, his skin a sickly greenish pallor. When she felt satisfied he would rest quietly, she eased out from under him. Climbing to her feet, she walked over to the entranceway and stared with a heavy heart at the rainstorm outside. The blowing wind forced the rain to fall sideways onto the green land. She looked over her shoulder at the stone ceiling and noted the lack of water seepage inside the great cairn. The gaps in the roof stone appeared filled with sea sand and burned soil for waterproofing. She needed to find a container to capture the rainwater for drinking.

The only possibility lay deep in the tomb, a place she did not want to go. With a heavy sigh, she moved back and cautiously stepped over Boyden.

The low growl was her only warning. A large hand locked around her booted ankle and yanked, tumbling her to her back.

Scota landed hard. He lay atop her, his body pressing her down, one forearm cutting off her airway.

"Boyden," she rasped. "It is I, Scota. You are too heavy."

Never-ending twilight pulsed in the deep depths of his fierce gaze.

She took a painful breath. "You were cut with a Darkshade dagger and battle an enchanted illness."

He eased a wee bit off her neck.

"That be not all I battle," he snarled with warning.

Gingerly, she touched his wrist. "Get off me, Boyden."

He eased some of his weight off her. Scota forced herself to hold his gaze, to reach for the honorable warrior within the dark enchantment. He had the most beautiful and unusual eyes she had ever seen, but at the moment they looked rather maddened.

"Boyden."

He flinched.

"I am here to help you. You must sense that."

He released her slowly.

Scota sat up just as slowly, rubbing her bruised neck.

"Do you remember me?" she asked. He watched her with an unblinking stare, threat coiling just below the surface like a sick and dangerous animal.

"Boyden?"

"I know you," he answered flatly.

She gave him a faint smile. "Remember? My name is Scota."

"Nay, I am not fooled."

She eyed him warily. "Who do you think I am?"

"Her."

His body promised retaliation, if she dare move.

"You must listen to me, Boyden. I am not this *her*. My name is Scota. You kidnapped me from my camp, nipped me on the jaw with some ritual bite and mated with me!" It took every ounce of willpower not to haul off and hit him. "Did you do that with *her*?"

She glared at him, eyes filled with a woman's fire, and he brought his hand to his head.

"Scota," Boyden said in abrupt recognition, eyelids closing in weightiness, the Darkshade madness releasing him. He took a deep breath.

"Who be this *her* creature?"

He chuckled low at her unexpected tone of covet-ousness. "You doona know her." He had no intention of explaining the deadly wind's claim on him and her body's likeness to the haunting in his dreams. "What are you doing here?" he asked, licking dry lips. "I thought I dropped you down a well."

"You did. I climbed out."

"I doubt it."

"I had help. Lie down," she commanded sternly, and he complied, having little strength to argue. Easing a forearm over his eyes, he breathed deeply, the misery in his blood continuing, yet lessening to tolerable levels. If the white blood of a true guardian born had flowed in his veins, he felt certain death would have claimed him long ago. Only the grace of his mortal ancestry saved him. Derina's herbal mixture was turning the tide, forc-ing the dark enchantment from his blood, changing pain to ache. He was no fool. He knew he needed help. It never occurred to him that it would come from Scota.

He heard her rise and after a long while, return.

"Boyden. Are you thirsty?"

He opened the one eye not encumbered by woolen cloth. He felt scorched inside and stank of Derina's con-founded herbs.

She knelt next to him, a slender warrior woman. Her white hands were cupped with clear rainwater. "You should drink this."

He pushed up on his elbow. Bending over her hands, he closed his eyes and drank from her as he had eaten berries from her, a kind of taming he recognized and accepted in need. Cool, life-sustaining water slid down his parched throat. His head throbbed mercilessly. His right shoulder itched with healing, and his stomach grumbled with emptiness.

"Stay, I will get more."

He nodded, remaining as he was, head bowed with thudding hurt, watery eyes closed, shutting the world out. The booming thunder and crack of lightning racked the land with fury and water, but it seemed far away.

"Here," she said with gentleness. She knelt before him once more, holding out her cupped hands to his lips. "Drink, Boyden."

Without looking at her, he drank, soothed by her nearness and attentiveness.

"More?"

He nodded.

She went away, returned, and again he drank from her offering. The fresh water glided down his throat in a resurging of life.

"Enough?" she inquired.

"Aye." He eased down to his back, feeling weakened but no less encouraged. "By the winds, I stink."

"Yes, you do. Can you eat before you rest?"

He shook his head, his stomach feeling unsteady, but it did not dissuade his pushy princess mate.

A piece of cold mutton pushed through his lips and arrived in his mouth.

He chewed, tasting no flavors, and swallowed.

Another followed and then another.

Cracking his eyes open, he grabbed her wrist to stay the next morsel. "My thanks, Scota. You eat this one."

Her sensuous mouth curved, and she nodded.

He released her.

A mistake, he quickly realized. Fingers pried his mouth open, leaving a piece of mutton behind.

He chewed, glaring his displeasure, even though he felt a wee bit better. "No more, Scota."

She nodded, and he eyed her suspiciously.

"No more, Boyden." She held up empty hands. "Sleep."

His eyes slid closed, the call of sleep painful in its demand.

"Rest and know you are safe with me," she soothed.

"Is that a promise?"

"Yes, Boyden."

Barely could he hear her response. A soft hand caressed his cheek, and he slipped into the realm of dark oblivion.

Scota watched over him a long while before getting to her feet and heading into the deepening shadows of the passage tomb. She needed to find something to catch the rainwater. Ancient burial places dotted the landscape, and although she had never entered such a grand tomb as this, she felt them all sacred and due respect.

She hoped the worshipers had left something behind she could use. An odd yellow light flowed with and around her, a feeling of magical direction and of trespass.

She paused and looked around. "Is that you?" she

asked, hearing the thunder outside and wondering if the wind would answer. The cool air did not move, and she turned back, inward bound, and entered a cruciform chamber at the end. It had a corbelled ceiling with upright gray stones. The musty scent of oldness permeated her lungs, a harking back to ancient times. The strange tiny lights continued to flow around her, lighting the intimidating shades. Near one of the three small recesses, she spied what she needed. Littering the floor around a basin stone, three chipped pottery bowls lay. There were also fragments of white quartz, water-rolled pebbles, bone pins, and four copper pendants with grooves in them. Scooping up the clay bowls, she ignored the other items and headed back out the chamber to the passage. Ornamental stone pillars, decorated with circles, spirals, arcs, star shapes, and chevrons, which were a form of zigzag lines she had never seen before, were everywhere she looked. The builders were expert craftsmen, intending this tomb to remain forever.

Stepping over Boyden, she placed the bowls outside the entrance. She cleaned them with rainwater, then drank of one when filled. Replacing the bowl, she returned to Boyden's side and inspected his temple. He did not move, but slept soundly. Sitting down next to him in the silence and the echoing call of the storm, she ate a small portion of the flavorful bread and mutton the druidess had prepared. Drinking another bowl of rainwater, she returned it to capture more rain and settled beside her sleeping enemy lover.

Closing her eyes, she sought the comfort of a much-needed rest and snuggled close to his heat. In the full winds and torrential rains, the captain would also seek shelter, thus delaying his search.

She felt they were safe for the moment. Resting her head on his uninjured shoulder, she fell into an exhausted sleep.

CHAPTER 11

SCOTA AWOKE WITH A START. She sat up and listened to the difference in the darkness, a fresh and extending silence caressing her senses. It was near dawn. She peered at the growing light spilling onto the entranceway floor of the passage tomb. The winds outside had lulled with the thunderstorm's passing, leaving behind a feeling of false tranquility that comforted. She took a deep breath and shoved the hair off her forehead.

Beside her, Boyden slept soundly, a powerful arm flung over his eyes.

Resting a hand on his firm stomach, she took a moment to study him, seeing only the lower half of his face. His nose fell straight, nostrils wide like most males. Full lips parted slightly in slumber, offering her a glimpse of white teeth. He had a strong, angled jaw. She peered closer and smiled at the tiny white scar under his chin. The shadow of a golden beard flowed halfway down his corded neck to the knob in his throat. That particular mark of maleness fascinated her, and she experienced a feminine urge to fit her mouth over it. Everything about him fascinated her. Her inspection dipped to the bronze torc resting on his collarbone. It looked old, the metalworking of a slender rope with two circles at the end. She continued her downward assessment to a body of muscular quickness and curled her legs underneath her. For a moment, she felt suspended in time, his breathing the only sound in her ears. Heat flowed in her woman's place, and her hand twitched on the crisp line of golden hair narrowing beneath his breeches. The gods and goddesses cast him to tempt and beguile the female.

Though he smelled of illness and battle, reckless wants curled inside her. Even so encumbered by a less than appealing scent, she found him extremely desirable. She needed to bathe him and found pleasure at the thought of . . . Scota's brows furrowed with puzzlement. What was wrong with her? Never did she bathe a male. Bathing another was a slave's duty. Yet, thoughts of a female slave touching the masculine slopes of him filled her with jealousy. Her thumb caressed the firmness of his stomach. He belonged only to her, her servant, her slave. *No*, she mused, shaking her head. He was neither servant nor slave, but equal in all ways to her.

Bending over him, she pressed a hand to his bristled cheek, the gold of a beginning beard rough against her skin. She found him cool, the fever gone. Easing from his side, she retrieved Derina's healing pouch. Careful not to wake him, she pulled his arm down and removed the bandage from his head. Cleaning the older green paste from his wound with her fingertips, she found the flesh surprisingly pink and healthy. Whatever made up this healing paste, it worked fast. He would have a thin scar from temple to brow, noting a victory hard won. Gladdened by his curing, she generously reapplied a portion of the remaining green paste. Using the dagger to cut another section from the hem of her woolen shirt, she wrapped his head. Next, she inspected his injured shoulder. Pushing some of the paste aside, she found the skin a pleasant shade of pink, too. With so little left of the druidess's curative mixture, she decided not to reapply any to the shoulder, saving what remained for the Darkshade wound.

With the needs of her own body pressing, she decided to venture out into the dappled dawn and walked toward the entranceway.

"Where are you going?"

Scota looked over her shoulder.

He regarded her from beneath lowered lids.

"How do you feel?" she asked instead of answering.

"Improved," he replied and asked again, "Where are you going?" There was a tone of ownership in his voice, a possessive quality that was both annoying and pleasing to her ears.

"Outside." She gestured with a wave of her hand. "I spied a small stream amongst the trees earlier and wish to bathe."

His eyes fluttered closed. "It is an underground spring, Scota. I suggest you watch out for the *undines*."

"Undines?"

"Water faeries."

"What water faeries?"

Those sensuous lips twitched with a male's secretive mirth. "They like to watch."

"Watch what?" She blurted out, suspecting the answer.

He licked his bottom lip and smiled.

"You need to bathe, too, Boyden."

"I know, later, when my head stops pounding."

"As you wish." Turning on her heel, Scota walked out into the brilliant land, butterflies appearing to drop out of the low-drifting clouds. The air was cool with the promise of warmth. To her right, sheets of gorse, golden flowers, lay across a wild meadow many horse lengths wide.

Mist rose from puddles and coated single areas of the moss-green land. She headed down the slope to the spring. After taking care of her needs, she removed her clothes and piled them near the purple haze of a hedgerow of rhododendrons.

Water sprang with exuberance from a grouping of triple boulders, ribbons rippling down into an ancient water hole unbroken in the shadow of time. The oblong pool curved sharply at one end. Testing the chilly waters with her right toe, she shivered and rubbed her arms. Resigned to a bathing, however, she made her way over slippery black pebbles and knelt where the water crested over the tops of her thighs. It was not deep. Wisps of mist moved insidiously all around her, casting unknown spells in the wavering line of bluebell and pink fuchsia flowers.

Breathing in whispers, she washed away the grime from her body and hair. She adapted to the cooler temperatures of the moving waters while keeping a careful lookout for any water faeries.

Convinced she was alone and no longer chilled, she rinsed out her clothes, stepped ashore, and donned them soaking wet.

Whoosh!

A terrible pain cut into her back bringing her to her knees. She grabbed frantically at her side.

Gasping for breath, Scota looked down at the crimson stain growing on the outer side of her left breast. The leaf-shaped flint tip of an arrowhead stuck out of her rib cage. The arrow had pierced her back, the wooden shaft lodging through her lung in painful permanence. In her mind, she knew arrow wounds to the lungs were fatal, causing massive blood loss, infection, and extreme restriction of breathing. No one survived this type of injury, and she had witnessed many to know. She had but a day before her air passages, swollen with yellow liquid and pus, closed. The bow and arrow picked off the enemy without creating an alarm. A silent killer, it had always been her preferred weapon of choice.

Pale and trembling, she attempted to inhale but a sharp pain cut off her airway.

Time seemed to slow and ebb.

A twig cracked beneath a heavy boot.

She could hear the beat of her straining heart.

The rushing sounds of the water . . .

. . . and a life near ending.

"Well, well, a pretty showing, Princess," Captain Rigoberto said, coming around to stand in front of her.

Lifting her head, Scota met her attacker's gaze.

"Lovely morn." The captain grinned, showing his yellowing teeth.

The wind began to pick up, shivering leaves and rolling twigs. She blinked slowly, trying to clear the haze in her vision.

Six hard-faced men, dressed in brown tunics and breeches, accompanied her killer. They remained apart and away from her, and she wondered which one of the four cowards carrying the bows took aim at her back.

"You have been a thorn in my side, Princess Scota, since I had the ill fortune to meet you."

Scota struggled to keep her wits about her. The captain wanted something of her or he would have impaled her heart immediately instead of her lung.

In sickly intent, his eyes roamed over her quivering breasts, clearly outlined by her damp shirt.

"You are a beautiful woman, Scota. It is a shame it has come to this. However, since you refused to share my bed, what use are you?"

She wet her lips before answering. "I am Amergin's emissary, not a whore."

"Are you?" he taunted. "Methinks the great bard did not know what to do with you and so dumped you on me."

"Not true," she said with denial.

"The Tuatha warrior's kidnapping of you provided an ideal solution for me." He smiled. "I will be grievously forced to tell the great Amergin that his emissary died in battle. Do you think he will remember your name? Do you think he shall grieve for the likes of you, a worthless woman?"

"I am not worthless."

"True," he agreed. "You are crafted for lying on your back while a man ruts between your legs. Your lovers have been exceedingly few, but speak hotly of your lust."

"Liar." Scota's hands pressed into the pain of her bleeding side.

"Tell me where the warrior is, Princess."

"Who?" she countered softly.

"Do not play me for a fool, Scota. Do you see my four bowmen over there? I could order them to aim their arrows for each of your limbs." He rubbed his chin. "Maybe a better convincer would be to toss you on your back and have all six of my men take turns on your sweet flesh."

She refused to flinch. "It matters not to me, I am already dead."

He knelt in front of her, the Darkshade dagger flashing in his hand. "I will make your death quick, a simple cut to the throat . . ." he made a slashing motion, ". . . if you tell me the location of the golden warrior. Where is he, Scota?"

"I do not know where he is," she wheezed, the colors around her gradually becoming lifeless and dull.

"Do not try my patience."

She had every intention of doing just that, every intention of setting off his temper for a quick death. She did not wish to linger in horrible suffocation while the men violated her body. Behind the captain, a strange glimmering in the air formed on the bank of the rippling spring. Scota wondered if the banshee, sensing death, had returned for her.

The strange glimmering was not the banshee.

"ENDING COMES," the reflection of herself whispered.

"Who are you?" Scota asked.

The captain's hand grasped her chin in hurtful domination. "Look at me, Scota."

Her gaze slid back to her killer.

"I am Captain Rigoberto. Tell me where I can find the warrior and I will make all this terrible pain go away."

"What pain?" she murmured.

He tapped the arrowhead peeking out of her side with the dagger's hilt, and she nearly fainted.

Fingers dug into her chin, holding her steady for the next torture. "Do not make me hurt you more."

Swallowing hard, she crafted a lie, hoping to misdirect. "The warrior left me tied to a tree. I have been trying to find my way back to our camp ever since."

"Lost, Princess? I do not believe you. I think the warrior is near."

"He is not."

"You protect him too swiftly. I saw the way he looked at you and you at him. He would not leave you, at least not before taking you." He leaned in close, releasing her chin and stealing more of her air. "I will not kill him, Scota. I only want the fey treasure."

Enough. She used what air remained in her lungs in a burst of fury. "There is no treasure except in your stupid and greedy little mind."

"Liar!" he roared, jumping to his feet in a fit of temper. A fist connected hard with her cheek, and Scota's head flew back, the warm taste of blood pooling in her mouth. Her right hand flung out for balance, fingers digging into damp soil and pebbles. Eyes tearing, ears ringing, she turned slowly back to the captain. Out of the corner of her eye, she saw an enraged tawny warrior silently slit the throats of two of the bowmen.

Boyden had come.

But he was too late to save her.

"Bitch," the captain growled, oblivious to the soundless attack going on behind him.

Scota crumpled to her side, the will to live spilling out of her in a cloak of red crimson. Cold wind blew hair off her face, and when she lifted heavy lashes, the captain had vanished. She blinked slowly, her body growing more and more chilled with each labored breath.

The reflection knelt before her, a willowy figure becoming more opaque than transparent. The faery, for that is what she thought of the slender creature, wore the sheerest white gown of crisscrossed cording. The clearest of crystals were embedded in the gown's weave and in the faery's black hair. Threads of pitch entwined in web crystal wings that folded against a small back.

"I AM HERE," the reflection murmured in her mind, impressions with no words.

Scota was no longer afraid of the unknowing, an easing gift bestowed with death's nearness. She met a hard gaze of faceted blue and rasped, "Who are you?"

Gaoth Shee came the reply, thoughts and translations meshing with her own.

"Faery Wind," she echoed low, the world pausing in an eternity of long moments.

The lovely creature bowed her dark head in acknowledgment.

Silence came to the land and Scota's ears.

Colors dulled in her vision.

The scent of the air and life dwindled.

Crimson wetness stained her quivering hands, side, and leg.

Her body felt blunted, numb, and colder than she had ever been.

"ENDING COMES."

Yes, Scota thought. *I am dying.*

"SAVE?" The Faery Wind's intentions entered her mind.

"Can you?" she asked in desperate hope, searching the smooth face.

"CLAIMING."

"Claiming?" She did not understand the meaning and heard a man's gurgle followed by a splash. Out of the corner of her eye, she saw Boyden kill her third attacker and throw the dead man into the moving spring. Three of the enemy remained, not counting the missing captain.

The faery creature tilted her head, eyes watchful and glinting. "Agree?"

"What do you mean by claiming?" Scota would rather die than give up her self.

"Become of you."

"No." She shook her head. She would not be a vessel for another, would never submit her mind and body to another's whim.

Rolling waves of desolation and terrible loneliness, not her own, engulfed her. "Stop," she gasped, her heart pounding. "I . . . stop."

A man's guttural scream pierced the air.

"If not claim, share?"

The faery creature's wants flowed swiftly into her.

The Faery Wind was a primordial being seeking release from a curse of a long and terrible isolation. Her one fragile connection to life remained with Boyden and now, with the babe growing in her womb. The mystical being wanted closeness, wanted Scota to share her body when Boyden mated with her. Not always, and not in a possession, but in the senses, touching, tasting, hearing, seeing . . . sharing.

"If I do not agree?" she countered in a breathless whisper.

"Ending then."

That was the alternative. If she did not agree, she would not live to see another twilight. Would not see her child grown, would not feel Boyden's touch ever again, would not end the war, but end herself instead.

She nodded. "So be it."

"AGREE?"

"I agree to share my body once, but only when I will it."

Not two horse lengths before her, Boyden dropped another man dead to the ground. Blood stained his arms and chest as he turned to meet the attack of the last man, one of greater height and girth, wielding a sword. The cowardly captain had gone missing, retreating to find reinforcements, a plausible excuse.

"SHARING WHEN I WISH IT," the faery creature's words forcibly entered her mind.

Scota's head lowered heavily between her shoulders. "No," she answered, losing the last of her strength.

A change came to the air, a sweeping to chilliness.

Scota forced herself to look up.

The Faery Wind, the ancient being, shimmered into circles of swirling mist.

Scota trembled and clutched her side. Her back felt like a mass of wet, red fire. *I am dying. There is no other way*, she reasoned inwardly, *no other way* and felt a momentary panic. *Boyden!* Her mind screamed with dread.

It was too late.

Bright colors danced before her eyes.

Icy cold sensations hurt her skin.

She wheezed, straining for air . . . and a glacial wind of incredible power, virulence, and mist flowed into her mouth, her nose. It stole down her throat, meshing with her heart, her lungs, her womb . . .

A silent cry of terror tore into her and, in that one defining moment . . . she became a being of dark purpose and enchantment.

Her life evaporated into the before days, leaving behind her life's knowledge, sorrows, and desires.

She became of the fey, *geayee*, of wind.

Off to the side, her enraged rescuer landed in the pool with a big splash, his dagger pressed against the bigger man's throat.

She did not blink.

Reaching behind her back, Scota broke off the feathered end of the arrow with a crack. Pushing the remaining shaft forward, she gripped the emerging flint arrowhead with her other hand and slid it clear from her bleeding body. She felt no pain. The Faery Wind within her protected her unborn child and preserved her lung.

Her lips parted, and the fey wind left her body in the exhaling of breath, leaving behind shades of ancient memories. In the bloodstained pool, three tiny *undines* watched her with fearful, jeweled eyes.

CHAPTER 12

THE EBBING OF THE DARKSHADE enchantment left him weakened, but the protective rage boiling in his blood more than compensated for it. Boyden shoved the dead man off his hips with a forceful kick and a loud splash. Rolling to his side, he pushed up in bloodstained waters.

"Scota?"

Her head was bowed in a tangle of wet black hair. She sat on her hip near the spring's edge, an arrow sticking out of her back.

He watched with frozen horror as she reached behind her back and broke the wooden shaft of the arrow at the point of the gray feathers. With a purposeful movement, she pushed the shaft through her body without sounds of torment, and his fist tightened on the dagger's hilt. *By the winds!* He could not believe her strength and courage. By the shaft's responsiveness to her insistence, he knew it was not lodged in bone. She grabbed the arrowhead appearing beneath her breast and pulled it out free and clear.

Her hand opened, dropping the bloody shaft to the ground near her knees, and she turned to the pool, no doubt seeking him among the dead.

He scrambled to his feet. In the next breath, he knelt before her.

"Scota," he said with an agonized whisper, jamming his dagger back in his waistband.

Black lashes lifted, and through a twist of hair, he stared into a waning sea of blankness. He gently tucked black strands behind delicate ears.

"I am here. You are safe."

Her eyes appeared dull and lifeless despite the tiny golden shards of light in their turquoise depths.

He let his breath out slowly.

Her eyes.

The marker of a fey claiming glittered in her eyes.

The sight of it caught him off guard. Never had he seen golden shards in the eyes of a non-blooded, but he would deal with this later.

For now, her life was threatened.

Reaching for her arm, he said the words softly, "Scota, let me see how badly you are hurt." She remained unmoving, breathing in and out, no wheezing or forcing.

He lifted the wet and bloody shirt, her lost gaze focusing on him.

"Easy, my warrior," he whispered.

With gentle fingers, he lifted her white breast and inspected the blackened exit wound beneath. A small opening appeared already congealed. He slid behind her and shoved wet hair out of his eyes. Lifting her shirt higher, he inspected the entrance wound under her shoulder blade. With the skin already purpling from the injury, he skimmed the black opening with his fingertips searching for shards of wood the shaft may have left behind.

"The wound looks clean, Scota. No pieces of wood left behind."

He came around and faced her.

Her shattered gaze, riddled with hurtful shades, drew him into her pain.

If her lung was punctured, and he suspected it was from discerning the arrow's angle, she would likely die. He did not know if he could survive without her.

Her gaze remained steady on his, trusting him to save her life.

"I must get you to safety, a place to rest and heal."

A spark of awareness flickered in the depths of her eyes.

"I am going to carry you back to the passage tomb, Scota. There remains some of Derina's magical healing paste, and I want to smear it on your wounds. If it can heal me of the Darkshade enchantment, mayhap it can heal you." He prayed silently for it to be true and scooped her up.

With slender arms locked around his neck and her head resting lightly on his shoulder, he made his way back to the Grange in the bright sunlight. The drive to keep her from harm beat at him strongly. She felt part of him, a linking deep in his bloodline. The only time he had ever felt such a connection was with the *Gaoth Shee*. She pressed her nose under his chin and he held her tightly, striding quickly up the grassy ridge.

He knew something had happened to her out there near the spring.

Never before did the faery marker of his brethren glimmer gold in a non-blooded.

Emerging from a strange dream of entangled sorrows and desires, Scota awoke slowly, trying to understand what happened to her.

Breathing in cautiously, she listened to the silence around her. Where she lay, fragrant herbs wafted in the air from a bed of green leaves and crushed wildflowers. Cool moist shadows soothed and waited, hugging close gray walls of stone. Her body felt . . . curious. No longer clenched in shock and hurt, she felt the pulse of life and yearnings.

Strange images flowed through her mind, images she did not comprehend. Her thoughts and heart remained her own except for a residual echoing within. It was a vault of knowledge of the long-ago times left over from a brief claiming of an ancient being. The Faery Wind had claimed her and just as swiftly, relinquished her. It was a promised saving and not a possession. She remained Scota, a woman of strength and decision, except . . . for the blood memories of the Elemental, except for the forevermore binding and sensing of the fey wind. Images continued to flow through her. She waited for them to dim. When they did not, she allowed them freedom and watched from within.

Many of the *Daoine Sidhe*, the faery folk, hungered for the surprise and wonder retained by their mortal kin who had not accepted, or yet passed from the inbetween. A few, like the ancient wind, ached for the experience of it.

She remembered seeing a gray seal once. When the animal popped his head out of a swell of foamy waves, she had jumped with surprise. A faery, sensing the presence of the animal, would not have been. Her thoughts returned to the primordial being who wanted much more than a simple sensing.

Scota understood the Elemental's desire for Boyden. He was the last of the mortals to carry the blood threads of her wind heritage, except for the unborn babe within her womb, and the Elemental had been too long alone.

Even the dark magical became lonely.

Slowly, Scota closed and opened her eyes in an inner shifting and acquiescence. She turned her head toward the slow cadence of male breathing, images fading into black mist.

"Good eve, warrior," he said.

"Boyden," she said achingly.

"Aye." He smiled, and her world centered into an inner glowing.

Her senses now keen in the ways of the fey, she could

hear the strong beat of his heart, the gentle rush of air in his lungs, and the grumbling of hunger in his belly. He smelled of berry sweetness, and her mouth watered to taste him.

Dark purple shadows and concern showed within his eyes along with a cold curiosity.

She suspected he sensed the change in her and took a calming breath, deep and full. He nodded.

"Derina's healing. I dinna know if it would help you." His fingers splayed over the bandage under her breast, and the heat of his hand comforted through her shirt. Any pain from the wounds was long gone.

Her senses told her they were no longer in the great passage tomb, but northeast in one of the lesser burial tombs dotting the countryside.

"How do you feel?" he asked. "You slept for three days."

"I am well."

"Does the wound hurt still?"

"It no longer hurts, Boyden."

Reaching out, she caressed his cheek tenderly.

Large fingers wrapped around her wrist, and he guided her hand back to her side.

She frowned.

"Rest, I have food and water when you are ready, then we talk."

She rose abruptly to her elbow. She did not want to talk. She wanted to taste him in her mouth, to reclaim the sweetness of life. Curling her hand behind his nape, she pulled him roughly down, her lips fitting over his in demand.

She could feel his surprise in her mouth, the tensing of male power and muscle. He tasted of fresh water, and she thirsted, her body humming.

He grabbed her wrist and pulled free. "Easy there, warrior." His voice was low in her ears.

She searched his face, not understanding.

"Why did the captain hurt you?" he questioned with quiet intensity.

She gingerly touched her side, more in nervousness than hurt. "He wanted you and I refused to tell him where you were."

"I suspected as much." He followed her hand. "Hurts?"

Scota shook her head. She knew she should be frail with injury, not restless with desire.

A long silence came and went, the rush of air and breath loud in her ears.

"What happened out there, Scota?" His voice dropped an octave, a command for information.

Truth or untruth? Her mouth clamped shut with indecision.

"You bear a fey marker in your eyes, Scota. The golden shards were not present before."

She blinked.

His head tilted with observation. "Your body heals faster than any I have ever encountered."

"Derina's healing," she offered with quick explanation.

A disdainful smile played about his lips before he answered. "Derina's healing canna add the shards of a fey marker in your eyes, Scota."

She looked away and thought that at least they were not amethyst like his, not a blooded claim.

"You were not born of this land or of the in-between of my faery kin, Scota. You are one of the non-blooded. What happened?"

She stared at the rock face, a hand's span from her nose.

"Look at me."

She turned back to him.

"What happened out there?"

"I am unsure," she murmured in truth, not fully understanding.

"Take your time and tell me what you remember."

"Pain." She turned back to the rock face and stared blankly at it. "I remember terrible pain shooting through my back and side. The captain's greed fouled my air so I could no longer breathe. His fist . . ." She touched her jaw. It was no longer tender.

"I am sorry I dinna come sooner, Scota."

She looked back at him warily.

"Think back and tell me all you remember."

"Does it matter, Boyden? Whatever happened, whatever magical intervention, it saved my life."

Some of the anger seemed to leave him and his nostrils flared.

"She did not hurt me, Boyden."

"She?"

"I sensed a female presence, not male."

His eyes narrowed with speculation. "It is true the

fey claim beauty for their own."

"A fey born shared of herself so I might live." She would give him a partial truth for now. A small part of her feared his knowing the full certainty of what happened.

He turned away and she forced calmness into her body.

"Who is this she? Give me her name. The fey doona offer kindness without reason, without want."

She looked away, unable to answer.

After a long, tense moment, he asked. "Are you hungry?"

She gave him a hesitant nod and climbed to her feet, swaying unsteadily.

He was there, supporting her, holding her close. Crisp, golden chest hair tickled her nose.

"I am sorry," he murmured into her hair.

Her arms slid around his waist, her cheek resting against warm skin.

He sighed heavily and turned her in his arms.

"Come, the food is back here, near the chamber. Can you walk?"

She nodded and leaned heavily into him.

He guided her to a deep bend near the front of a small chamber and helped her sit.

"I am not very hungry," she said, her stomach muttering with disagreement. She tugged at the hem of her woolen shirt fluttering loose above her waist, shortened from the frequent need for bandages.

He stepped away with a low chuckle. "Your body disagrees, warrior."

Mesmerized, she watched him bend on one knee,

offering her an appealing view of a tight male bottom. His height was mostly in his legs and the rest of him continued to enthrall her. The muscles in his lower back and arms flexed while he gathered his offering to her. She licked her lips, pausing, sensing . . .

Inhaling deeply, Scota lifted her nose in the air. Standing stones lined the small span of a passage outside the burial tomb. This passage grave was empty except for the moldy scent of . . . she turned and met the green jewel gaze of a large-headed spriggan. She recognized the fey born instantly, misty images of form and consciousness from the blood memories left behind by the primordial wind being. Apparently, she left some of her superior senses behind, as well.

The rock faery sat cross-legged on the oval mound to her right. He wore a green, rock-encrusted coat and pants the color of soil. Fey borns remained invisible to mortals unless they willed to be seen, and this one most definitely did not will to be seen. Yet, she saw him and attributed it to the magic of her connection with the Faery Wind.

Spriggans were minders of burial tombs and dolmans, sacred places of the Otherworld. The spriggan, a bringer of mischief, tugged on his coarse black beard. Confident of his invisibility, his green eyes studied her with vile curiosity. She could taste the creature's lust in the air. He was anxious to witness the mating of the large male with the dark-haired female.

She tilted her head, met his gaze, and smiled.

The rock faery peered at her, unsure.

Scota waved at him.

He jumped to his bare feet and winked out.

"What are you looking at?" Boyden asked, pulling her attention back.

Scota smiled warmly at her mate. "A hairy-nosed spriggan."

"A hairy-nosed spriggan," he repeated dully and looked back at the mound.

"He has left, Boyden."

Her handsome mate nodded without comment and placed food in front of her.

CHAPTER 13

BOYDEN SAT BACK ON HIS haunches, studying his lovely mate as she in turn studied the stale bread and cold mutton he had stolen from the food bags of the dead men. The tattered remains of her white woolen shirt hung from slender shoulders, unmarked by blade or dagger. The frayed laces were undone, and he caught a tantalizing view of white breasts.

His gaze slid back to her face. He did not consider himself a fool. She should have died. He had seen wounds of that type many times before in battle and in accident. Death always occurred a day or two after. He fingered the leaf-shaped arrowhead in his right hand, warmed by his skin. The smooth flint impaled flesh, but it was not magical, not spell cast, and he set it aside.

The shirt slipped farther down her arm, exposing the sleek line of her. Laces rested on the crest of a breast's tantalizing peek. He licked his lips. The Darkshade scar at his temple continued to itch in healing. It was a withering of the dark enchantment that had nearly spoiled his blood and taken his life. A true guardian born would have died swiftly in progressing misery and pain. He was not true born. The dagger attacked only the magical blood threads within him, bringing upon an eventual death. Ending did not happen because of Derina's spellbound herbal concoction and because of Scota's courage.

With a quick tug, she yanked the shirt back over her shoulder but not before a pebbled nipple poked through the laces. His lower stomach clenched, and he shifted to hide his arousal. Her efforts had saved his life. He knew it well. Since ending did not happen, he chose to no longer ponder it. He was a warrior who lived in the here and now. He breathed in. Another fragrance mixed with hers. Light and easily missed, it was a scent born of the winds. Suspicion gnawed away at him. Answers skirted his senses just out of reach. His warrior mate was a peculiar mixture of courage and vulnerability, providing a strong attraction for him. He would know what happened to her out there.

He caught her looking at him, the tip of her tongue tracing a delectable bottom lip.

"Eat." He gestured.

With a single finger, his fussy mate poked at the bread.

Reaching out, he tore off a small piece of the stale bread, plopped it in his mouth, and took a swig of water from a leather pouch. The pouch was another confiscation.

She watched him, her turquoise eyes full of strange golden intensities.

"Thirsty?" he inquired and offered the small pouch to her. She took it, her movements slow and unsure in continuing weakness. As he watched, she fumbled and nearly dropped it. They could not afford the spilling of the precious water upon the ground.

"Not like that." Scooting closer, he took the leather pouch out of her hands and held the narrow lip near her mouth.

"Open your mouth," he commanded.

Head tilting back, her lips parted in obedience. He poured the cool, life-sustaining spring water into her. The scent of his mating bite made him sweat.

Cool, white fingers wrapped around his wrist, needful in their purpose.

She drank from his offering, her gaze cast downward, her mouth and throat working until the bag was empty.

"There is no more, Scota."

She released his wrist, dropping her hand to her lap.

"I have another pouch of water," he offered, but did not reach for it. "Methinks you should put food in your belly first to get your strength back."

Beads of water dotted her lips, and when her tongue darted out, he turned away.

"Eat," he grumbled again, grabbing a leg of cold mutton for himself. He took a bite and met her hungry gaze. Barely swallowing the meat, he held the mutton leg out to her. "You want this one?"

Leaning forward, she took a small bite near his finger, the plump softness of her lip grazing his thumb.

The muscles in his stomach tightened even more.

She chewed in pleasure as if she had never tasted cold mutton before.

He could not look away from her.

She leaned forward again, the woolen shirt slipping, exposing the curve of a white shoulder. Small teeth nipped free another piece of meat. He felt caught and spell cast with covetousness.

Another bite and he broke out in a sweat.

He held the leg for her, his hand a platter from which they shared.

In amazement, he watched her go from fussy princess to ravenous warrior. One hand locked around his wrist with fierce strength while the other guided the mutton leg to her mouth. He hoped she would leave his fingers intact. She cleaned the bone, her teeth ravaging and chewing the plain fare. Finishing it in a few more bites, she sat back with a huge sigh, sated and full, clutching his wrist.

He gave a little tug and she released him with a shy smile. Tossing the bone aside, he turned back and found her eyelids fluttering closed. Hunger appeased, sleep called her to a deeper healing.

"Time to rest, Scota." Scooping her up in his arms, he returned her to the bed of leaves and healing herbs he had made for her. She lay on her back, her head lolling to the side, away from him. Gently slipping his arms free from under her back and legs, he sat down next to her in the shadows. Pressing his back to the stone wall for support, he adjusted himself, then rested an arm on a bent knee.

"Do not leave, Boyden," she whispered.

"I am here, Scota. Go to sleep and regain your health."

Her hands curled protectively in front of her face and her body relaxed.

Closing his eyes, he rested his head against the hardness of stone, his hearing tuned to the sounds of possible threat.

"We are safe," she said softly, convincingly.

"Aye." He wished he could believe her, but knew better. Somewhere outside, the captain searched for them, driven on by greed and resentment. He needed to get back to his tribe and prepare for the battle to come. He ran a hand through his hair. What was he going to do with her? She was his mate, a mistake made in the heat of the moment. Though she came from a faraway land, intent on invasion, she felt tantalizingly familiar, even more so since the arrow wounding.

He exhaled. Fatigue pushed all troubling thoughts aside. Eyes closing, he let sleep take him on a recuperative journey, the old nightmare unknowingly lost in the breath of the one he guarded.

Scota opened her eyes after a short time of rest and breathed deeply of the twilight shadows balanced outside the tomb. As long as she sensed the outside land

and air, the fear of small places remained confined. She always disliked closed-in places, but she could tolerate them if need be. Life's choices were not always formed of sunlight but sometimes of clouds and storms. And she preferred life, in all its forms, to death.

The weakness of her body felt nearly gone. She rolled to her side and admired her virile mate. His eyes were closed, lips parted in slumber. He sat with his back propped against the wall, a most uncomfortable position from the looks of it. Head tilted back, supported by a wedge in the wall, he rested. He breathed in and out in a slow cadence.

He was beautiful in the ways of a sleeping male, a poised strength, an explosion of quickness only a breath away. Lines of fatigue edged his mouth, increasing her desire to get closer to him.

As her need rose . . .

. . . so did the cold, living wind.

Strands of hair danced in front of her face, a feathery touch of recognition in swirls of glittering mist.

Boyden's name echoed in her mind along with the word *share,* laced with an Elemental's excitement, an anticipation of a mating.

Scota's fists clenched. It was time to honor her vow. "SHARE?"

"Do him no harm," she whispered with firmness.

"NEVER," came the reply.

"I remain who I am," she added quickly, staring at the circling mist.

"Always."

Her brows drew together. "You will not hurt my babe."

"Never."

She nodded. "Afterward, you will leave me be."

"Always."

"He may not want to mate," she added. "He sleeps."

"Make him want."

Pushing aside her trepidation, Scota nodded abruptly.

"Breathe." The word lingered in her mind, a stream of awareness.

Closing her eyes, she inhaled deeply. Chilled air swept inside her lungs, inside her body, an ancient being's sharing of desires and wants combined.

Scota blinked.

She pushed up on her knees, a breathing flame rising within her womb. Her white shirt dangling open, laces trailing on the ground, she crawled silently between Boyden's outstretched legs. Pausing at the apex of his long limbs, she immediately noticed the large bulge there. This was how he gave her earthly pleasure last time, his thrusts sending spiraling sparks of light and darkness through her blood. She quivered with remembrance.

The laces of his brown breeches were loose, offering her a tiny glimpse of his flaxen nest. Her fingertips brushed the tip of his root, and he stirred in sleep. Arms braced under her, she leaned in lustfully, and inhaled the light musky scent of him. Through the laces, she fitted her mouth over his thick shaft and . . .

Hands locked in her hair.

He dragged her up a hard chest.

"By the winds," he muttered in a ragged breath before his mouth clamped down on hers.

Thrill and desire arched through her womb like bolts of lightning in a gathering windstorm.

Lightning flashed through Boyden, too, and he crushed her slender body to him. Never had he awoken with a female's mouth sucking hard on him, and he reacted instinctively. His kiss, anything but gentle, reached for her passion, as she in turn demanded his. Tongues entwined, battling, plunging, he kissed her fiercely and put her on her back though he suspected she wanted him on his. She tasted of storms, a craving that could not be contained. Something untamed rose up to claim him, and he shuddered, roughly breaking the kiss.

"Doona let me hurt you, warrior," he growled low, staring down into glazed eyes.

Scota quaked within, wanting him desperately. She wanted him forceful, taking and giving. Never had she felt such yearning for a male to pleasure her. In the deep reaches of her mind, part of her recognized another's desire, but it was a small part. The rest belonged wholly to her, the passion, the yearning. She had fallen hopelessly and intolerably in love with the enemy. Unfamiliar tears stung her eyes, and she blinked at the swift understanding. *By the gods and goddesses, I do love him.*

"Scota, I am sorry." He misinterpreted her tears. Pushing back, he inspected her side, his hand tenderly tracing. "Did I hurt you?"

"No, Boyden," she answered huskily. Burying her hands in his hair, she reclaimed his lips. She would not let him withdraw, not while craving for him gnawed a hole inside her womb. She dragged him back, taking his tongue inside her mouth and suckled. Through the clothes, she felt his man root flex against her belly and wrapped her legs around his lean hips. She pushed up against the hardness of him, rubbing her throbbing cave against his root. A growl of excitement vibrated in his throat, into her mouth.

In the next moment, large impatient hands held her face, fingers tightened, and his kiss turned demanding. He tilted her head, his mouth ravenous, taking her as she wished to be taken. She battled a male's command for submission. Within her, the Elemental struggled for domination, her hunger sharp and ancient, recognizing no superior.

A ripple of unease flowed through him, and Boyden forced himself to slow down.

She was gasping for breath, and his tongue stroked across her cheek, teeth scraping her jaw where the scent of his mating claim reigned. Her legs abruptly tightened around him, sending a surge of hot lust into his blood. Grabbing her shins, he forced his release.

Scota helped him remove her clothes, pulling the tattered shirt off first. Her boots and breeches followed. Next, he quickly removed his clothes and tossed them aside. Her heart nearly stopped at the raw power of him returning between her legs. Veins clearly outlined in muscular arms, he was covered in a fine sheen of sweat, a male storm fierce and ready for her. One knee parted her legs, and his large body blanketed hers.

"*Tá tú go h-álainn,*" he murmured, his mouth returning to devour hers, matching hungers, matching dominances.

The olden words, *you are beautiful*, echoed in her mind, knowledge from the Elemental, then evaporated into yearnings. Scota shifted, reaching down firm stomach muscles for his man root. Her fingers grazed the purple tip, only to be caught, held, and prevented. Air escaped her lungs in frustration. He pulled her hands above her head, imprisoning her with greater strength, his relentless mouth moving to her breasts. His tongue swirled, teasing, suckling, driving her beyond madness.

Gasping, she fought imprisonment, hands aching to lead him to the place of hurtful needs. His root pressed against her cave, and she nearly wept in relief. Again he pressed, hard, insistent. Spreading her legs apart, she tilted her hips.

Boyden needed no further incentive. Releasing her breast, he poised above her and thrust into moist heat. She jolted under him in a cry of pleasure. He gauged her resistance and released her wrists. Bracing for balance with one hand, he cupped her curvy bottom, lifting her white hips to plunge deeper. Her body clenched hotly around him, and he fought his body's savage release, his mind tuned to the cries and tension within her. He would make her forget the existence of all other males.

Scota barely breathed, her nails scoring his shoulders and arms attempting to get closer, his body commanding hers. He thrust relentlessly between her thighs, building tension. Veins pulsed in his neck, and her world narrowed to him. Her body gripped his root with insatiable want and he answered. Deeper and faster his hips moved, answering her calling.

Tension mounted and expanded.

She could no longer breathe . . .

Light dimmed to her innermost essence, centering in her womb.

Her mouth opened in a silent cry of ecstasy and agony.

The air and all that she was went up in flames.

His body surging, Boyden thrust harder and deeper to the very edge of his control. She stiffened under him, her body strung taut in a female's provoking release. He continued pumping to keening cries muffled against his forearm, his body reaching for the unbearable explosion, raging, coiling . . . and . . . it . . . came.

Teeth clamped shut.

Head flung back.

His seed spilled into her milking womb, the world shaking within him, his body a cauldron of flames and pain, a male's tormented release.

Arms trembling, he collapsed beside her, his face buried in a bed of green leaves and wildflowers.

Sated, Scota held her mate close and waited for the Elemental to release her.

"I kept my word. Leave me now," she commanded silently.

Nothing happened.

Scota felt a fleeting panic and wondered if Boyden sensed it. Taking a deep breath, she exhaled forcefully, enacting the power of her will over a superior being.

The Elemental rose in her throat, leaving behind the faint bitterness of her reluctance. All at once Scota felt herself again.

"Did I hurt you?" her mate asked.

She kissed him gently on the lips. "No, Boyden," she reassured.

He gathered her close and rolled onto his back. Scota rested her head on his shoulder. Her arm eased across his chest, and she buried her fingers in wiry chest curls. They lay in each other's arms, hearts beating a similar rhythm, and she thought him asleep.

"Scota, I must return to my tribe."

Scota barely heard him.

The scent of mold stung the air, an announcement of arrival. Bolting upright, she glared her displeasure at the interruption materializing in the air.

Her mate was right beside her, dagger in hand, instantly alert and ready to defend. "What . . ." he muttered.

"Coming!" A green-eyed spriggan pointed, hopping on his bare toes in obvious distress. Reaching out, Scota rested her hand on Boyden's wrist, pushing the dagger down. "Boyden, I do not think he threatens, but warns us instead," she whispered.

"Coming!" the rock faery said with a voice turned gravelly with urgency. He jabbed his finger toward the tomb's entrance, his rock-encrusted coat flapping about his short frame. If she stood to her full height, the top of the creature's head would barely reach her hips.

"Calm yourself, Master Spriggan," Scota said, unknowingly tapping into the olden knowledge within her. These creatures tended to slip into frenzy when overly excited.

"Follow me." The spriggan ran past them, heading into the tomb, gesturing impatiently and muttering, "My home. No want blood spill here. Follow."

When they did not move, the rock faery yanked fretfully at his black beard. "FOLLOW!"

Scota reached for her shirt and found Boyden scrutinizing her.

"It is a spriggan," she explained, shrugging into her shirt.

"I know, Scota. I have seen them in the past. I am curious as to how you know."

She tossed him his breeches and quickly put on her own.

"He wants us to follow him," she said with a rush, slipping her feet into her boots.

"Aye, I can see that. Get dressed." Shrugging into his breeches and boots, her mate secured the scabbard onto his back with quick grace and thrust the dagger into the waistband of his breeches.

Outside the small tomb, the impatient bellow of Captain Rigoberto could be heard in the wind, way above the sounds of the other men.

CHAPTER 14

TAKING HER ARM, BOYDEN GUIDED Scota after the fretting rock faery. Though fey borns were kin to his tribe, he did not trust them, as their motives were ever a mystery until too late. As one born of the in-between, he shared neither fey nor mortal fate, but walked an unconnected path. The territorial goddesses told Derina that one of the in-between would fall from grace. He let his breath out slowly. He was not with his tribe, not defending his people, not battling the invaders. Instead, he took one to his bed, claimed her in the way of his tribe, and spewed his seed into her clenching womb. He was the one falling from grace.

"Follow," the spriggan said with annoyance, heading down the narrowing passage into shadowy darkness.

He released his unbreakable hold on her arm.

Rubbing the tender spot, she stared back at him, eyes dark with uncertainty.

"Follow," came the command from ahead again.

Boyden looked around her. "Lead on, Master

Spriggan," he answered, using her address. "Go, Scota. Follow the spriggan."

"Are you coming?" she asked with a low voice.

"Soon."

She remained as she was, an outline against sloped rock etched with circles.

"Boyden, I . . ." she ended with a stifled voice, her hands fisted at her sides.

He sensed dread in her and fought to keep from gathering her in his arms. He turned away and doubled back to check the progress of their pursuers. Men shadows were cast over the entranceway. His mouth flattened. They had run out of time.

For a moment, he thought about attacking their pursuers, then decided against it. He bolted back into the dimness on silent feet.

Rounding a narrow bend, he pushed himself between a protruding rock shaped like a dog and the craggy surface of the stone wall. These underground passages were not meant for males built to his size.

Up ahead he saw the rock faery pause between two, midnight-gray standing stones. As he came closer, he noticed the edges were carved with notches in ancient writings. The fey creature looked up at Scota. He patted the inscriptions fondly, stepped through the trickle of running water between the stones and . . . disappeared.

Water, whether a puddle, raindrop, or stream, allowed passage to the Otherworld of the fey realm.

"Follow," a gravelly voice called from the beyond.

Water provided a gateway to the fey borns of the land and to those born of the in-between, although he never traveled through water.

He looked at Scota. His warrior mate was mortal born and would be unable to follow. He would not leave her behind. Glancing over his shoulder, he realized the only way out would be to attack their pursuers and hope the element of surprise would give them an edge.

"Boyden."

He looked back.

His mate gave him one of those rare and uncertain smiles, a spreading darkness sinking into her eyes.

He tilted his head. "Scota?"

"This way." She stepped through the trickle of water to the unknown beyond.

"By the winds," he muttered with a quick look over his shoulder. Behind them, the excited voices of men on the hunt were closing in for the kill.

He bolted toward the trickle, ducked, and stepped through a cold stream of water. A strong sense of dislocation and air disruption swirled around him. His next step brought him into a small chamber of stolen treasures, and he hit his head on the edge of a low ceiling rock.

"Ouch," he snarled, grabbing his temple, and nearly tumbling backward into a pond.

Scota grabbed her mate by the arm and yanked him down into the cool shallows of an underground pool where she crouched. The gray rock ceiling, sparkling with pinpricks of starry white light, hung low even for her, but the magical luminance provided enough light to see by.

"Are you injured?" she asked and received a low growl of displeasure in response.

"Follow. Not stay here." The spriggan stood in the middle of his chamber cave, waving wildly.

"He wants us to follow," she whispered and received a withering glare from her mate. She gave him a cautious smile and faced the low chamber—and her fear of small places. Alarm entered her bloodstream, a feeling of panic washing over her. As long as she saw a way out into the light and air, the dread was contained. This chamber, however, existed in the deep shadows of the below. She blew air out of her lungs and bit her bottom lip.

"Scota?" he asked, no doubt picking up on her distress.

"I do not like the below," she offered a quick explanation and swallowed bile in her throat. Never had she felt the dread so intensely as at this moment, and she wondered briefly if the child growing in her womb magnified it. Not that she meant to lay blame on an innocent, but she heard breeding women remark of teary emotions for no apparent reason.

"If you doona like the below, then let us leave the cave as quickly as possible," Boyden said, and she could not agree more. Stepping around a white stone pillar, they climbed out of the crystal-black pool onto slabs of flowing rock. Limestone icicles, frozen in time, sprouted from the floor, rocky tables made ready for the piles of stolen neck rings and bracelets, a spriggan's horde.

Struggling for composure, her legs cold and dripping wet from the pool, Scota turned to Boyden for direction.

Boyden adjusted his bronze torc, making sure it remained on his neck. The neck ring had belonged to his older brother, who died from an unfortunate tumble off a horse. He would not part with it willingly. He took Scota's arm and guided her forward.

"I think it might be a wee bit easier on our backs if we crawl rather than try to crouch," he advised.

She dropped to her knees, pale and trembling, worrying him.

"Scota, are you ill?"

"No, Boyden. I care not for this place and wish only to return to the light of the land."

The spriggan approached, and Boyden rose on his knees to meet the creature's level gaze.

"All mine," the fey born said.

Boyden pointed to Scota. "That mine," he replied in kind to the challenge.

"Rest mine."

"I doona want your treasures," Boyden remarked firmly, adjusting the dagger at his waist.

The spriggan looked at Scota, the menace leaving his eyes and replaced by a fey born's appreciation for beauty.

"I have no need of your treasures, Master Spriggan," she reassured, and Boyden was once again reminded of her highborn heritage. He took an enemy princess as mate. His tribe would not be pleased.

The spriggan walked away and demanded loudly,

"Follow."

"If he says that word one more time, I will swat him like an insect."

Beside him, his warrior mate laughed shakily.

"Spriggans can be annoying," she murmured, automatically tapping into olden blood memories.

"He wants something," Boyden countered, wondering how she knew a spriggan's foremost trait.

"Maybe," she replied, anxious to leave the chamber.

He felt anxious, too, but for other reasons. Spriggan tales, like many of the fey borns, were passed down from father and mother to son and daughter. Scota was not of this land, not of the *Tuatha Dé Danann*, yet she demonstrated knowledge of their ways. He shifted the leather straps across his shoulders. *How did she pass through the trickle of water?* he wondered. She was blooded, not fey. Who was this warrior he claimed as mate?

He touched her elbow to get her moving. "Let us follow the rock faery before he throws a fit."

She crawled forward in the murky light, remaining close to his side, a kind of nervous laughter bursting out of her. "Talk to me, Boyden." It sounded like a plea for help, her voice tense and low. "What is your favorite food?" she asked.

"Mead."

"Female?" she asked, her shoulder brushing his.

"Dark-haired and stubborn."

She laughed unevenly. "Weapon?"

"Sword." He crouched lower so the sword hilt at his

back would not catch on a wedge of rock.

"I prefer the bow and arrow," she replied. "It makes males and females equal. We do not have the strength and quickness of males."

"Females are definitely weaker and slower," he agreed.

"In some things," she countered. "In others, we are better."

"Aye," he said, continuing to crawl over slabs of rock and packed soil. "Are you any good with the arrow?"

"Better than you."

He arched a brow. "Do you challenge me, Scota?"

"Do I?" She looked at him through wayward strands of black hair, their banter, for the moment at least, replacing her fears.

"At times," he admitted, enjoying her swift mind.

"I think you have it too easy, my tawny one."

He gave her a wicked smile. "How easy do you want me, Scota? Methinks a female like you needs dispute and challenge in a male."

Her eyes glimmered in memory of their mating a few hours before. "Next time, we see who dominates."

His stomach clenched at her seductive implication, and he hit his head on a protruding rock. "Ouch." He pulled back, rubbing the tender spot.

"You need to pay closer attention to the encroaching ceiling, my love."

Boyden caught the endearment and was unable to acknowledge it. "Well said," he mumbled.

"FOLLOW!" In the ragged darkness ahead, the

rock faery stomped his foot. He stood beneath clusters of yellow crystals that looked ready to drop and impale him at any moment. The spriggan pointed to a dark-purple crystal embedded in the wall several paces from him. It was nearly man-sized and shaped as a half-moon rock. Shafts of blue light spilled to the floor in a magical and living radiance.

Though he had never traveled one, Boyden knew a feypath's signature when he saw one.

Scota recognized the faceted marker, too, from the olden blood memories. Feypaths were dark tunnels sprawling under the land and lochs. Tremors of fear added to the anxiety already clutching at her. She forced herself to crawl into the shafts of cool light, tingles of ancient magic pulsing against her skin, a feypath's signature of deception and promises waiting beyond.

"Go," the spriggan commanded, reaching for the hidden indentation beneath. The crystal half-moon rock slid open in silence.

"Where does this feypath lead?" Boyden asked.

"Outside soon," the spriggan answered.

"Good enough. If you deceive me, Master Spriggan, I will come back and remove your head from your body."

The rock faery squealed and grabbed at his short neck. "No appreciate you."

"Oh, I appreciate your help well enough. Stay away from the passage tombs for a few days."

"Can you not wink us out to the land?" Scota asked quietly, desperately.

The spriggan looked appalled. "Nay, him too big. Flatten me."

"He is a youngling, Scota."

"Youngling?" She looked from Boyden to the spriggan and his straggly beard.

"An adult might be able to wink us out of here, but I doubt it. I am too big for them."

"Give payment now." The rock faery held out a small hand with dirty fingernails. "Pretty bronze torc."

Her formidable mate leaned into the short creature, his teeth gleaming in a menacing smile. "Think again, youngling."

The rock faery, sensing confrontation and danger, quickly winked out, and Boyden turned to her with bemusement. "Methinks he shows exceedingly good judgment for a spriggan."

His smile quickly faded.

Scota could only imagine how dread and alarm strained her features.

His warm hand took her cold one with reassurance.

"I know you dislike this place, Scota. We must continue in the below for a wee bit longer."

Panic rose, nearly choking her. "I want to go back," she said, battling revulsion, and gripped his hand tightly.

"Walk with me," he coaxed in a voice changing to gentleness and pulled her through the half-moon opening into purple smears.

The temperature immediately dipped, and he helped her to her feet in the moving shadows.

The passage was narrow but high. She heard the half-moon crystal rock close behind them in a thump of finality. Her throat closed, and Scota covered her mouth and gagged. It would be easier not to breathe.

"It smells of rotting crops in here," Boyden snorted. "Faery spitefulness, a provoking scent." He coughed, scanning the path ahead.

Scota stood transfixed. Carved out of rock and stone, the feypaths were not meant for mortal passage. A tangled canopy of brown vines and silver thorns climbed the walls to the ceiling. In the distant reaches of her mind, she knew the vines to be faery cursed, needing no sunlight for the growing.

"Come, Scota. Let us find our way out of this."

She could not make her legs move, a primordial howling rising within her bloodstream.

"Scota?"

"I can not sense the above," she croaked, nearly sobbing.

Boyden had never seen her so pale. He caught her wrist, his hand slipping down to hers. "Scota," he said, calm and low. "I willna let anything here hurt you."

She looked vulnerable, a whirlwind of fears reflected back at him.

He moved closer and stroked her hair. "Come, walk with me." His hand drifted purposely down her back, soothing and propelling her forward into the eerie dim. Drawing her trembling body nearer to his, he whispered encouragements.

She obeyed him, silent and tense, nails digging into his arm.

They walked on, a bit of force here and there keeping her moving forward. She allowed it, and he continued, her breathing rapid and loud in the silence. The absence of day and night unnerved him, but he kept going.

"I wish to go back," she said on the edge of panic, giving him a firm tug of rebellion.

He held on to her hand. "Nay, we keep going. There is no back. Walk with me. Put one foot in front of the other. Good. Keep moving."

Thick vines soon gave way to gray walls draped with folding rocks, the walls closing in.

"I want to go back, Boyden."

"I am sure Master Spriggan would not welcome our return to his home. The only way is this way. Think of the wind in the trees. Fill your mind with open fields and running streams. Walk, Scota. You are doing fine."

"There is no ending to it," she mumbled, trembling.

"There are always endings. See? Look ahead."

A few steps beyond and a bend in the passage led to two white pillars of tapering stalactite, hanging from the roof. Embedded in the wall between them, a crystal half-moon rock sparkled dully, a return to the living world.

"I see it." She covered her mouth and coughed.

He released her and stepped between the pillars. Running his hands down sharp facets, he searched for the release of the magical half-moon rock. "If I remember what Derina told me, there is a . . ." His fingers caught the indentation on the smooth underside, and he pushed the surface in. The rock slid back from his hands in a burst of cool air, and a feeling of dislocation flowed over him.

"What do you see?" she asked, arms wrapped around herself in protection.

"Darkness." Reaching back, he grabbed her hand and pulled her with him.

CHAPTER 15

SCOTA THOUGHT THE SKY TO be the prettiest blue she had ever seen in her entire life. They stood in the warm golden light of the summer sun, an easterly breeze lifting strands of their hair. "The fragrance of the land smells sweet to me," she murmured.

"Aye," he agreed heartily.

Scota glanced over her shoulder. A grouping of five horn-shaped boulders stood in a wild meadow. In the magical ways of the fey, gray-green vines crept back over the largest boulder, covering the secret of the embedded half-moon rock crystal.

She returned her focus forward and breathed deeply of the outside, the panic inside her dwindling. Ribbons of running water crossed an embankment of green pastures disappearing into purple hedgerows as far as the eye could see. In the glow of late afternoon, horses grazed with ease, noble heads bowed and tails swishing.

"I doona know this hilltop village," her mate remarked quietly to himself.

"Is it safe?" she asked, studying the small herd of white goats near a crumbling stone wall.

He shrugged.

Flowers named Meadowsweet sprang on reddish purple stems along the edges of the tiny streams, and she could see a wavering line of tall trees in the far distance.

"It is beautiful here," she remarked and felt the return of her composure and . . . the humiliation and shame of her dread.

She glanced at him, speculating on what he thought of his warrior woman now. He had seen a weak and panic-driven part of her no other ever had, or ever would.

"Are you feeling better?" he asked, simply.

"Yes," she answered and thought to explain her earlier behavior. "Boyden, I . . ."

He held up a hand. "Small places make me uncomfortable." He gave her a grin. "I tend to bump into things."

And that was the end of it.

I love you, Boyden, whispered inside her. *I love you.* She tucked stray strands of hair behind her ears. She thought perhaps she should tell him about his unborn babe, then quickly decided against it. Instinct told her to wait. It was not yet the right time to mention his babe or the sharing of her body with a primordial being who lusted after him.

He stood to her right, sniffing the air, hands easily gripping the leather straps anchoring the scabbard at his back. He was untamable, her very own tawny-maned stallion scanning his surroundings.

"What do you smell?" she asked.

"Not scent, but presence," he murmured. "I feel the *Gaot*—" He rolled his shoulders, catching himself.

"The Faery Wind?" she finished for him.

He glanced at her sharply.

"I know the *Gaoth Shee*, Boyden," she answered honestly. *I know the magical from the wind guardians flows in your blood. I know you are a descendent of long-ago Wind Kings*, she thought but did not say. They were two lineages, both demanding, both pulling him apart.

"What do you know?" he countered, and Scota felt a living hatred emanating out of him. "Tell me what you know, Scota."

She answered carefully. "My people heard tales of a lethal enchanted wind coming down from the mountains to kill."

He turned away. "The wind doona come from the mountains."

"Do you know this wind?" She asked the question, knowing the answer.

"Aye, I know it, and it knows me. The blood threads of her claim stream in my blood."

"Those blood threads are what make you who you are." *And our babe.*

"Scota, you doona know of what you speak."

"I do know."

"What do you know, invader?" he lashed out. "You come to a land to enact vengeance upon many for the death of one. You attack indiscriminately and burn whole villages."

"It was not I who ordered the villages burned."

"Who, then?" he demanded.

"Amergin."

"Your bard leader?"

"Yes," she replied.

"He will be among the first I kill."

"You will have to go through me, Boyden."

He strode to her, fury glittering in his eyes. She refused to cower, refused to back down. Catching her upper arms, he lifted her off her feet. His mouth swooped down on hers, demanding submission. It was a hurtful kiss, meant to dominate. His body pressed aggressively into hers with a potent heat, creating intolerable need.

"Never stand between, Scota," he rasped against her lips. "You canna hope to best me."

He pinned her wrists behind her back with one hand.

She allowed it, seeing the shimmer of savagery in his eyes.

"Is this how a destined king treats his mate?" she asked, reaching for his reason.

His gaze narrowed. "You have spoken to Derina." It was a statement, not a question.

"She told me you are *rigdamnai*."

"Derina is daft," he said firmly, releasing her as quickly as he claimed her, and moved away.

"Is she, Boyden? I give you that she shares little of what she knows. She is a fey born after all. Both of you told me that. But there is truth to her words, if you listen."

"Doona trust fey borns, Scota. They follow different rules than we poor unfortunate mortals. I carry the blood threads of guardians and an ancient lethal wind in my body. I am not a destined king. I am of the in-between."

He turned back to her with unblinking eyes. "Doona ever stand between me and the enemy."

Her stomach in knots, she countered, using his inflection, "Doona ever stand between *me* and the enemy."

"Confrontation comes?" A brow arched.

"Yes," she agreed.

He looked away. After a moment, he sighed deeply and held his hand out to her. "Walk with me, my willful warrior."

It sounded like a royal command and so she obeyed.

They walked across flowing meadows of feathery grasses up the slope of a hill to the rough-hewn and primitive village. A grouping of stone circles, belonging to some druid no doubt, lay to the right. In the round cottages ahead, she hoped to borrow some soap made from tallow or ash and wash every pore of her skin and every strand of her hair.

"Brush your hair in front of your face, Scota."

"Why?"

"Your eyes carry the fey marker, and these people will recognize it and be leery."

"What? Your eyes are not fey marked?"

He looked at her, the amethyst hue returning to the silvery gray as when they first met. The golden shards remained, but they were dulled and unnoticeable.

"How did you do that? Your eyes changed back."

"I am learning control."

"Does that include your temper?" she prompted.

"Nay," he said in a seductive caress. "Only you control that."

She snorted. "I doubt it."

His slow smile warmed her before he turned away.

Up ahead, a group of villagers gathered around a wooden plough, watching their approach with blank faces.

"We are farmers, Scota. Our village was burned, our home was destroyed, we barely escaped, and are seeking food and shelter."

"You do not look like a farmer to me," she offered, observing the thickness of his arms. Those muscular slopes came from sword wielding, not ploughing soil.

"Indulge me. Keep silent and let me speak to them."

"I wish to bathe."

"You need it," he offered, pulling her close with a wicked grin.

Using a spear as a walking stick, one of the village men moved to greet them. Plaits of graying hair swung about his shoulders. He wore a farmer's working tunic and breeches, woven of wool and horsehair.

They met at the crest of the hill near a stone shaped like a giant's foot.

"I am Boyden. This is my mate, Scota. We seek food and shelter. Our village and farm were burned."

"I am Aedan, village leader. What tribe are you from?"

"The *Tuatha Dé Danann*," Boyden replied easily.

"I thought so. Your female carries the shards of the fey in her eyes."

If he only knew the truth, Scota thought and stared defiantly back through her hair.

The man turned back to Boyden. "We doona want the magical here in our village. It brings trouble."

"We seek only food and a place to rest for a while, Leader Aedan," Boyden reassured. "We have traveled far and my female is in need of rest and food."

Her stomach rumbled at just the precise moment, and Scota clamped down on her teeth. The older man looked at her, nodded, and gestured them to accompany him. "Come, then. We have food."

Aedan led them through a village of small round houses and various food and herb gardens. She could smell the cooking of meat, and her mouth watered. They paused outside a small cottage littered with tools for milling grain in the side yard.

"Nia," the village leader called, tapping the edge of his spear against the doorframe. "I bring strangers in need."

A woman with flowing brown hair emerged from the cottage dressed in a gown of blue wool.

"Our simpler, Nia, will care for your female while we speak."

Scota glared at Boyden, then nodded sweetly to the simpler.

"Come inside," Nia offered, taking her arm gently.

Scota allowed the healer woman to lead her inside a cozy main room.

"You come from the faery tribe?" the healer asked as she moved about her dwelling gathering clothes and soap.

"Yes." Scota nodded. She waited near the dying embers of a fire circle.

"You doona speak as we do."

"No." She offered no further explanation and locked her hands behind her back.

"Your mate dinna look much the farmer to me, either."

"He is not, Nia."

"Good, you doona lie."

The older woman handed her the soap.

"I try not to lie." Scota sniffed the soap. The scent pleased her. It was a mixture of fragrant herbs that calmed the spirit.

"What is your name, child?" Nia asked.

"I am called Scota." Clothes settled in her arms.

"Many of the Tuatha tribe have strange-sounding names."

She did not know if it were true and so simply agreed. "Yes."

"How old are you, Scota?"

"Twenty-one summers come the end of season," she answered.

"You look younger."

"It is the dirt."

The simpler nodded, laughing softly. "You answer my questions without impatience. A woman of true spirit. Come, this way, Scota."

Scota followed the short simpler into a tiny back

room framed with colorful bunches of drying herbs.

"When I heard strangers were coming, I asked the village boys to bring buckets of water from our streams for your bathing. Aedan always brings me the grimy ones."

"My thanks, Nia." Scota walked into shafts of fading sunlight spilling onto the plank floor from the window. Warmth caressed her weary legs.

"Those pots are for you." The simpler pointed to three extremely large clay pots. "Those others be for your mate and the boys are bringing more. They will leave the water outside and wait to empty the dirty water."

Dropping to her knees beside one of the pots, Scota looked up to see Boyden looming behind the simpler.

"Help your mate and wash yourself." Nia shoved him gently forward. "I must prepare more food. I dinna think you would be so big."

Boyden nodded, his gaze troubled. "My thanks, Nia."

The simpler disappeared back into the main room, leaving them alone.

Walking around the clay pots, Boyden immediately placed the scabbard, sword, and dagger aside, then stripped out of his clothes.

Grabbing the soap out of her hand, he broke it in two and handed the smaller piece back to her. Kneeling next to one of the larger pots, he bent and splashed water onto his chest and arms.

Only the bronze torc remained about his neck, and without clothes he looked larger, much larger.

"By the winds, it is cold." He shivered and ducked

his head in the water, washing his hair with soap and rinsing. Straightening, he flung his head back, spraying her with water. "Do you plan to stare at me with needful eyes or wash? I doona think Nia would care if I spread your thighs here."

A flicker of displeasure crossed her features. "I am not needful."

"I am." He watched her with hooded eyes, an inner fire coming to flame.

With great effort she looked away from him and quickly removed her clothes. Doing the same as he, she gave her hair a thorough dunking and washing.

"When you entered, you looked troubled. Is something wrong?" she asked, trying not to shiver from the cold water.

"Aedan has seen a band of warriors roaming near the trees."

"Do you think it is the captain?" Scota asked, tossing her wet, clean hair over her shoulder.

"Aye." He washed under his right arm. "The pig nose hounds me like the blasted wind."

Scota nodded at his description of the captain. "They track us quickly."

"I suspect this village is not far from the passage tomb we were in."

"Captain Rigoberto searches in ever-widening circles. That is our way." Scota offered in explanation, washing her neck and breasts. "I would not expect him to search the land without first checking the tombs, though."

He washed under his left arm. "He may have done that. Instead of hours, I suspect many days have passed while we were in the feypaths. Derina told me time moves differently when in the fey realm."

"Days? How many days do you think?"

He shrugged. "Methinks at least a sennight."

"Seven days," she murmured without questioning him. The ancient knowledge inside her confirmed his words. "We do not have much time and should leave as soon as possible. I do not want to bring blood spill to this village."

"Agreed." He washed his lower stomach. "I must find a way back to my tribe."

She met his gaze, her hands full of soap. "Boyden. That is not the way to end the war."

"How would you end it?" He continued with his washing.

"First, you must give me your word not to kill Amergin."

"I willna give it, Scota." He rinsed himself off.

"Then I can not share my thoughts with you." She soaped her stomach and splashed water onto herself.

He dropped what was left of his piece of soap into one of the clay pots, watching her with agitation. "Tell me, Scota. I will listen to your words."

Indecision warred within her, her heart and mind battling. "Amergin can bring ending to the war. Kill him and all hope is gone."

"Go on."

"I am Amergin's emissary, Boyden. He will listen to me."

"What are your words?"

"The Tuatha tribe are innocent, as many in this land are innocent. Seek the ones who wronged us and stop the killings across the land."

"True words," he murmured with approval. "Will the bard leader listen to you?"

"I will make him listen . . . if you tell me who killed Lord Íth."

"I told you I was not there, Scota. I doona know the truth of what I heard."

"Tell me what you heard, Boyden. Trust me."

He blew air out of his nostrils, his gaze searching her face and finding what he needed. "In the north part of the land, Íth was met by three tribal kings, MacCuill, MacCecht, and MacGreine. Received in honor among them, a misunderstanding pertaining to the land somehow occurred."

"What misunderstanding?" she prompted.

Boyden cleaned the rest of the soap from his lower body and legs. "I am told Íth greatly admired the beauty of our lands. When he left to go back to his ship, the kings reflected on his words and grew worried. They believed Íth meant to return with many men and claim the land for his own."

"They killed him, thinking he would bring invaders," Scota said with understanding.

"Aye."

"MacCuill, MacCecht, and MacGreine," she whispered the kings' names aloud. "They know what happened, three men for many lives ended."

"Aye."

"We must find these kings and bring them to Amergin," she said firmly, scrubbing her legs.

Boyden climbed to his feet, clean and greatly refreshed. "Nay, Scota. We must go directly to Amergin. If he is the man you believe him to be, then he will listen to you and stop the invasion. With the help of my tribe, we then find the kings and bring them to Amergin to hear their truth or untruth."

Their gazes met and held, and Scota nodded. "Agreed."

Footfalls approached, and they both turned.

"I willna have rutting here," Nia commanded, mistaking the intensity of their glances for a sexual dance. She walked back into the room unannounced, carrying clean brown breeches and a tunic. "These should fit you, warrior who is not a farmer." The older woman laughed softly, scooped up their dirty clothes, and disappeared once more into the main room.

Boyden picked up the clean breeches. "Misunderstandings seem to happen more often than I thought."

"I suspect your condition has something to do with it," Scota offered.

Fully aroused, his body gleamed with returning health.

He looked down at himself and quirked a brow at her. " 'Tis what happens when I am near you, my warrior."

Scota plunged her face into the cold water, battling a smile. She hurried to finish up. Using a cloth to dry herself off, she reached for her clothes. "We must make haste," she remarked and paused. Instead of sturdy breeches and tunic, her hands clasped a linen gown spun from flax.

"I can not wear this," she complained, holding it up for inspection. A simple farm-girl gown, it was embellished with a thin belt under the seam for the breasts.

Boyden chuckled behind her and she glared her annoyance at him.

" 'Tis the farm gown or nothing, my warrior. Put it on."

She eyed his rough woven clothes with envy. "How about you don the gown and give me those brown breeches and tunic you are wearing."

He slipped his feet into his boots, straightened, and splayed his hands over his chest, the sleeveless tunic showing the breadth and muscle of his shoulders and arms.

"Nay, Scota. I like the feeling of finely crafted wool." His tone dripped with sarcasm. "Besides, I doona think the gown will fit me. You are shivering, Scota. Put on the gown and let us eat, rest, and be off."

"I will not wear a gown." She stubbornly refused.

"Put it on before I help you put it on."

"Try it," she challenged, teeth chattering.

He took a threatening step forward and stopped.

Outside, the sound of boys returning could be heard, and Scota hastily shrugged into the wheat-colored gown. Tying the leather belt under her breasts, she found the cloth surprisingly comfortable, the hem falling to her ankles.

She tossed damp hair over her shoulder, found a comb carved from wood, and ran it through her tangled mane until it shone.

"*Tá tú go h-álainn*," her mate murmured, watchful, and she turned to him.

"You are beautiful, Scota."

She smiled warmly. "As are you." She handed him the small comb and gestured to his wild mane while she went and retrieved her boots.

He put the comb aside. "Aye," he agreed with low laughter and ran his hands through the tangles. Scooping up the scabbard housing the sword, he shrugged back into it. The dagger returned to his waistband, as well.

"Come, eat, the two of you," Nia called from inside the main room.

"We eat, rest, and leave at dawn," he said, taking her arm.

Scota nodded, anxious to return to Amergin and stop the bloodshed.

CHAPTER 16

SHE ATE MORE THAN BOYDEN and released a loud burp to prove it.

He chuckled, squatting down to adjust their makeshift bed of white sheepskins and hay. "You ate enough for two, my warrior."

"I was hungry," she mumbled in explanation, rubbing a slightly bloated stomach.

"Aye, I saw you were. Stew, roots, mutton, goat's milk, and *drisheen*," he said with bemusement. "I enjoyed the blood pudding, too." Sitting down on the bed, he patted the edge. "Come and take your rest with me. We leave early on the morrow."

She started to untie the gown's leather belt and paused in thoughtfulness. "We should remain clothed in case of rude awakenings."

"Aye, 'tis my thought, but doona let that stop you."

Her eyes narrowed at his innocent look, and she retied her belt.

"Do you think of nothing else, Boyden?"

"I am a male." He grinned and extended his hand, murmuring, "Come, Scota. 'Tis time for sleeping."

She slid her hand in his warmer one and settled down next to him, unresisting and quiet.

Shifting to give her more room, he lay on his back. When she settled down, an arm wrapped around her, holding her close. She eased her head upon his shoulder, feeling strangely cherished, the strength of him real and solid beside her. His clean scent filled her lungs with whiffs of the simpler's herbal soap. She probably smelled the same, she thought, smiling. It was a lightly fragrant scent sprinkled with the touch of a wild meadow.

"Sleep, Scota," he murmured with a tender press of lips to her temple. "Our day will be long on the morrow, and we may not have another chance to seek our rest again. I wish to reach Amergin soon. Do you know where to find him?"

"Yes, Boyden." Warmth from his body seeped into hers, pulling her down into weariness. "He stays at the bend of a large river, near Tailtiu. Do you know this place?" She yawned, covering her mouth.

"Aye, I know it well. A land of northern hills and a river bountiful with salmon flowing northeast out to sea."

"A fine place for battle?" she asked.

"Aye," he agreed, "a fine place for battle. We will talk more on the morrow."

"Aye." She yawned, imitating him. *Aye* sounded more lyrical than a plain old, *yes*, she decided and snuggled close. After a while, his arm relaxed around her as he slipped into sleep.

They rested within an unfinished cottage next to Nia's home. The interior smelled of freshly downed trees. Aedan, the village leader, commanded they sleep here. Although she preferred the outdoors, she was too full of food to argue with him. Through the unfinished roof of twigs and labor, she watched a half moon waning in a black sky dotted with tiny stars. Warm light winds crossed the lands and lochs in a wooing of nightly enchantment. Eyes fluttering closed, she listened to her mate's slumber. It was a soft snoring, which slid into the silence of nightly animal sounds. Peace settled within her body, and she slept for a few precious hours.

Scota did not know if the nausea or the insistent whisperings of a dark dream were what woke her. In either case, it mattered not, and she eased from her sleeping mate to take care of her necessities outside the cottage. She refused to vomit in a villager's unfinished home. It would be a bad omen.

Placing her hand over her mouth and with her stomach cramping, she slipped quickly outside into the cool darkness. She made it to a grouping of three trees before the delicious meal she had eaten last eve decided to leave her stomach.

Shivering with inner chills, Scota pressed back against the rough tree bark, her body soaked in a cold sweat. After a few more dry heaves, the queasiness released her. She wiped her mouth with the back of her hand, having a greater appreciation for what females endured while breeding. She hoped this was the end of it. Never did she feel sick, never weak-kneed or trembling, and attributed it to the finicky demands of the growing babe within her womb.

"No more of that, little one," she pleaded silently on shaky legs. She took a deep breath of recovery, reluctantly admitting to a fleeting feebleness. Tucking strands of hair behind her right ear, she lifted her gaze to the horizon. Dawn trickled across the distant peaks, a gift of solitude in floating pinks and gold. She stood at the ragged edge of a wild and enchanted land, marveling at the beauty of it, and wondering if Amergin, the great druid bard, would listen to her words and end an invasion that should never have begun. "MacCuill, MacCecht, and MacGreine," she whispered the kings' names aloud and vowed to find them.

Slowly, she became aware of the absence of bird songs, and the hair on the back of her neck bristled. A blast of cold wind nearly pushed her off her feet. The word SHARE floated inside her mind, a lingering demand of lust and desire.

Scota straightened, searching for the ancient wind.

"SHARE HIM."

"Show yourself," she demanded.

The air glimmered, and a reflection of herself materialized with a silvery blast of air. The *Gaoth Shee* stood in a sheer white gown woven of crystals, mist moving in circles around her.

"Show your true self, not a version of me."

An answer of emptiness invaded her mind, of presence and need without form. The Elemental presented reflections of her intentions. She did not have a real body.

"SHARE."

Scota shook her head. "We agreed, and I allowed you to enter my body and share my senses when he touched me. I will not do it again."

The air around her vibrated with the anger of a primordial being.

"No, I will not betray him again."

"WANT HIM."

"You can not have him," she snapped.

"Oh, but I intend to," Captain Rigoberto said, grabbing her hair and thrusting the tip of the Darkshade dagger against her throat.

"I intend to have him and his fey treasure."

Foul breath brushed her cheek. In the corner of her eye, Scota saw the reflection of herself fade, abandoning her to the fanaticism of the pig-nosed captain.

"I did not recognize you in that simple farm gown, Princess Scota." Superficial charm rolled off his tongue. "You look quite young," he murmured, "like one of the girls from my village."

His lips pressed to her ear. "I like innocence. I find it exceedingly attractive to my tastes, you know."

Instinct warned her to caution. She could feel the magical babe within her womb coiling away from the press of the Darkshade dagger to her skin. Scota knew debauchery when it stood before her and unconsciously calmed in the warrior way.

"If we had more time, I would show you exactly what I like from a female." He moved behind her. "I can assure you that you would enjoy it, too. All females like what I do to them. But this morning my interest is for far richer fare. The fey treasure will bring me great wealth. Wealth to do with as I wish, for as long as I wish, and you are going to help me find it."

"Release me, Captain. You have no right to hold me with a dagger. I am Amergin's emissary."

"You are Amergin's whore." He drooled on her neck. "I care little for what you think you are."

The rustle of bushes sounded behind them. "My men grow anxious with our delay." He pressed into her, rubbing his arousal into her buttocks. "If only there were more time to show you what I like, but, alas, I must wait." He sighed. "Greed calls insistently to me, and I must answer." His hand tightened in her hair, and he pushed her forward. From the bushes, ten men emerged and followed them silently.

"Tell me where the yellow-haired faery is."

Scota refused to answer, and he gave her hair a hurtful yank, causing her to nearly lose her balance.

"A sudden thought puzzles me. I do believe we have done this before. Did I not have one of my men shoot you with an arrow?" His brows joined together as he examined her body in detail. "Why are you not dead, Princess Scota?"

"Your bowman's aim was off," she countered, seeking his anger. Anger made men foolish. "You ran away like a coward before confirming it. You are not a leader of men."

"Do not tempt me to kill you again," he sneered. His hand wrapped around her throat while the other continued to press the dagger under her jaw.

"Walk, Princess."

"You are a coward," she hissed. "Sneaking up behind me while I vomited in weakness. Give me a sword and meet me on the honor field as a warrior."

"Warrior?" He snickered in hearty disagreement. "You are not a warrior. You talk to the air and nothingness, your mind touched by the fell winds of this boggy land."

He forced her to walk into the center of the sleeping village. In the distance, an orange dawn brightened into blue skies.

Captain Rigoberto called over his shoulder to his men, "Wake the entire village. Drag every yellow-haired male of age, out of bed, and bring him to me. I will have the faery."

"Leave these people alone," Scota said.

"Shut up!"

Hearing the commotion outside, frightened families emerged from their homes with the mothers clutching their children close.

Scota hated to see fear on their faces. "Leave them be, Captain. They are innocents."

"No one is innocent in this land, especially females. Now shut up before I make you shut up." Fingers dug into her neck, and he forced her to walk forward.

"Where is the golden faery?" he demanded loudly, clasping her tightly in front of him. "Where is he?"

"I am here, Captain," Boyden answered, his tone radiating the menace and dark power residing within him.

In hurried whispers, the villagers parted to let him pass, more afraid of what he might be than of the mortal males threatening their village.

Panicking, her captor dragged her backward a step before regaining his composure.

Scota's heart went cold with what she saw.

It was Boyden, and yet not him. He appeared to be a primordial hunter of the long-ago times, one of those pledged to the dark powers, and that darkness was now stalking them. The wind swirled in gusts all about the invaders. It was a mystical guarantee of deadly purpose.

Scota lifted her gaze to eyes of amethyst rage radiating promises of retaliation. She had seen many gazes in times of battle, none compared to this.

"*Titim gan éirí ort,*" Boyden said the ancient oath aloud, letting the curse roll off his tongue. *May you fall without rising.* He took full note of the Darkshade dagger pressed to his mate's slender neck, and the fury within coiled to strike.

"If you fear meeting a warrior woman on the honor field of battle, mayhap you willna fear me," he taunted. "Come, Captain, show your men you are not a coward."

"I am not a coward!"

Boyden tilted the tip of his weapon in response.

"Prove you are not. Come and test my sword."

Air slashed the skin with sudden chill, and a child cried out in fright somewhere to his right. Boyden felt the *Gaoth Shee* lingering near, a companion of death, waiting for his summons. He could end it all with merely a thought and struggled to contain his torrid fury.

"Come, Captain." Boyden smiled invitingly. "Come meet me like the warrior you pretend to be." He circled the bastard holding his mate captive, the rogue band of males giving him room. He knew what they saw, a male of dark and dangerous enchantment, his hair blowing in wind gusts they did not feel. It had been a blast of wind that awoke him, a blast of bone-chilling howling and warning of his mate's endangerment.

"I can best you, faery," the captain said violently, "if you do not spell cast me."

"There is no need for spell cast," Boyden replied firmly, though he knew not how to weave one. "If you hurt her, I willna tell you the location of the fey treasure *ever*." *Because I will impale you with my blade, you coward!*

"You vow to battle me fairly?"

Boyden spread his arms wide, his right hand wrapped around the hilt of his sword in a lethal balance. "I always vow to play fairly, Captain. 'Tis the way of the fey. Best me and I will reveal to you what you seek." The untruth left his lips easily.

"I knew it," the captain said excitedly, never noticing the golden shards of the fey in his captive's lovely turquoise eyes. "I knew you were one of them." He shoved

Scota hard to the ground and threw the Darkshade dagger at him.

"You are mine!" the captain roared.

"No!" Scota cried.

With a quick turn and swipe of his sword, Boyden battered the ancient dagger aside. The weapon flipped, end over end, the tip embedding in the rocky soil behind him.

On the ground, he heard Scota breathe a sigh of relief. Only she knew the true threat of the dagger should it find his flesh again.

"You missed, Captain Rigoberto," he said calmly.

"I will not miss with this." The captain launched at him, his sword drawn.

Boyden easily sidestepped his opponent, centuries of swiftness pulsing in his blood. With a downward thrust, he slashed the shorter man across his ribs.

Sucking in his breath, the captain came back at him, face contorted in frenzy, yelling for his men to help him subdue the weakling faery. "Help me, and you will have more treasure then you can imagine!"

The men stepped forward, faces pale, yet assurances of wealth overriding their trepidation.

Boyden bared his teeth and attacked.

Scota did, too. Grabbing the Darkshade dagger, she slashed the back of a male's leg, bringing the aggressor down to his knees and cut his throat swiftly. She reached for the dead man's sword, climbed to her feet, and tripped on the hem of the infernal gown. Recovering quickly, she advanced to protect Boyden's back.

"It is me," she yelled, giving him notice before she met the swords of two of the captain's greedy companions. Gripping the bronze hilt with both hands, she feinted at one and slashed the neck of the other. She dropped to one knee and propelled her sword upward as the other sought her death. He held his blade high above his head with the intent of slicing her in two. A mistake. She plunged her blade into his heaving chest, a quick thrust in and out. Jumping up, she pivoted on the balls of her feet, and met the downward sword thrust of the spineless captain. Parrying his blade, she forced the furious pig nose to back up.

"I knew you would attack me from behind, Captain." She deflected his next attempt bringing her sword down to protect her stomach.

"Whore, I do not wish to fight you," he said, seething with anger. "It is him I want. Him! Get out of my way." He sought to slash at her. "Give me the magical dagger, whore, and I will not kill you." He was sweating profusely in the warm air.

Jammed in the belt beneath her breast, the Darkshade dagger throbbed with sickly darkness through the cloth of her gown. She could feel the essence of power threatening her womb.

Battling against the ill sensation, she regarded the captain steadily. She knew that as long as the blade did not cut her flesh, it could do no harm to her or her babe.

The captain attacked and she deflected all attempts to remove her head from her neck.

"Give the dagger to me, whore."

She advanced, extending her sword arm. "Try and take the dagger from me. Come, Captain Rigoberto, see if you can best a mere female." She goaded him, wanting him to strike. She would not be bested, not by him.

"Scota!" Boyden called from somewhere behind her, the clang of swords ringing in the air.

"I am fine," she reassured, her eyes never leaving her enemy.

The captain feinted right, intent on impaling her heart. Knocking his foolish effort aside with a quick swipe of her sword, she stepped around him, forcing him to balance on his weaker side. She had seen him in battle and knew how he fought. She counterattacked with serene ferocity, a warrior true in heart and diligence, a female shielding her mate.

"You stupid bitch!" He came after her, his face mottled in rage. She evaded, deflected, and dodged with accuracy and grace.

"I am the stronger here!" he yelled. "You are worthless." All his charm had long ago disappeared. His cheeks grew more crimson, and he changed tactics, plunging to avoid the engaging force of her sword and . . . she had him.

With a loud chink, their weapons met. Forcing his blade high, she reached for the Darkshade dagger at her waist . . .

. . . and another stepped into her field of vision. She pivoted and flung the dagger into the other attacker.

It left her side open.

Spinning back, she tripped on her hem, a breath too late to defend herself.

A loud crack resonated a hand's length in front of her nose. She blinked at the silvery blade dripping with blood.

Boyden.

His sword blocked the captain's swipe from taking off her head.

With superior strength, he shoved the smaller man back.

"Coward," her infuriated mate snarled. "Attacking her from behind!"

In the next moment, Captain Rigoberto screamed a bloodcurdling cry of surprise and rage. He stumbled back. His sword toppled out of his hand and landed on the ground with a loud thwack.

With eyes bulging in astonishment, the captain coughed crimson spittle down his chin. Blood shooting out of his throat like a waterfall, she watched him fall backward, dying almost instantly.

Spinning around, she pulled the Darkshade dagger out of the chest of the dead attacker. With a sword in one hand and the dagger in the other, she planted her feet wide . . . breathless and intent for the next attack.

None came.

The battle was over.

She looked to Boyden.

Boyden walked over to the seven dead men on the ground, their arms sprawled wide in a last fruitless attempt to claim their prize. The three remaining attackers, cowards in all, were running away down the slope of the hill, never looking back.

He looked over his shoulder and his blood-spattered mate grinned triumphantly at him.

Against greater numbers, they had fought and won.

He could easily wrap Scota in his arms and kiss her fiercely in joy. However, since hostile villagers surrounded them, he decided to wait on their celebration.

"You have brought blood spill to our village," Leader Aedan said angrily, walking up to him.

Taking a deep breath, Boyden prepared to face the irate older man calmly. " 'Twas never my intention to bring harm to your village, Leader Aedan."

"Yet, you did," the leader grunted, some of his initial anger waning.

"I canna control the actions of others and ask you to consider this in your decision of us. Were any hurt in your village?"

They both turned, searching the worried faces, and Boyden grew thankful at what he saw.

"It dinna seem so," Aedan answered for his people after a moment. "Frightened, but not hurt."

Boyden nodded and wiped the blood from his blade on the brown tunic of one of the dead men. "Invaders come to our lands, Leader Aedan." With a quick shift, he slid the sword back into the scabbard at his back. "Your people have been blessed that war has not yet reached your homes."

"We are safe here," the leader agreed wearily. "The

hill protects us."

"You are not safe. It is foolish to believe it so," Scota challenged, joining Boyden. She felt a bit shaky and jammed the Darkshade dagger back into her belt.

"Scota." Boyden motioned her to silence with a warning glance and turned back to address the concerns of the upset leader.

It was a good thing for she felt weakness coming over her.

"We will leave your village," her mate offered while the world seemed to gray and dim around the edges.

"Aye, methinks it best you do."

Scota heard little else. She tried to reach out for Boyden but found she could not lift her arm. Her world tilted, and her legs gave out from under her. She crumpled in a dead faint.

CHAPTER 17

"Scota!" Boyden caught her before her head could hit the ground. His heart pounded in his chest, as it never did during battle. Kneeling, he cradled her protectively. Suddenly afraid, he searched her body for any kind of injury.

"How bad is she hurt?" Aedan asked, leaning over him, casting shadows across his mate's face.

"I doona know. I canna find any wound."

"Boyden, bring her to my home," the simpler Nia said, touching his shoulder. Her tone was laced with the sympathy of a healer. "I will see to her care."

"They canna stay." Aedan straightened, addressing his concerns with the simpler.

Nia greatly disagreed, though nodded. "I understand Aedan. I ask only for time to see to her well-being before you send them away."

"Do it swiftly, simpler. More trouble follows them, and I willna have our people caught in the between of it. They are fey cast, and you know my feelings about the magical."

"I understand." Nia nodded again with patience.

Having stated his preference, the leader walked away and motioned to several of the villager men, calling them by name. "Come and help me bury the dead far away from our village. Beyond the trees, methinks. I doona want their stink leeching into our crops."

Boyden ignored everyone but his unconscious mate. Her cheeks were pale, and her skin far too cold to his touch. He checked each of her limbs for wounds. Finding nothing, he focused his search on her shoulders, breasts, stomach, and then lower. Turning her over, he inspected her back and bottom, running his hand over every curve.

"Come, Boyden." Nia tapped his shoulder.

Ignoring the simpler, he turned Scota over, whispering a silent prayer to the gods and goddesses to heal his mate of the unseen injury. He buried his hands in her hair, searching her scalp.

"Boyden, I ask you to bring her to my home so I can tend to her. You can do nothing here."

He gave a quick nod and lifted Scota in his arms. Her head rolled listlessly to the side. Shifting her slight weight in his arms, he scanned the surroundings for threat. Many villagers turned their faces away in apprehension of him. They reacted this way because an outsider had named him faery and he was once again reminded of their prejudices against the fey.

"They fear what they doona understand, Boyden. Doona judge them too harshly," the simpler tried to explain.

He had seen this reaction often times before. Most of the other tribes feared what they did not understand, feared the warriors of the *Tuatha Dé Danann*.

Cradling his injured mate in his arms, he looked down at the simpler. "Do you fear me, Nia?"

"Nay, Boyden." She pulled on his wrist. "Come, your enemy be gone. You are safe for now. Carry Scota to my home, away from these gawking faces."

Holding Scota close, he followed the simpler back up the trodden slope to her round cottage. He listened to her breathing and with a quick adjustment, tucked her head under his chin.

"Doona leave me, Scota," he said low, barely above a croak. "I canna breathe with the thought of you gone from me."

Eyelashes fluttered feather light against his chin, and his heart lurched within his chest.

"Why would I leave?" she mumbled, not fully awake. She blinked up at him, momentary blankness dulling the turquoise hue of her eyes.

"What happened?" She rubbed her temple. "Why are you carrying me?"

"You fainted," he replied, his heart easing.

"I do not faint," she grumbled with denial and rested her head back against his shoulder, arms wrapping around his neck. "Put me down."

"In a moment." He managed a smile at her curt command and walked into the simpler's cottage. It was shadowy inside, and he followed the healer to another one of her small, herb-scented rooms to the left.

"Place her on my bed, Boyden." The simpler gestured with a wave of her hand and turned to move a wooden table of decorated combs and bones out of the way.

"I am fine," Scota protested, which he ignored. Avoiding a pair of simple, one-piece, rawhide shoes on the floor, he gently eased her down onto a bed of colorful woven blankets and moved back.

"This is needless," his warrior mate groaned aloud. "I want only some water to quench my thirst."

The simpler sat down on the edge of the bed. "Boyden, I have water in the main room. If you would be so kind as to fetch some, I will look to her."

"I do not need looking after."

Boyden ignored that comment, too. His lips quirking, he went in search of goblets or leather bags to serve as containers for the water.

Ready to argue, Scota turned her attention to the simpler.

"Hush now, Scota," Nia commanded, taking charge in the time-honored fashion of a village wise woman.

Undaunted, Scota continued to glare in rebellion at the older woman. As a warrior, she had experienced many wounds in battle, but never did she faint for no apparent reason. It was . . . embarrassing. The problem, she quickly decided, was the unborn babe stealing her strength and the simpler watching her with an all-too-knowing gaze.

"You doona seem to be cut anywhere."

"I am not," she replied firmly. The fragrance of herbs wafted in the air, and she detected the soothing scent of almonds. Meadowsweet, she thought. The creamy, white-flowered plant was favored among all healers, and she remembered it growing down by the tiny streams. Her people's wise women dried the plant and added it to warmed water flavored with honey. It cleared many a stuffy head and made the senses joyful. These people, she mused, were not so different from hers.

"My thanks, Nia, but I am well and do not need tending." She tried to sit up, but the healer pushed her back down. It was a gentle but firm command for obedience. "Rest a moment, Scota. Do you hurt anywhere?"

Scota shook her head, reluctantly admiring the stubbornness and compassion of this woman. "No," she answered, expecting that to be the end of it. Unfortunately, the simpler did not seem to understand.

"When was your last moon time, Scota? When did your womb bleed?"

Scota's bit her lip. "Why would it matter?"

"Methinks you know why."

She clasped her hands on her stomach, the hilt of the Darkshade dagger pressing into her wrist with a nauseating heat. "I do not remember," she answered and changed the subject. "Do you have a cloth?"

"Why?"

"I wish to wrap my dagger."

It was obvious the simpler thought her response odd, but she reached behind her for a scrap of clean wool. Scota took the cloth, pulled the dagger from her waist, wrapped it thoroughly, than safely wedged it back at her waist.

"Why do you wrap that dagger?" the simpler asked, curious.

"To keep it safe." *And away from me.*

The simpler studied the wrapped dagger with a furrow to her forehead. "It be fey?"

"Yes," Scota answered, offering no further explanation.

"I understand." The older woman folded her hands in her lap. "You left last eve's food under one of my trees this morn."

Heat flushed Scota's cheeks. "It has been a difficult few days, and my stomach bothered me."

"How do your breasts feel?"

Scota pulled back. "What?"

The wise woman leaned forward. "I asked, how do your breasts feel?"

Tender. "Fine."

Scota disliked seeing that knowing smile.

"Methinks a fey babe roots in your womb from Boyden, and this is the reason for your unaccustomed weakness. As this appears to be your first, mayhap you doona recognize the signs."

She did not know how to respond to that and sat up abruptly. Looking over the woman's shoulder, her gaze collided with dark shadows of amethyst.

"Boyden," she said softly, wondering how much he heard.

"She is with babe?" he asked, his gaze a physical touch on her face. He stood unmoving, a thin veil of emotion smoldering just below the surface.

A silent exhalation of air left her lungs. She could not tell if he was pleased with the news or affronted.

"Aye, methinks so, Boyden, but it be too early to tell." The simpler rose from the bed and went to him. She touched his sinewy forearm. "She be well enough to travel if you go slow. I will prepare food for your journey."

He bowed his head. "My thanks, Nia. You have been generous to us."

The simpler patted his arm and left them alone.

Scota looked away, chaos streaming within her. She knew battle and sword, knew the taking of life. She knew nothing about nurturing life. The simpler's awareness of her condition made it more terrifyingly real. Boyden's awareness filled her with apprehension for no reason she could name.

The bed dipped with his weight.

He held a silver goblet out to her. " 'Tis water."

Taking the goblet of water from his steady hand, she found to her great chagrin that her own hands were trembling. Staring dejectedly at his knee, she sipped.

"My thanks for your aid, my warrior. You saved my life."

"Yes," she agreed without conceit. He had been one warrior against ten. "You killed the captain," she murmured.

"He deserved it. He was . . ."

". . . evil," she finished for him and lifted her face.

A terrible tension pulsed behind the calm facade of him. His hand grasped her chin, a calloused thumb stroking her jaw, stroking the mating bite of claim forever marking her flesh with his scent.

His mouth lowered, finding her lips with a tender, heart-wrenching kiss.

" 'Tis my babe, Scota?" His question muffled against her lips, and she pulled away from him in hurt outrage.

Boyden stared into wide, turquoise eyes, the silence lengthening between them, and chose his words carefully. "At the spring, you were . . ."

She waited, unblinking, the golden shards within her eyes shiny with indignation.

He reformed his thoughts. "When an arrow impaled your lung, you said a fey born saved your life."

"Yes," she replied cautiously.

He hesitated. "Did the fey born leave something behind?"

"Yes."

He nodded, a great glacial disturbance rising within him.

Her chin tilted upward with temper. "But not what you be thinking of, you big oaf. The fey born was female. Remember? I told you this."

Her hair was suddenly bunched in a big hand, tilting her head gently backward.

"Tell me the truth, Scota."

"Tell you what?" She grabbed hold of his thick wrist, ready to do battle.

His eyes shone dangerously. "Doona tease me in this."

"I do not tease. The babe is yours, Boyden."

The tension eased in her hair, but he did not release her.

She remained passive to his silence, his body pressed against hers. "Do you not believe me?" she whispered.

"I believe you." His mouth lowered to hers with a tender kiss of possession. "When it comes to you, I am undone." Boyden drank of her, his body throbbing in need. If the fey born of the spring did not claim her womb, then it was his seed rooting. Joy and terror washed over him in equal waves.

Joy, at the thought of having a son or daughter with Scota.

Terror, at the thought of passing on the accursed blood threads of his line.

Small hands pressed up against his chest. He kissed her cheeks, her throat, her ear, her chin. He could not get enough of her.

"Boyden," she gasped with tantalizing laughter. "Your kisses steal my air."

"And you have stolen my heart," he whispered without thinking against her temple. He froze, a great release of relief washing over him. He loved her? Why had he not recognized these feelings before?

Fingers dove into the hair at his temples, holding him still.

She stared up at him and he waited, desperate to hear her return vow.

"I love you, Boyden, but I believe you already know this."

He grinned, his heart near bursting. "Aye, Scota. I know it." He caressed her face. "I always knew I would win your heart."

She rolled her eyes. "Arrogant, brooding, impossible . . ."

"Aye," he agreed silkily.

"Kiss me."

He framed her face with his hands and took her mouth, took her breath, her heart, and her spirit into him for all and the forever time. He could taste her heartbeat, her lips soft and inviting against his, calling him. His body stirred, hardened, a compelling need, coiling low, as old as time itself. He wanted her wild and hungry under him. The war and his private struggle against the lethal Faery Wind faded until only she remained in his arms, warm and alive.

Hair lifted from his shoulders.

A cold gust nipped at his flesh, and she tore her mouth free with a strangled refusal, pushing out of his arms.

He let her go, not understanding.

White mist swirled behind her, forming . . .

"Scota?"

He stared at a reflection behind his beloved, a sudden and terrible comprehension taking hold of him. Passion and desire waned into chill, blood threads swirling, thickening, pulsing into ancient memories of betrayal.

He rose from the edge of the bed, backing up slowly, a sickening rage coiling in his gut.

"Boyden," Scota called, unable to reach his hand.

"Why do you look at me so?"

The reflection returned his unblinking gaze, pinning him with illusionary heat in challenge and demand.

CHAPTER 18

IN A CRIMSON CLOUD OF mist, the shadowy blood memory of a dead king rose up from his bones—as if it had been waiting for him all the years of his life. He stumbled back, coming hard up against a wall. The heavy weight of betrayal and anger washed over him, the inherited feelings claiming him for their own. He gazed deeply into the cold, jeweled eyes of the reflection, of the *Gaoth Shee*, and said with deeply felt bitterness, "I remember . . ."

In the long-ago time, before the reign of the gods and goddesses, a Wind King was brought to his knees, bleeding and tainted from the treachery of a once-loved brother and his greedy lover.

Unease rippled through him and Boyden took a shaky breath. The muddled visions faded to a single night of glowing flames and cruelty. In his mind, nightmare became memory . . .

. . . a golden and widowed king was sweating and straining against rope restraints, the light of a fire at his back. Wrists tied to stakes in the ground, his head high and defiant, Boyden glimpsed an image of himself in his ancestor, Conall. A daughter, young and vulnerable, lay crumpled a few paces away. She was sobbing, her oval face streaked with dirt.

Darkness and rage engulfed him.

"You were foolish to reject me," the dark-haired woman said with quiet violence. She regarded. It was a brief connection, a seductive gaze meant to entice. It only made him hate her more. His brother's whore.

The tingling numbness in his right hand muted, and he tightened his fist. They stayed that way, gazes locked in a test of wills and awareness.

Neither gave in.

"Must we battle like this? Do you not understand that you belong to me?" she murmured, a faint curve to her pink lips. "All is not lost, tell me the wind vow."

Conall said nothing, and Boyden breathed the fury with him, nerves pulsing.

The woman's head tilted, and she lifted her short sword to him. The tip grazed his shoulder in a threatening and fleeting caress, making his blood boil.

Within Boyden, Conall answered her with mutinous silence.

Anger leaped into her eyes. "Give me the wind vow, Conall!"

Rage rose in this throat. "You want the wind vow

to secure the power to rule my realm. Nay, I willna give it," the king growled in reply. "Only I control the lethal wind, a male blood vow of promise to the land you could never understand."

"I doona need to understand it. I only need to wield it. Besides, your brother's blood be the same as yours." She pointed behind her to a white-faced man astride a great, brown, horned bird, a creature of legend. "He be *rigdamnai*, of kingly material, the same as you."

From Conall's blood memories, Boyden recognized the falsehood spilling out of the woman's mouth. Her lust was centered on control, power, and greed.

"The Elemental wishes freedom from your constant restraint. She came to us and pleaded our help."

"The wind never pleads," the king snarled, his jaw clenching.

"Give your brother the vow. He willna be so forceful as you in his rule." She pointed her sword at the weeping child. "I promise to release you and your daughter. When I stand beside your brother, I will be Wind Queen and promise to offer you both pardons. You may live the remainder of your life far from here, but your line must end with her."

Conall laughed caustically. "Foolish female. You know little of what you speak. My brother and I have different mothers. Even if I lied about our mothers, the weakling standing behind you canna control the wind. He canna even control his lust for a scrapping whore."

"Wind bastard!" the woman screeched and lashed

out ferociously in frustration.

Her sword arm rose.

Resolve settled deep in his chest, and Boyden felt Conall take his last breath of free air.

Pain and fire sliced into his side.

"His blood be the same as yours," the woman snarled, jerking her blade out of kingly flesh.

"Nay," the younger brother protested, dismounting quickly. "Not this way. Hurt the daughter."

Conall roared in rage and pain, summoning the *Gaoth Shee* to do his bidding. A blast of glacial wind swept across the fire. The warriors surrounding them scattered like insects, running away in terror, deserting the rebellion to save their miserly lives.

The woman screamed, falling to her knees.

"Stop, Conall!" The brother's command ended abruptly in paralysis, a strangled sound erupting out of his throat as he attempted to reach his bird mount. No longer able to pull breath into his lungs, he collapsed to the ground and turned to look at his wheezing lover. In the final moments of their ending, they glared hatred and blame, turning upon each other.

The bird mount shifted uneasily, unharmed by the lethal wind.

"Daughter," the king called gently, his head falling low between his shoulders, a bowing in death's coming.

The child scrambled to her feet, hugging him close with skinny white arms full of desperate strength.

"Listen to me, daughter. With my death, the lethal

wind goes free and our realm enters into chaos. Doona ever think of her or summon her. You have not the strength to control her, and she kills all she touches if unchecked. Live your life away from here. When a male child returns to our line, the blood vow will stream in the reclaiming. Now go with my love and never look back . . ."

Boyden stumbled, his back hitting a wall. The misty image of the sobbing daughter holding on to her dying father slowly faded into waves of grief and loathing.

"Boyden?"

He shook his head, trying to clear it. Scota's voice sounded far away.

The *Gaoth Shee* had wanted freedom in the long-ago times and had used others to kill her Servant King. The daughter escaped into a life of simpler days, raising a daughter of her own, and passing her father's blood down the inherited line.

In time, knowledge of the lethal wind faded in the daughters of the line. He was the first and only male ancestor of the Wind Servant King. The only one able to force his will upon the Elemental, a powerful and ancient being. None of the daughters of the line possessed the ability, only the sons.

Only the males.

Only him.

Lifting his head slowly, he stared hard at the reflection.

He alone had the ability to control her, to ask her to kill one, instead of many or all, and she knew it. Locked away in the inaccessible blood memories within him, he would relearn the wind vow.

"Boyden, whatever you remember, I allowed her only once to share in you."

His gaze dropped to his mate. He did not understand. "Share?" he said dimly.

She stared at him through a glistening of tears. "Yes. At the spring, when I was dying, she offered me a choice of life or death."

"Choice?" His voice sounded hoarse to his ears. "What did you forfeit, Scota?"

"While you battled the captain and his warriors, I agreed to let her enter my body. She filled me with strength and saved my life," she explained, sounding hopeful.

"The fey doona save without reason," he replied firmly, reclaiming his wits.

"Boyden, the arrow lodged in me in a way none have ever survived. That wound meant certain death. You know this," she argued.

He knew it. "What did you give in return?" he asked cautiously. The magical always wanted.

She hesitated and a warning chill slid down his spine.

"When last we mated, she entered my body, and shared my senses. You made love to us both."

He made love to his . . . ancestor's killer?

"Boyden. Did you hear me?"

"I heard you."

Scota felt him physically withdraw from her, felt the emptiness rising like a sea between them. Clenching her hands in her lap, she fought from flinging herself off the bed and going to him.

He pushed away from the wall in lethal grace, a lover turned predator, eyes hard and cold.

"Leave us," he snarled, wild and tense, ready to destroy.

Beside her, the reflection vanished.

With an unsteady hand, Scota tucked a few strands of hair behind her ear. A sickly sensation settled in her stomach but she needed to know what her actions had wrought between them.

"This fey creature is your enemy?" Scota asked slowly, watching his response.

"Aye."

That one simple word told her all she needed to know.

By sharing her senses with the Elemental, she had betrayed Boyden irrevocably.

He walked to the doorway, not once looking back at her.

"Nia says you are able to travel. Are you?" he asked, his tone distant.

She climbed from the bed and went to him. "Yes," she said, reaching for his arm.

He avoided her touch, and Scota dropped her hand to her side in rejection.

"Will you still help me end this invasion and speak to Amergin on behalf of my people?"

She looked up at him with confusion. "Yes, Boyden.

Why would I not?"

"I will stay with you until the babe is born, Scota."

"Then after?" she asked.

"There is no after. The child goes with me."

"You would take my babe from me?"

"Aye," he answered and left her standing alone, ill in heart.

Over the next few days, Scota felt hysterical sobs trying to well up and choke her. She battered the wayward emotions down, struggling for balance in an unfamiliar land of blue skies, rolling hills, swirling mists, and decadent enchantments. Her depression had not lasted long as she sought ways to solve her dilemma. Maybe it would be best if Boyden took the babe, she reasoned, trying to find a way out of the hurt. She knew little about the raising of children, and infants frightened her. She would not know what to do with a small and easily injured babe. Dread and anxiousness tightened within her chest when she thought of giving up her child. She tried to shake off the feelings but to no avail. The sad fact was, she wanted this babe.

"Are you ill, Scota?"

She glanced right. He had walked along in brooding silence since their journey and *now* he wanted to know if she were ill?

"Scota?"

"What?" She snapped a small branch off a green bush as she passed.

"I asked if you were ill."

"I am with babe. I do not consider it an illness."

He nodded, turning away from her. "Do you wish to rest? Twilight comes."

In answer, she plopped down on a gray boulder and grimaced.

"Are you in pain?" he inquired, his gaze watchful.

She shook her head.

"You frown."

"I sat on the edge of a rock. You would frown if it jammed you, too." She tossed the twig away. "Are we near the river yet?"

"Have you not heard the water?" he countered, pulling Nia's food bag from his shoulder, and pointed toward the trees.

She turned on her hip and listened. The sounds of a flowing river echoed in the darkening air.

"We are close to the river," he murmured and settled down a ways from her. He opened the bag, probably ready to offer her food *again*. Lately it seemed she ate more than him and was twice as tired.

She scanned their surroundings. They sat among gaping ruins of fallen pillar stones and clumps of weeds and rocks. Bright splashes of yellow gorse dotted the countryside in a lovely display. In the distance, she saw an elongated ridge and a large passage tomb rising.

"Is that the tomb?"

"Aye, 'tis the Grange," he answered.

"It appears we have come full circle."

"Aye."

She looked back at him. His rage was a living breath soiling the air around them. "I found you there, dying from the Darkshade enchantment, Boyden."

"Aye."

"I saved your life," she said softly, adjusting the Darkshade dagger at her waist.

"Aye."

She braced her hands on either side of her. "Can you not say something other than 'aye'?"

"Aye."

Scota's eyes narrowed, and she blew air out of her mouth in irritation.

"Are you hungry?" he asked, his tone remaining aloof.

"No, I am not." She stood up and walked over to him. "Boyden, I will have this silence between us gone. Tell me what I have done so I can understand. I allowed the enchanted wind to share in you only once, a bargain made to save my life. You would have done the same. Is life so meaningless to you that you cannot consider my choice?"

He stood so quickly she stumbled back. Power emanated out of him, and a gust of cold wind nearly took her feet out from under her.

"Do you know what that wind creature is, my warrior? 'Tis death. With one thought I could take your life, and the lives of all creatures, in payment for the betrayal."

"Is that what you wish, Boyden?" she asked. "To

take my life and the life of your unborn babe?"

He pulled back, a sudden inner horror crossing his features and turned away. "Nay, Scota," his voice lowered, and he ran a hand down his face. "I wish no harm to come to you or the babe."

She grabbed his arm and faced him. "Yet, you hate me. How did I betray you, Boyden? By sharing my body with an ancient being in order to save my own life?"

He looked away, and she grabbed a handful of yellow hair.

In the next instant, she was on her back with a large and angry warrior propped above her.

"Stop this, Scota. I canna control the rage filling me."

"Tell me what I did wrong," she demanded, staring into dark amethyst eyes.

"I doona want to hurt you."

"You brooding oaf, I will not stop until I have my answer. Who betrayed you?" She studied his face and formed her own conclusions. "The ancient wind is your betrayer."

He did not answer.

"You think I would have willingly shared my body if I knew she betrayed you?"

His gaze narrowed, and she took a deep breath. "Boyden, I would rather die than betray you. You must believe me."

He pulled back in rejection of her claim, and she managed to catch him off balance. Clipping his arm, she rolled him to his back and straddled him like a horse.

"By the gods and goddesses, you are a thick-headed

goat." Grasping his wrists, she pinned his hands above his head.

They stared at each other, heat and storm arcing between them like lightning.

His hands clenched, a gathering of power.

Hers tightened on thick wrists, a promise of strength.

A demand for submission.

A relinquishing of dominance.

"Boyden . . ."

"What did you feel when the lethal wind joined with you?" he interrupted.

Scota knew her answer important to him. "I felt grief and desire . . . and a hurtful need to be close to you."

"Grief and need for what?"

Scota eased her grip on his wrists. "She is lonely, Boyden."

"Her choice," he growled, barely accepting her dominance. "The wind used others to kill and gain her freedom."

"As I would," Scota offered in truth. "As you would, Boyden. Freedom means everything. It is a gift hard won and should never be taken lightly."

His eyes darkened.

"Even now, you chafe under me, a minor restraint," she said quietly.

Scota felt the force of his anger return with his continued silence. He was one of those warriors who brewed inwardly before exploding. "These others the wind used to kill and gain her freedom, who were they?" she asked.

"A king's brother and lover," he answered low.

"You know them?"

"The betrayed king is my ancestor. His blood memories fill me."

"His emotions fill you, too?"

She saw a shifting within his gaze.

"Aye," he replied after a pause.

"These emotions are of a magical blood linking between the two of you?" she inquired, barely above a whisper. She was feeling her way here, a treacherous and magical path of bloodline emotions.

"Aye."

"These are feelings of *his* betrayal, Boyden, not yours." Her mouth lowered to his, kissing the edge of his firm lips. "I did not betray you, Boyden. I would not betray you. If I knew how deeply you felt, never would I have agreed to share my body and senses when you touched me. Feel with your emotions, Boyden, not his, and tell me you hate me."

Deep inside, Boyden reached through the residual turbulence of a dead king. His feelings of betrayal came from her sharing of the mating. Yet, what choice did she have? She would have died.

Her hips rocked against his manhood, halting his thoughts.

He looked into her eyes and saw desire's smoldering flame.

"Tell me you hate me, Boyden." Her hot, tight mouth fastened on his, asserting female dominance on an aggressive male. "Open for me," she murmured with command.

His lips parted, and she kissed him fiercely as if every breath in her body depended upon his. Her tongue darted in his mouth, and fury blurred into passion. He tilted his head to give her better access and she took it.

Need clawed into his lower belly.

Drops of sweat beaded his brow.

He flexed his hips, and she moaned in his mouth.

"Tell me, Boyden." Her decadent mouth moved to his jaw, leaving a trail of moisture. "Is it I you hate?"

His body tightened still more, and he flipped her onto her back.

"Nay, I doona hate you." Drinking in her gasp, he reclaimed her mouth and feasted on what belonged to him with a primitive and possessive growl.

In the next instant, a hand yanked his head back, a rope looped tight around his neck, and he was dragged off her.

CHAPTER 19

THEY WERE IN AMERGIN'S CAMP. Beneath the light of a full moon, night seeped across the land known as Tailtiu. The bloodbath of a wrongful invasion was nearly over.

Scota walked in quiet contemplation between two Milesian guardsmen. She must be prepared to state her beliefs firmly and with rightly cause, she reasoned. Any attempts to sway the leader with hysterical emotions, exaggerations, or falsehoods would not work.

With the strong northerly breeze whipping strands of hair across her nose, she accompanied the guardsmen through the fire-lit camp. The warriors they passed spoke in whispers among themselves. Some nodded to her, others remained silent in their judgments. Above the crackle of the fire circle's flames, the chink of sword, armor, and spear could be heard in testings of balance or endless cleanings. A group of large warhorses roamed about the small meadow to the right, seeking rest from a hard day of battle. The air smelled of exhaustion, both from warrior and from beast.

Scota pulled the stray strands of hair behind her ears. Near the end of the camp stood a solitary warrior. Hands were locked behind his back in quiet observation of the night. Shiny bronze beads decorated brown plaits hanging down his back. The brown warrior tunic and breeches of her tribesmen hugged his tall frame.

The two guardsmen brought her near, stopped, then drifted back.

She was alone with Amergin.

"In the suspended time of this land, the winds blow in threatening possession," the druidic bard said low.

"The winds blow in threatening possession due to your prisoner, Amergin."

The Milesian leader turned to her. He took in her wheat-colored gown with a curious twist of his lips.

"It is no wonder my warriors did not recognize you, Princess Scota." He folded his arms across his chest, the bronze cuffs on his wrists dark in shadow. "Besides rutting under an enemy's sword, you wear the farm clothes of a villager."

Scota glanced down at herself. "What I wear is of little importance."

"Is that so?"

She straightened her shoulders. "Amergin, may I speak?"

He nodded, and she began her defense of Boyden's people. "The warrior you captured and hold is not your enemy, Amergin." Grasping the folds of her gown, she approached him and stood by his side in shafts of moonlight. She knew he could not see the change in her eyes in this dim light and felt thankful for it. "Amergin, these people are not the enemy."

She heard him exhale.

"That may be, but I vowed to find the murderers of Lord Íth and I mean to do it." He turned away from her and headed back to the fire circle, effectively ending their conversation.

She went after him, the guards trailing close at her back. "I have the murderers' names, Amergin, but the one you hold captive knows who they are and where to find them."

He stopped and turned back to her, his focus penetrating.

"Summon him," Scota offered, the heat of the fire circle warming her right side.

"Coll," Lord Amergin called over his shoulder. "Bring the problem prisoner to me."

A guard nodded and disappeared into the fire-lit night.

Scota waited anxiously, hoping her feelings would not betray her.

"Does this warrior mean something to you, Princess?" A single dark brow lifted in question.

For a long moment, she looked into her leader's face and decided to err on the side of truth. "Aye, he does," she replied, inadvertently mimicking Boyden's speech.

"'Aye'?"

Immediately, she corrected herself. "I meant yes."

"I see." He turned away and strode closer to the flames, the orange light all but engulfing him. "You

needed to travel across the sea to find an acceptable
warrior for your bed. None of mine would do," he complained. "This one must be exceptional for the warrior
princess to defend him."

"He is, Amergin," she answered quietly, unsure of
the druidic bard's changeable moods. He was known for
his flashes of temper, yet he always dealt fairly with his
warriors and she trusted him, trusted he would be fair to
her, as well.

He returned to her side, looking down at her specu-
latively. "Is this captive one of the tribal kings?"

"He is the Wind Herald of the *Tuatha Dé Danann*."

"The Wind Herald of the faery tribe? I have heard
of the faery tribe, but never did I hear of a warrior called
the Wind Herald."

"It is difficult to explain, Amergin." She saw the
concentration in his face.

On the other side of the fire circle, a man grunted
with pain.

Lord Amergin's head came up. "Like the rest of
these stubborn and prideful people, your herald refuses
to submit."

"Only with me is he submissive," she offered and bit
her lip, not meaning to give away an intimacy.

"I see," he murmured again, and she wondered if
he did.

"I hope you do. I hope you will listen to us."

"Us?"

"Yes."

Hard intensity stared back at her. "Tell me the names of the murderers, Princess Scota."

"I will tell you their names," Boyden declared loudly, his hands bound together in front of him with ropes.

The Milesian leader turned to him, eyes large and black. "You are the Wind Herald?"

Boyden glanced at Scota and nodded. "That is what I am named."

"Why?"

He did not pretend to misunderstand. "I am blooded to the winds."

The leader lifted his eyebrows. "You are one of those fey creatures?"

"He is of the between," Scota presented in explanation.

"I have heard of this *in-between*." The druidic bard nodded and scratched his chin thoughtfully. "Blooded to the wind is the fey part of you. I imagine that is why your eyes reflect the color amethyst with the golden shards of light. The rest is mortal. You are a mixed-blood."

"Aye," Boyden replied, surprised by the bard's understanding of his heritage.

The Milesian leader came and stood before him, a man of near equal height.

"I am Lord Amergin of the Milesians."

"I know. I am Boyden, Wind Herald of the *Tuatha Dé Danann*, tribe of the goddess Dana."

They measured each other's worth and substance for long moments.

Reaching behind his back, the druidic bard pulled something from his waistband.

Boyden looked down at a dagger with ancient etchings and went very still inside. *The Darkshade dagger.*

Behind the bard leader, he saw Scota clutch at her belt in realization of the missing dagger.

Amergin held the dead captain's dagger up to his face. "Wind Herald of the *Tuatha Dé Danann*, I ask my question. If I impale you with a sword or cut you with this dagger, your blood spills red and not the true white of faery?" he inquired. "I would know of who or what I am speaking with."

Boyden did not answer. It seemed Amergin only understood part of what was. Both red and white blood flowed in the veins of the fey realm. Guardians had true white blood, but some, like the territorial goddesses, bled crimson. Not all fey bled white blood. Not all fey died from the cut of a Darkshade, only guardians . . . and him.

Holding the hilt, Lord Amergin turned the dagger over in his hand. "I heard strange tales about this dagger." A finger traced the etchings on the blade. "I am told it is named Darkshade, a blade of sinister enchantment. I have never seen the like of it before and admire the talent of your craftsmen."

Boyden met the leader's cold, calculating glare.

"Princess Scota was kind enough to give it to me." Amergin leaned forward and smiled gently. "You do not mind if I cut you, Boyden? I understand fey creatures spill white blood. I must know who or what I am speaking with."

Boyden stiffened, but before he could speak, his warrior mate pushed herself between them and grabbed the enchanted dagger out of Amergin's hand. "This is a ceremonial dagger and worth much if not soiled with blood." She wrapped it quickly in cloth and held it under her arm. "Use another dagger to cut him." Swiping one from a guardsman standing near, she returned, took his hand, and nicked his palm before he could protest.

"Scota!" He glared at her.

"See? He bleeds red, Amergin," she said clearly, tossing the dagger back to the guardsman. "Boyden is not fey born. You can trust him."

"My thanks, Princess Scota," Lord Amergin said with a tone of mild displeasure.

She released his wrist without apology and stepped back. Bringing his arms up, Boyden licked the small cut below his thumb while holding the leader's intense gaze.

"You have a defender, Wind Herald."

"That depends on your perspective," he replied.

The Milesian regarded him with suspicion and strong curiosity, good traits within a leader, Boyden decided.

"Princess Scota does not choose her lovers lightly. I know of only one other than you."

He read the challenge within the leader's voice.

"She is unique," Boyden offered in explanation for his interest. He would not share his feelings with an enemy.

"Unique?" The leader smiled slowly, considering his comment. "Well said."

They stared at each other, a battle of wills between aggressor and defender.

"I brought you here for a reason. Princess Scota feels you have answers for me."

"I know."

"Who killed Lord Íth, Wind Herald?"

"Kings MacCuill, MacCecht, and MacGreine, but I doona know the truth of it," Boyden answered. "We must bring them here to discover the certainty."

Shaking his head with disgust, Lord Amergin stepped back. "That would prove difficult, as these three kings are dead already."

"Dead?" Boyden echoed. Without the kings, how could he hope to prove his tribe's innocence? "How?" he heard himself ask.

"Did you not know?" Lord Amergin chuckled darkly. "Their wives betrayed them in order for this land to bear their names under our rule. They made me promise, foolish whores."

Fury consumed Boyden. If Lord Amergin had killed those kings, knowing them as murderers, then why did he continue with the invasion? "Did you know they killed Íth?" he asked, his jaw tight.

"They denied it, as all the others do."

"The other tribes are innocent," Boyden said firmly.

Lord Amergin did not reply but went to stand near the fire circle, presenting his back in answer.

"My tribe is innocent," Boyden said forcefully and stepped forward. The guards were at his side immediately, staying him.

"Your tribe?" Lord Amergin murmured. "The faery tribe, an interesting people. Not many are left."

Gloom and futility settled in all around Boyden in a cloak of black suffocation. Shadows of death danced among the orange flames casting blue sparks into the night.

Near the end of his tolerance, he looked to Scota gravely and released a slow breath. Either she reason with the bard or he would end it here in bloodshed.

Their eyes met, one hot with frustrated fury and one with calm understanding.

Scota walked over to Amergin and touched the leader's arm. "Amergin, you must stop the bloodshed. Lord Íth would not want this. You have your vengeance. Kings MacCuill, MacCecht, and MacGreine are dead. Find a way to end the blood spill and speak to Boyden's tribal king and the other kings if need be. It is time to end it."

"Do you believe those three kings killed Lord Íth, Princess?"

"I do," she replied with soft insistence.

"I am uncertain."

She gripped her hands in front of her, wanting desperately to shake sense into him.

Lord Amergin released a slow breath and frowned, rubbing his temple. "Perhaps it is time to end it. I grow weary of the slaughter. I did not anticipate the stubbornness of these people. Despite our superior numbers and weapons, they would fight me until the last child drops from my blade—and I am not a killer of children." Lifting his head, he looked over his shoulder at Boyden.

"Do you think your kings will speak to me, Wind Herald?"

Boyden nodded. "I will bring my chieftain to you. He can speak for all of our tribes."

"Untie him," Lord Amergin commanded with a wave of his hand.

The guardsman Coll stepped forward and removed the ropes from Boyden's wrists.

"My thanks, Amergin," Scota whispered, struggling not to show her elation.

"Do not thank me, Princess. We have other matters to discuss."

He walked over to Boyden and she joined them.

"You will leave this eve and bring your chieftain to me before the next full moon," Lord Amergin said firmly. "The princess remains with me."

Scota stopped Boyden's protest with a swift embrace. Burrowing against him, she pulled his head down and kissed him passionately, pouring her heart into him. "Go, Boyden," she whispered against his lips and jammed the cloth-wrapped Darkshade dagger low into his waistband where it could not be seen. She stepped back, her heart aching. "I am safe here with my people."

He looked down at her, his gaze searching. "I will return."

With a nod to Amergin, the holder of her heart turned and walked away.

Swallowing hard, Scota watched until he became but another shadow in the moving night. The winds seemed to calm, and the stars appeared brighter in the night sky.

"Will he return with his chieftain?" Lord Amergin asked after a time.

"Boyden is honorable."

"We shall see."

She lowered her gaze to the ground. "What other complaint is against me?"

"First, tell me the why and the how of your eyes changing."

She exhaled. "You do not miss much, Amergin. One of the fey beings of this land saved my life and left the golden shards of claim in my eyes."

"What fey being?"

"The wind," she replied in truth.

"Ah, Boyden," he chuckled low with misunderstanding. "I am told these fey born males leave something of themselves behind."

Yes, she thought, unwilling to correct him. Boyden was much more than fey born. "Tell me of the complaint."

"How did you know there exists a complaint against you?"

"I saw Captain Rigoberto's men and overhead grievances before you summoned me."

"What did you hear?" he asked.

"I am to be charged with the killing of Captain Rigoberto."

His black eyes bored into her. "Did you kill him?"

She thought of Boyden's defense of her and lied, "Yes."

He sighed. "You know my rules, Princess. Dispute among my warriors is forbidden and addressed in direct combat between them. I know you did not like him, but Captain Rigoberto proved efficient for my needs."

Scota nodded, silent and tense, waiting for judgment.

His face strained. He spoke firmly as if the words tasted foul in his mouth, "I will not make exceptions for you."

Something deep inside her closed off. "I understand," she replied without looking at him.

"At dawn, your life ends."

She stiffened at his swift, harsh judgment and said, "I am with babe, an innocent."

His eyes narrowed at her disclosure.

She met his gaze. "I ask you to allow me to give birth before my life is forfeit."

"Is Boyden the father?"

"Yes," she replied. "I would have the babe given into his care and ask your word on it."

"Given."

Scota nodded her thanks, her legs shaky. In nine months she should be able to convince him to spare her life.

"When Boyden returns, you will tell him you wish to remain among your own people. The babe will be brought to him upon birth, and he will be told you died in the child-birthing."

Scota nodded. She stood rooted to the spot as

Amergin walked over to the guardsman Coll and spoke quietly. Raising her eyes to the moonlight, she pressed her lips together.

She had managed to give the dagger to Boyden without Amergin noticing. The enchanted weapon could never be used against him again. The possibility of peace loomed in the enchanted land, and she had nine months to convince the druidic bard to spare her life. All in all, it was a fruitful day.

CHAPTER 20

SCOTA CHOSE TO SPEND HER time quietly until Boyden returned. It was worthless to worry about things she could not control, and so she did not. *Like people,* she thought. All her life, she experienced difficulty getting close to people. Most men thought her too outspoken and confident for a woman, ruffling feathers where she should not. Some women commented she was too self-assured and blunt, and she experienced several jealous confrontations because of it. Most thought her too strong . . . all except for Boyden. He valued her with an intensity that surprised her.

She stood under the bough of a large oak, watching the arrival of dawn spread across the sky, and listening to the dull roar of the flowing river beyond. The sound felt like a forever echoing in this emerald land of mild but changeable weather. She had been told the river rose from a bog, a cloud-fed wetland of acidic peat and dead plants. Black waters poured east like a herd of wild mares mating with the stallion of the sea. It was a river brimming with life, particularly salmon. The fish was a delicacy for the warrior who experienced the good fortune of capturing one. Roasted over a fire, one ate the salmon with honey. The Milesian warriors believed the flesh of the salmon bestowed restorative powers, a much-needed influence in the days of battle ahead. Strength meant survival. She knew this well, though she could not make herself eat. For the moment, her babe wished only for water. A problematic encounter yesterday with bitter stew and *drisheen,* or blood pudding, left her weak-kneed. No longer did she choose to eat whatever she wished. Her babe's preference would dictate her likes in the coming months. *Boyden's babe.*

She did not have to close her eyes to see him, strong and wild like this unconquerable land of mist and hill.

"Princess," the bearded guard called from behind her.

She bent her head in acknowledgment. *It is time to return to my tiny prison*, she mused. Turning her back to the dawn, she walked up the gentle slope between patches of feathery ferns to her tent.

Supported by wood poles, her small tent of animal skins had been hastily erected about four horse lengths from Lord Amergin's tent. He wanted her near, a lure for Boyden, she suspected.

Walking around a hip-high boulder, she nodded to the second guard posted to watch her. Lifting the flap of cloth draped over her tent's entrance, she entered. Three unlit candles waited beside her bed of wool blankets and tufts of grass.

A pensive sigh escaped her, and she changed into a more comfortable brown tunic. Her fingers unaccountably clumsy, she laced up the front over her tender breasts. To her right, a green frog hopped into her tent. Not liking the accommodations, he hopped out again, seeking freedom, as she could not.

As the days gave way to nights, she had watched the changing stages of the moonrise and moonset, gibbons, half moon, and crescent waning, followed by the new moon rising, the darkest of dark. Time was passing.

She had slept little the night before. With a final tug, she adjusted her tunic.

Shouts came from outside.

Pushing aside the entrance cloth of her tent, she took a step into the cloudy gloom of dawn. Immediately, the two guards blocked her.

She stood silent and tense, her bare feet ankle-deep in morning dew.

Out of the mist, newcomers appeared like vaporous spirits.

Accompanied by a group of fierce-looking warriors, Boyden entered Lord Amergin's large tent without a single glance in her direction.

Glancing at her toes, she nodded to herself, and returned inside her tent to wait for the inevitable confrontation. She must be strong and make Boyden believe she no longer desired him. If Amergin ever suspected Boyden had killed his favored captain, she dared not think of the consequences.

She ate little of what the guards brought her and set the bowl aside. Sitting cross-legged in the trampled grass of her tent, she decided to wait. Patience was not her usual course of action, but it would be this day. The temperature was comfortable, not too hot or too cold. She did not mark the passing of time for it went too quickly to suit her. By late afternoon, the two guards posted outside spoke of an agreement reached.

She leaned forward and listened to their conversation . . .

The Milesians would rule the above while the Tuatha ruled the below and what land remained untouched by invasion.

Scota released a sigh of relief.

As long as it ended the blood spill, she cared little for who ruled which hill and loch. Closing her eyes, she strived for inner calm.

He would come to her soon.

She must be ready.

Lifting the flap of brown cloth, Boyden stepped inside Scota's small tent with a frown. He thought a princess would demand better accommodations.

"Why are there guards posted outside?" he inquired, seeing her meager surroundings of two blue blankets for a bed and three spent candles.

She rose gracefully to her feet, a warrior cast in dimness, and turned to him. He hardly recognized her. Gone was the vitality he so admired, and in its wake stood a pale and lost creature.

"How did you get in?" she asked.

He pointed to the entranceway covered by the flap of cloth.

"The guards allowed you to pass?"

His brows drew together. "Why would they not?" This was not the return welcome he expected. He studied her, feeling the sharp bite of her coldness.

His warrior wore her black hair in plaits, pulled away from a face masked with stillness. A brown tunic and breeches hung about her frame, giving her a thinner appearance than he remembered.

"Have the leaders come to an agreement?" she asked with a clear voice. "Is it over?"

"Aye," he replied, giving her a steady look. "Neither liked what the other one said, but they agreed. Your people are to hold the land they conquered, a concession we made. My people are to hold what remains, a concession Lord Amergin made."

"Including the faery realm below?" she asked thoughtfully.

He was deliberately slow in responding, trying to understand her. "Including the fey realm below," he answered. "The High King of the Faeries will be most pleased that he willna have to kill your people." He smiled gently.

She did not smile back, her gaze instead shifting away. "Amergin does not comprehend the mystery and riches that reside in the fey realm."

"Methinks he understands well enough, Scota. He

chooses to ignore it, at least for now. We would never give up the fey realm, Scota. It belongs only to us and our brethren."

"I am glad, Boyden." She glanced back at him, something strange and terrible living within her eyes.

He moved to take her in his arms, and she stepped violently away, turning her back to him.

"Since you left, I have thought much about us and changed my mind about many things," she spoke quickly, filling the air with her rejection.

He stared at the back of her head. He had thought about them, as well, and wanted her in his life despite all that came before. Given his blood ancestry, forgiveness came exceedingly hard for him, especially when combined with thoughts of betrayal. However, a life without her proved inconceivable to him.

"What things?" he responded ruthlessly.

"My people need me to guide them in the times ahead," she explained with a normal-sounding voice and faced him once again. "You told me you would stay with me until the babe is born. There is no need, Boyden. I will send the babe to you upon its birth. I do not want it."

His features grew hard from hurt.

"I do not want the babe," she reiterated, a forcing of belief. "We come from two different lands," she continued stiffly, looking past him. "I feel it is better this way, Boyden."

"You little liar," he accused softly. "I am not deceived. State your true reasons. You have never been one to give up without a fight. Doona play submissive maiden with me, my warrior."

She came at him with a ferociousness he never expected.

Plowing into him with a hard smack, she flattened her hands against his chest and attempted to shove him out the tent.

"Get out!"

He would not be shoved until she gave him the truth. Leaning into her, he planted his feet, refusing to budge, using his superior strength and weight.

"Get out!" she choked, tears streaming down her cheeks.

Grabbing her wrists, he yanked her arms wide, unbalancing her. A horse whinny sounded somewhere outside, adding a sense of normalcy where there was none. It stunned him to see her undone like this.

Her knee came up swiftly, and he barely avoided being brought down.

She fought him, cursing and hissing like a trapped and injured animal. A frustrated screech rent the air.

"Scota, you had better tell me what is going on," he growled back. He flipped her around, his chest pressing into her back, trying hard not to hurt her. An elbow slammed into his ribs and he doubled over in pain. With a swift kick, she took out his legs from under him, and he fell backward with a loud thump, his body hitting hard ground.

Slightly dazed, he felt her climb on top of him. Small hands pressed against his chest, strong thighs locked around his hips.

Holding his palms up in surrender, he waited, yielding to her unexplained rage.

She was shaking all over and breathing in rapid bursts.

He was afraid if he moved she might break in two.

Slowly, his hand moved up her left arm. "Tell me what upsets you, Scota."

Her mouth opened and closed, a strangled moan escaping into an unending silence.

She shook her head despondently, black plaits falling to his chest. He watched a single tear trail down a flushed cheek and felt it plop on his throat.

"Scota." He pulled her down, cupping silken temples, feathering kisses across her eyes, cheek, and chin, tasting the salt of her grief. "What is wrong, my warrior?" Her breath was warm with remembered sweetness, and he captured her mouth. She made a queer sound in her throat and rocked against him. He could not restrain himself and drank of her, taking her air into his body, and offering his own.

Scota clung to him in trembling misery and desire. He tasted of life and dreams she would never experience again. Her one remaining joy was her babe. The child would grow up in its father's world, a land of mysterious beauty and enchantment. In her heart, she silently wished for a son to be born as valiant and golden as the father.

Abruptly his body tensed below hers, warm lips stilling in their passion.

A male-sized shadow fell across her, and she pushed sharply off Boyden, nearly knocking the thick candles over with her foot.

"I see he can be submissive when he chooses to be," Lord Amergin noted tonelessly, standing just inside the tent.

Boyden climbed slowly to his feet and glanced over his shoulder at Scota. She stood staring at the ground, blinking hard. *What hold does he have over her?* he wondered.

"Your chieftain awaits you outside, Wind Herald."

He nodded, but did not move.

"The princess wishes to remain with her people. Did she not tell you?" the druidic bard inquired.

"Aye, she lies poorly."

The Milesian leader folded his arms across his chest. "Do you think so?"

"You doona know her," Boyden said with a voice of open challenge.

"Indeed." A brow arched with disdain. "I know she protects you, Wind Herald."

"No, Amergin," his lovely and troubled mate disputed. "It is as I answered you."

Boyden looked back at her, questioning. "What did you say to him?"

"I asked her who killed Captain Rigoberto," Lord Amergin answered for her.

"I did," she exclaimed, her jaw working. "Please have him leave, Amergin. I grow weary of his presence."

Amergin replied with a mocking tone, "You did not look weary a moment before while you thrust your tongue down his throat, Princess."

"Amergin, I accepted your judgment without protest,

please let him leave."

Boyden looked at her in astonishment and growing anger. Never had he heard his warrior princess beg, never saw her near to breaking. It enraged him, and he faced the leader.

"I took the sniveling coward's life," he growled low and brutal. "He threatened what was mine."

The Milesian leader unfolded his arms, his lips thinning with anger.

"He lies!" Scota cried, stepping in front of Boyden. "I killed Rigoberto, Amergin."

The leader looked at both of them, his face unreadable. "Guards," Amergin called over his shoulder. The two men posted outside entered the tent. Each gripped a sword in readiness. "Bring Captain Rigoberto's men to me."

The guards nodded and ducked out of the tent, first one, followed by the other, to do their leader's bidding.

"Outside, the both of you," Lord Amergin commanded, uncharacteristically turning his back and leaving the tent.

The instant the leader left, Scota felt large calloused hands cup her face. She looked up and said sharply, "You made a mess of it."

"Obviously."

He kissed her fast and fierce, a terrible instant of dread clutching at her heart before she burrowed into him. Worse his kisses made her feel, until she could no longer breathe, and pushed forcefully against his chest, seeking her freedom. She turned to dart outside, and his hand locked around her wrist.

Breathing heavily, she turned back to him.

He looked at her, golden shards glittering with dark amethyst fire, a faint scowl creasing his handsome brow.

"We face whatever this is together, my warrior."

No, she thought wildly.

He pulled her firmly to his side and guided her out of the tent into a fading afternoon lit by fire.

Choking back an objection, Scota swallowed down turbulent emotions and let him lead. She doubted she could free her hand even if she wished it. Joined by four more guards, they were escorted to the camp's center fire circle, a bonfire of orange flames and raging light. Her mind raced for a solution.

"The fire god senses blood letting," Boyden murmured, skimming the faces of the gathering men. Some men stood only in breeches; others were fully armed with sword and shield. He felt their vehemence, but also their curiosity.

"Your chieftain stands there," Scota said softly and Boyden looked to his right.

Several paces away, Lord Amergin spoke in confidence with the chieftain. Surrounded by tribal elders and several other tribal kings, the Dark Chieftain of the *Tuatha Dé Danann* nodded, and Boyden knew the two leaders had agreed to his fate.

Whatever deemed, he mused. He would protect Scota in spite of herself.

"You were foolish to lie to him, my warrior," he admonished her, seeing the turbulent emotions below the surface.

Her cheeks flushed the color of a summer rose and her chin lifted. "My intention was to kill the coward, therefore it is not a lie."

He did not answer, attempting to follow her reasoning.

"Besides, I was trying to protect you, you big oaf. You are . . ."

". . . devoted to me?" he finished for her.

She hissed between her teeth, not even looking at him.

He was glad to see the return of her feisty spirit and could not help the twitch of a smile.

She swore at him beneath her breath, words he never heard before.

They stood on hard ground, the low clouds of an incoming storm shutting out the growing brilliance of the stars. The tops of the trees swayed with the wind, leaves gesturing wildly to the call of the moving air. He lifted his gaze and felt the *Gaoth Shee* waiting in the shadows beyond the fire, a silvering of the air.

"The lethal wind waits near, Boyden."

"Aye, I feel her." He glanced at his mate. Like him, Scota was now attuned to the wind. His fiery mate was linked to the ancient darkest sister of the winds, as he was, a link never to be broken, a link already forming with the growing babe in her womb. His babe, he thought, fiercely defensive of them both.

All Scota could think about was protecting Boyden. She knew Amergin, knew his swift justice would not be stayed. She had nine months to convince him to spare her life, nine months before the babe entered the world. Now the blessed end was coming, and she could do nothing to stop it.

Amergin returned to her side. Moments later, the three spineless warriors of the captain were brought before them, one with a beard, one slender, and one broad. All had faces flushed red with mead and whoring. They smirked at her, confident of their place. These were the men who filled the Milesian leader's head with untruths about her.

"I am told the Wind Herald never lies," Lord Amergin addressed his people loudly, "therefore he is removed from my judgment."

Two guards grabbed Boyden by the arms and pulled him roughly from her side.

Scota did not move or offer objection. She knew what was to come and prepared herself.

"Except for our guests, all here know of my rules." Lord Amergin locked his hands behind him. "I do not tolerate deceit among my warriors. These three men told me Princess Scota killed Captain Rigoberto out of spite." He lifted his head higher. "When confronted, Princess Scota agreed with them, though I suspected differently. She accepted my judgment meekly, which immediately told me she protected another." He glanced at her. "As we all know, Princess Scota is never meek."

To her right, someone snickered with agreement.

"Amergin," Scota started to dissent, and he held his

hand up to silence her.

"Except around the Wind Herald, it seems. He has somehow managed to tame her."

Scota flushed apple red and chanced a glance over her shoulder.

Barely contained between three guardsmen, the Wind Herald burned silently with fury while treetops bowed to stronger winds.

"These three warriors lied out of spite and vengeance," Lord Amergin continued and one of the so-called warriors blinked bloodshot eyes at her. "I believe this as their tongues have grown loose with mead and feelings of false security. Reports came to me even before these three arrived in my camp. Captain Rigoberto left his post to pursue a yellow-haired enemy warrior, one he believed to be fey born, and one he believed would lead him to a great fey treasure. Is that not right, Wind Herald?"

"Aye," Boyden growled his response behind her.

"You are that enemy warrior, Wind Herald?"

"Aye," came the angry response again.

Lord Amergin nodded, and the three men before her shifted uneasily, understanding slowly rising above their inebriation.

"Captain Rigoberto attacked Princess Scota to get to the Wind Herald. Is that not so, Princess?"

"Yes," she replied. Out of the corner of her eye, a guardsman with a mass of red hair approached. In his hand, he held the hilt of an unsheathed sword.

"At first, I did not understand why one of my captains

would attack one of my emissaries. I understand now. Princess Scota lied to me to protect her mate, the warrior we have come to know as the Wind Herald."

"Amergin," Scota protested.

He ignored her. "Since truce is struck this eve with the *Tuatha Dé Danann* tribe, I will not pose judgment on a misguided loyalty. Quiet, Princess. I am not done." The druidic bard looked over his shoulder and addressed his firm command to the guards. "Hold the Wind Herald. He is not to interfere."

Scota did not turn around to the sounds of the scuffle behind her, but focused inward. Flexing her arms to ease the tension in her shoulders, she stood ready for combat. Quickness, she knew, would be her only chance for victory.

"Since all lied to me, I deem the fates to decide judgment."

The guardsman with the red hair tossed her the sword.

Scota caught the bronze hilt easily. She swept into the glow of the fire, the blade in perfect balance, an extension of her arm.

Encumbered by mead, the men were slow and clumsy in reaching for their swords and responding to her attack. One even dropped his weapon. She chose him to be the first to fall and sliced open his neck without malice, then dropped and rolled. There was no room for vengeance here, only survival. Swinging her sword in a low arc, she clipped the back of another's leg. Cursing, the bearded man fell sideways toward her. Avoiding his flailing arms, she jumped to her feet. With two hands gripping the sword's hilt, she swung hard, lopping off his head, and spun to meet the threatening blade of the third.

Less encumbered by mead than the other two, the broad warrior proved more of a challenge. His weight and strength nearly triple hers, she knew she could not meet him face-to-face and win. The mead made him sluggish, but filled him greatly with temper. She took advantage, dancing around him as if wings sprouted from her back. He was a slow goat trying to catch a graceful dragonfly. Redirecting the strength of his swipe with her weapon in a loud clash, she twirled, dropped to her knee, and thrust the blade of her sword upward and into his chest. Breathing heavily, she let go of the sword's hilt and stepped back into the sounds of crackling flames.

The dying man staggered back and fell to his knees.

As the last breath left him, she looked over her shoulder. Four guardsmen had Boyden pinned to the ground and were even now having trouble containing him.

"Even in this moment you look to him instead of me."

Scota lifted her eyes and gazed into a face shadowed by orange light.

"Yes, Amergin," she said, feeling faintly regretful.

"In this victory, you earned the right to live. I give you back your life, Princess Scota, but I can no longer trust your word. You lied to me."

She would not argue the truth. "Release the Wind Herald," she replied in answer, their once close association slipping away.

The Milesian leader studied her before moving away.

In the glow of firelight, Lord Amergin spoke so all could hear. "The fates chose Princess Scota. She has won the right to live, but she has not won the right of my returned trust. I therefore ban her from her people and give her unto the care of the Wind Herald. Never will she live among us again."

Scota felt her chest go tight, but stood her ground.

The druidic bard walked around her to his fuming captive.

With his arms and legs pinned to the ground, Boyden glared up at the leader. "If she died, I would have killed you."

"I know." Lord Amergin gestured his guards away with a flip of his hand and Boyden jumped to his feet.

They stared at each other.

One pensive.

One angry.

"Where is the magical Darkshade dagger, Wind Herald?' Lord Amergin asked, missing little.

"Where it belongs, with my brethren," Boyden replied firmly.

The leader nodded, silence opening between them.

After a long moment, Lord Amergin said, "Take good care of her, Wind Herald," and walked away.

CHAPTER 21

MANY DAYS CAME AND WENT since leaving her people's camp. A kind of sadness moved through Scota as the old familiarities were left behind. She considered herself a daughter of the emerald land now, and . . . of the winds. Old allegiances were gone, not by her choice, but by Amergin's. At first, his banishment hurt and angered, but when Boyden took her arm and whispered, *"Come with me, Scota. I love you,"* all fury dissipated as if it had never been.

His love warmed her. He made her feel wanted, made her feel incredibly alive.

She went with him willingly. Walking out of Lord Amergin's camp, she never looked back.

That part of her life was over.

Scota pressed her hand to her stomach with a secretive smile. A magical babe grew within her, bringing promises of new beginnings. She looked forward to holding their daughter or son in her arms. She looked forward to growing old with Boyden in the land of his fey brethren. There were so many new things to learn and experience. She was excited by it all. Beside her, the Wind Herald walked in silence while the others of his tribe kept several paces ahead. The large group of men who first accompanied Boyden into Lord Amergin's camp parted many days before with simple nods. Four men remained. Two accompanied the Tuatha chieftain, while the fourth, the wind warrior, remained protectively by her side.

They were moving deeper inland toward a place where the faery woodlands were said to be. As they walked a grassy path, Scota thought about the mysterious faeries. Lavender shadows crept across green rolling lands and crystal-clear lochs. The ending light seemed to turn the living realm into the dominion of the magical.

In the near distance, woodlands rose from swirls of white mists, treetops kissing a gray, cloud-filled sky.

Anticipation stirred within her.

No one in her tribe knew of the existence of the magical fey woodlands, no one but herself. She felt like a traveler, on her way to a hidden and ancient discovery. "Do these woods have a special fey name, Boyden?" she asked quietly.

"Nay, we call them simply the fey woodlands. Disappointed?"

"No."

He smiled. "These woodlands are verra old. They are an enchanted place where the sound of flutes can be heard, if one cares to listen."

Her eyes widened with awe. "Have you heard these flutes?"

"Aye, I have," he answered mysteriously, adjusting the torc at his neck.

"What do they sound like?"

"It is a kind of music that has no words to describe it. Delicate notes reach inside you, telling whispers of newborn flower petals or a bee's journey to a bush. Your heart will hear it and you will understand. Many things will be new to you here. Deep within the woods, white roses grow in impenetrable thorn thickets of silver and gold, and faeries can be seen riding on the backs of snails, hares, or wolves."

"Truth?" she prompted, giving him a curious look.

"Always truth, Scota. Look for yourself." He pointed.

In the reflecting rays of the ending day, a tiny rider approached astride a blue hare with white ears. The rider, a white-cloaked faery with yellow hair, held a bridle of golden twigs.

"One of the piskies," Boyden explained, shielding his eyes from the last rays of the setting sun.

Scota shielded her eyes too. She recognized the tiny faery from the Elemental's blood memories within her, but awe still welled up inside her throat at seeing the little fey born with her own two eyes.

Boyden paused beside her at the crest of the slope, and Scota breathed in the wonder of the charming land. Ribbons of gold and silver danced in the wind-scored hills, marking the woodland's border of enchantment.

Reaching for the sky, giant trees slipped in and out of faded colors and white mist.

Her focus returned to the tiny herald astride the white-eared hare. "Boyden, the rider seems to be speaking harshly with your chieftain."

"Aye," he commented, his focus on the exchange, as well.

"Do you not wish to hear what he says?"

"The rider is a she," he corrected, a smile tugging at the corners of his mouth. "If the tiny one wished to speak with me, she would ride to me, but the wee piskies doona care much for the wind."

He glanced at her with mischief before returning his attention to the tiny faery. After a moment, his brows drew together in a frown. "I am surprised she comes to meet us in the high meadow. Normally, they willna reveal themselves in this way."

"Why do you scowl, Boyden?"

"Something is amiss. My chieftain argues."

The piskie pointed at them and gestured wildly.

"She appears to be unhappy with our presence," Scota said in observation, a falling feeling in her stomach.

"Extremely," he replied slowly. "My chieftain waves for us to go on ahead. We will wait for them at the abandoned place."

He touched her shoulder, guiding her gently forward.

"Boyden, do you . . ."

He shook his head. "I doona know, Scota. Let us wait and see. The fey react differently than one expects, and I willna say until I know the truth of their quarrel."

She pushed a few strands of hair off her face. "Although I am excited to become part of your fey brethren, I do not think the faeries want me here."

He looked at her. "Why do you say that?"

She shrugged. "Derina said they consider me an enemy."

"You are my mate. You go where I go." He took her hand. "Come, let us enter the mist together. Let me show you a wee bit of the magical."

He pulled her forward, taking a path different from the chieftain and the tiny rider. They entered the swirling white mist of the woodlands. Cool dampness caressed her face; the fresh scent of tree bark and freedom entered her lungs. Everything was beautiful.

"Boyden, never have I seen such olden trees. The trunks are so large."

"I am gladdened. The trees have seen many a time pass. Come, 'tis this way."

They walked into shadows of amber light, and he led her to the edge of a large sylvan thicket where an abandoned fort of circular homes stood. Some of the homes were built of oak timbers, but most were made of poles, stakes, twigs, and tree branches bound with clay and mud. Hazelnuts woven into musky old animal skins hung over many of the door entrances.

The air in the thicket smelled of moisture and decay, but it was not offensive, only sad. Pausing beside one of the circular homes, Scota lifted the brown animal skin and looked in. Broken acorn shells littered the floor. In the center of the room, a circle of small gray stones lay in wait for a fire long ago extinguished.

She stepped in. In the back, a large bed of old white sheepskins and woven blue blankets had been left behind. The place was sprinkled with wolf hair, and she surmised the cottage was already taken. To her right, a trestle table with a broken leg stood precariously above reaching green vines.

She returned to Boyden's side, outside.

He stood near a crumbling stone wall entwined with thick brown vines.

"Is this a faery place?" she asked, slightly disappointed.

"Nay, Scota," he chuckled. " 'Tis belonging to my tribe and abandoned from the times of the Kindred war."

"The Kindred war?"

He nodded. "Long ago, the chieftain of my tribe fulfilled a prophecy to mate with a territorial goddess to save the land. It is a long story."

She looked down at her hands. Vicious memories from her joining with the primordial wind, flickered within her. They were shades of the Kindred battle, and what had almost been.

"Scota, are you feeling ill?"

She pushed the troubling shades aside, unwilling to taint her happiness. "I am well." She was with her mate; all else mattered little to her. "You must share the chieftain's tale with me sometime."

"Sometime," he smiled in reply, offering nothing more. She did not pester him, but instead surveyed the crumbled homes with hands on her hips. "Do we rest here and wait for the others to come?"

"Aye, we rest," he replied.

Neither moved.

Instead, they stood listening to the hum of frogs and crickets greeting the growing darkness. She knew he was troubled by the appearance of the tiny faery, but remained silent. What would be, would be; she had no control over fate. She lived in the moment and would face what came when it presented itself.

To her right, a decayed ruin of fallen stones was buried beneath a massive thicket of silver thorns. Brown wrens foraged through the undergrowth, unconcerned by their presence.

"The birds do not fear us," she remarked with fascination.

"In the fey woodlands, the wild creatures doona fear, but walk among us. Wolf, pig, wren, it matters not, Scota." He pointed to the active birds. "They search only for spiders and bugs to sate their hunger." He took her hand again. "Come, let us select a cottage to rest in."

"Not that one," Scota pulled him back. "A wolf has claimed it."

"Do you think the wolf would object to us confiscating his home?" he teased.

"Yes," she tugged him back, "especially when there are so many other ruins to choose from."

"Agreed. How about the ruin near the double boulder?" He gestured toward a smaller round house.

"Let us first check availability," she advised.

He laughed and pulled her with him, the incoming night close on their heels.

The morning of the next day, they made the small round house theirs, filling it with usable pieces. From one abandoned home, they claimed a table; from another, a basket of candles; and still another, four clay pots, one large and three small. The animal skins proved more of a challenge. Old and dirty, Scota shook them out against the boulder and washed them in a nearby stream. She did not know how long the fey intended for them to wait and decided to keep busy. In the waning afternoon, Boyden went to meet with his chieftain. She did not know how long he would be and decided to take this time for herself and bathe in the black waters of the stream.

Surrounded by ancient trees draped in moss and white flowers, she dropped her clothes on the shore. Testing the cold waters with her toe, she shivered, bit her lip, and waded in. She knelt on a soft bed of rounded pebbles with black waters rising to her waist in cool caresses. After a while, she stopped shivering and began to wash.

She did not expect company.

But company, she had.

A twig broke, and a hooded figure appeared beside a tree.

"Derina," Scota greeted the ancient woman. "I did not expect anyone."

The druidess stood beneath the boughs of a large oak, leaning on a walking stick. She wore a white, hooded robe that fell to her ankles. "I brought you my soap, Princess. I thought you would like to wash from your journey."

"My thanks, Derina." Scota went to get up, but the druidess waved to her to remain where she was.

"Open your hand, Princess."

Scota caught the thin bar of green soap easily. It continually unnerved her the way the ancient saw with no eyes, but she shrugged the feeling off. "My thanks, Derina." She sniffed the soap with appreciation. The combined scents of lavender and rosemary were soothing.

"Wash and we talk." The druidess grabbed the folds of her robe with one hand and with the walking stick in the other, made her way between feathery stalks of grass. She paused to stand at the edge of the shore.

Scota dipped the soap under the moving waters and began to wash her arms and shoulders.

"You wish to speak with me alone? Without Boyden?" Scota surmised the fey might consider her an enemy still. She fervently hoped not.

"Aye," Derina replied, saying nothing further.

Freeing her hair from the plaits, Scota dipped her head under the water. In the continuing silence, she washed and rinsed her hair and her body, but the anxiety slowly built within.

She flipped her wet hair back. "The fey do not accept me, do they, Derina?" Scota murmured her question.

"Nay, the High King of the Fairies willna accept you, Princess."

Through wet lashes, she met the druidess's empty eye sockets. "Even after all that has happened? This king who judges without meeting me still considers me an enemy to his realm?"

"Aye."

"Why?" she blurted out angrily.

"You and your people invaded our land, Princess. The fey can be spiteful in their ways. They doona forgive or forget. The king accepts the unborn babe in your womb because the child be belonging to Boyden, and he wants Boyden. The Wind Herald be verra special to the faeries though he refuses to acknowledge his heritage."

Scota took the rejection deep inside and pushed it down so it would not hurt. She looked away, her once bright and hopeful future dimming into murky shadows. "He is an unwise king."

"Mayhap," the druidess replied. "The High Queen of the Faeries allies herself with you, as do I."

She looked up in surprise. "Why would she? Why would you?"

The ancient clasped the walking stick in front of her. "Without you, we both believe the line of the Servant Wind King ends. I doona think Boyden will ever claim another as he has you."

"Am I merely a vessel to you?" she scoffed, full of hurt.

"Nay, Princess. You be his heart and . . ." she smiled warmly, ". . . I hope, my friend. I am old, Princess. In my time, I have seen much and know life be not fair. When the moon rises high in the sky this eve, a rider comes to summon you to the High King. Your fate be decided then. Whatever happens, Boyden must not break away from the fey realm." White brows furrowed, and Scota felt the close regard of those empty eye sockets. "Do you understand me, Princess?"

She understood. "If I am banned from the fey, you wish me to shun him and leave." It was a statement.

"Aye, you must."

She shook her head. "What you ask . . . I can not do." She stared down at the lathered soap in her hands.

"I doona ask this lightly, Princess."

"Do not ask me at all, then," she said, holding on to her temper.

"Boyden must learn to control the lethal wind. The daughters of his line have lost the knowledge, and so he must find it within himself. The fey can help him regain it."

"He will find it," Scota murmured, believing it so.

"He must, Princess. If he canna relearn the ancient blood vow within him, the lethal wind be forever lost to us."

"Would that be so terrible?" she asked softly.

"Aye, Princess. Doona ask me why. Know only that it be a most terrible thing. Boyden must remain with his faery brethren and rediscover his blood vow of the wind."

"What of me, Derina?"

"Whatever the king's decision this eve, you carry the Wind Herald's babe, a bloodline never to be broken. If the High King decides against you, you must accept his decision."

"Where would I go, Derina?"

Derina tilted her head. "Far from here be a place known only to a few. It be called White Fells, and I will take you there. In time, you will become a distant memory to Boyden." She did not add the High King's intention to wipe the Wind Herald's memory clean of her.

"You act as if I am banned already. What of my babe?"

"When birthing time arrives, I will come to you and take the babe. I will give the babe to the father and tell him you died."

Scota studied the soap. "Your words speak the same hurt to me as Lord Amergin. He promised to give my babe to the father and tell him I died in birthing. I am not wanted on either side."

"You are caught between, Princess."

"Between," Scota repeated softly. "Is there no hope for me, Derina?"

"Methinks only a wee bit."

She nodded. "I will think on what you have said to me."

"You will come to know what I say be the way of it," Derina murmured.

"The way of what?" Boyden stood at the edge of the trees, looking inquisitively between them.

Quickly dunking her head, Scota came up sputtering. "Derina says I will like her food. After she described the tripe to me, I said I would think on it."

A single brow arched. "Do you lie to me, Scota?"

"Yes," she replied stiffly.

He gave the druidess a long stare. "You bring mischief, Derina."

"Do I, Wind Herald?" Hiking up her white robe with one hand, she leaned on her walking stick and turned away. "I go now, before the nasty wind topples me over." Without further comment, the white-haired ancient disappeared among the shadows of the trees.

"What did she say to you, Scota?"

The leaves fluttered in the day's light winds, responding to his disquiet.

"Did you speak with your chieftain?" she asked rather than answered.

"Aye, he told me the High King of the Faeries shall summon us when the moon is high this eve. You did not answer my question."

"Come into the water and I will."

"Scota," he warned.

"Come into the water, Boyden. It feels wonderful."

He moved closer, taking a step down the slight embankment.

"Without your clothes," she directed and leisurely soaped her breasts.

The tunic came off first.

She was not afraid of his temper and needed his

passion right now.

Next came the boots. One boot toppled down the embankment and landed near the water. The breeches came off next, followed by a splash.

When large hands caught at her shoulders, she pulled him down into the cold waters with a fierce kiss of possession.

Boyden went willingly. His mate was wild and hungry, battling an inner tempest she refused to discuss.

He managed to get them both to shore before she pushed him onto his back. Every muscle in his body tensed as she climbed astride him.

He stared up into the smoldering fire above him. "Teaching me your rein, Princess?"

She tilted her head, water dripping from her hair down her breasts. Her perfect mouth curved into a mysterious and tantalizing smile.

Without answering, she bent down, retaking his mouth, her lips soft and warm in their demand for his passion. Her teeth tugged gently on his lips, soft breasts crushed against his chest.

"What did you say to me?" she whispered.

His mind blanked. "When?"

"To you am I bound . . . your claiming of me."

"To you am I bound," he repeated his Claim of Binding to her with as much felt meaning as he did before. "To twilight. To honor. To land."

A cool hand slid down his stomach and wrapped at the base of his throbbing manhood.

"To you am I bound," she said, guiding him to the entrance of her woman's place.

"To twilight." She squeezed tenderly, a fingertip grazing his sensitive tip. A guttural response rose in his throat.

"To honor," she murmured against his lips.

A bead of perspiration formed on his temple.

"To land."

She pushed down upon him, and he exhaled sharply. His hands fitted over her hips.

Scota nearly wept at the exquisite stretching. Bracing her hands against his shoulders, she began her ride on her untamable and tawny stallion. Rocking, pumping, she needed to fill every part of her until she thought she might explode.

The hands on her hips challenged her authority and dominance. She grabbed a wrist and pinned his hand above his head, forcing compliance by offering him her breast.

His head lifted, his free hand reaching for her breast. An insatiable mouth settled on her. Heat pulled on her nipple, stealing her entire existence.

Releasing his wrist, she cupped the back of his head, holding the fire close, her hips driving up and down his length, reaching for the agony of female completion.

Thoughts of giving him up pierced her heart, and she rode him harder.

He released her breast with a harsh oath, hips surging upward, reaching the cliffs of a male's pleasure. She could feel him swelling within her. Nails digging into his shoulders, she ground down onto him.

Boyden flipped her over, commandeering the rhythm. She went rigid for a moment then fought him, as he knew she would, his beautiful and tormented warrior. Pinning her hands above her head, he kissed her mouth, enticing her to comply with his dominance. "My turn, my warrior."

Her gaze flashed angry fire, and he gave her deeper, longer strokes in answer, covering her slender body with his.

The shards of fey light gleamed in her eyes before black lashes fluttered closed.

Her thighs slowly spread wider.

His strokes deepened.

Friction grew between their bodies.

Wet.

Consuming.

Heightening.

His teeth clenched, refusing to give in to his body.

"Scota," he rasped.

Hips surging, she stiffened under him with a soft cry. Her cave tightened around his shaft, milking him in a female's release.

He surged forward, hardening, giving her all the pleasure he could before he lost the battle.

Eyes closing, he jerked above her, spewing his seed into her womb in a roaring windstorm of claim.

Boyden flung back his head, air leaving his lungs in a rush. His body went weak, and he lay down beside her, fulfilled.

Soaked in sweat, and after a few recovering breaths,

he spoke low, "Now, will you tell me what Derina said to you?" Her gaze moved over his shoulder. "You might want to speak with the spiky-haired faery first."

Shifting his weight, he lifted his head and met jeweled eyes. Astride a blue hare with white ears, a piskie with thorny white hair stared back at him, her tiny face unreadable.

"You are early," he muttered.

"COME NOW," she piped. Reining her mount around, they hopped away into green stalks of downy grasses.

Boyden pushed to his feet and reached for Scota's hand.

CHAPTER 22

SCOTA LIFTED HER FACE TO the warm breeze. She stood next to a massive tree fashioned with three intertwined trunks. Interlaced boughs reached ever outward, creating shade and grace, and cupping the blue sky in graceful lengths. A songbird peeped behind her and flew away on tiny blue wings. Touching the coarse, brown-black bark of the tree, she looked up into a sea of green leaves. They fluttered with silvery undercoats in respect of the afternoon air currents.

"She be an olden tree goddess," Derina remarked quietly beside her, her face turned upward. "The trunks be named Maid, Mother, Crone."

"Yes." Scota patted the triple trunks of the goddess tree with fondness.

Dressed in an ethereal gown of crimson rosebuds, she felt more like a false queen than a warrior, and turned her attention to the long ridge known as *Teamhair na Rí*, the Hill of the Kings. It was Tara, the faery's enchanted home.

"This is the seat of all enchantment, is it not?" she

asked with awe.

"Aye, in the below and in the above."

Light winds caressed the sun-kissed land, blowing floating veils about her bare calves.

"Many died here in the before-time and in the present-time," the druidess said softly. "It be a place of standing stones and ring forts, a land of moving waters, and of kingly dwellers with troubled hearts."

Scota nodded. *Troubled hearts all*, she thought. Three months had come and gone since the summons of the faeries' High King Lugh. It was now the month of *Lughnasa*, August, the season of harvest, the season of the High King. Many of Boyden's tribe believed the High King to be *samhioldanach*, equally-skilled-in-all-arts. She pulled at her lip, hoping he was at least skilled in fair judgments.

Gathering the delicate folds of the gown in one hand, she stepped away from the goddess tree, her gaze resting on a small group of birds flying north. "Ravens fly in the sky this late afternoon. It is a bad omen, Derina."

"Doona mark the birds," the druidess replied, adjusting the belt of brown horsehair over her white, woolen robe. "They fly always near Tara."

Scota curled her arm over her rounding stomach, a faint color of rose in her cheeks. "I mark all things of late, Derina," she said gravely.

The High King and Boyden continued to disagree, their battle over her future turning the fey realm dull and lifeless with dissent and weary tempers.

"I heard the king threaten to spell cast Boyden into forgetting me. Is it true, Derina?"

"Aye."

She nodded, distraught and angry. "Give me a sword and I will spell cast off the king's head."

"That may be the way of it," Derina cackled, and Scota frowned at the druidess.

"I do not find it amusing, Derina."

"I do. The High Queen may thank you." The ancient switched her crooked walking stick to her left hand.

Scota gave the fitted veil covering her stomach a strong study. "I hear the King and Queen do not get along."

"Nay, they doona get along. It be the way of it sometimes. But enough of them, how do you feel?"

"Besides angry and frustrated, I am hungry all the time."

"Aye, even Boyden commented proudly upon your appetite. You should eat small portions many times a day to keep up your strength."

She shrugged, feeling faintly guilty, and tugged on the double-puff sleeves of the gown. "I feel famished all the time, Derina. It is worse in the eve when I lay down to rest."

"Eat a wee bit then, too. Doona worry about it overly much."

"Do other women who are breeding eat as much?"

"Some," the druidess replied. "Methinks your womb be crowded with more than one babe and you must eat accordingly."

"Maybe," she whispered, a small tremor in her voice.

"Princess, I attend all the magical births of the tribe. There be no need to fret."

"I do not fret," Scota whirled away, stifling her trepidation of a multiple birth and wishing to vent her irritation on a stubborn king.

The ancient tapped her walking stick on the ground. "You delay, Princess."

"I am no longer a princess, Derina."

The druidess's eyebrows lifted in supreme skepticism. "Princess," she said forcefully. "Blood and heritage doona change because you move to a different land. I feel the approach of twilight in my bones. 'Tis time to go. You canna delay any longer."

Scota looked over her shoulder and met those empty eye sockets directly. "Derina, it does not feel right to handfast to Boyden before an angry king."

"Ah." The ancient folded her hands on the top of her walking stick, a peculiar frown tugging at her mouth. "Be this why you came here? To get away?"

"Yes."

"Do you run away?" Derina gave her a disappointed look, and something inside Scota roared to life. "Never do I run," she nearly shouted.

"I wondered for a moment where the warrior princess had gone."

Scota judged it prudent not to curse on the day of her handfasting and drew a deep breath. "I am here," she said.

"The King willna attend, Princess, and Boyden willna wait any longer. He wishes to claim you for the entire fey realm to see. Come. 'Tis time. Walk with an old crone."

With careful attention, Scota lifted the hem of her delicately woven gown and walked with Derina through the blades of grass, her feet bare against the warm land.

"My thanks for the gown, Derina. It is unlike anything I have ever seen or worn." Scota felt the sheer fey gown revealed more than it should, but it felt enchanting against her skin. Red rose petals hugged her body, offering glimpses of white skin. The round neck bodice, showing the swells of her breasts, was accented with ribbons of tiny white roses. Double-puff sleeves fell off her shoulders in scalloped veils draping over her hands. Crimson layers of light sprinkled with glittering crystals attached to her high hips and floated down to her bare ankles, trailing outward behind her. The hem, embroidered with tiny sprigs and webs, gave the gown a hint of weight. Her feet were bare except for the anklets of ivy.

"The Wind Guardians gift it to you, not I." The druidess leaned behind her and adjusted the long translucent drape, which attached to the center of her back. It drifted behind her, caught in the warm breezes of the day.

"The Wind Guardians? I thought they did not approve of me." She adjusted the crown of roses resting atop her head. Her straight black hair fell down her back in a soft waterfall of movement.

"Make no mistake, Princess. They doona approve of you, but neither are they foolish. They can no longer deny the female carrying the seed of the Wind Herald. They walk a fine path between displeasing the High King and alienating the Wind Herald."

"What does Boyden think? They have not allowed me to see him for near a sennight."

"Ask him yourself. He stands there." The druidess pointed off to the left and dipped her head. "I will wait for you beside the stone circle. Doona delay, twilight comes and you must handfast to Boyden during the time of the between."

"My thanks, Derina."

The druidess touched her arm in an offering of comfort before she disappeared amid the shadows of two trees.

Scota lifted her gaze to Boyden, and the land felt as if it moved beneath her bare feet.

In the shafts of fading sunlight filtering through the branches of trees, he waited. An unmoving god of power and silence rising from the below realm of the faeries, he was unfathomable. His hair shone gold even in the shadows, the bronze torc a glimmer about his corded neck. He wore a sleeveless, purple tunic with laces up the front and the sides. Fitted black breeches and boots showed the muscular length of his legs. He looked the mysterious Wind Servant King, charming, dangerous, returning from the long-ago past to steal away her heart.

Boyden gazed intently at her face, his center swelling with pride and awe. She was beauty and strength to him and all that remained good in the land. He extended his hand, and she came forward, an ethereal creature of crimson veils and glittering crystals.

"You look beautiful, Scota." He caught her smaller hand, her palm nearly as calloused as his.

She smiled, and the day brightened for him. "As you," she replied calmly.

"How do you feel?"

"Hungry."

A smile curved his lips. "There will be food and celebration after the ceremony. Can you wait?"

"Yes, Boyden," she squeezed his hand. "I only tease."

"I missed you and ask forgiveness for my absence these past days." He kept his eyes on her face, silently cursing the king. "The High King and I doona agree."

"I know."

He nodded, trying to form the right words. Trying to think of how to tell her about his heart, about how he felt. Swordplay and battle came easier for him. He was not one to bring a maiden into a garden and spout poetic phrases like a bard.

"I would have it differently between us, Scota."

Her silence was not making it any easier, and he shifted on his feet, a slight movement.

"Tell me, Boyden."

"I wish to handfast with you," he said.

She nodded. "Derina came to me last morn and told me your wishes."

He fought from fiddling with her fingers. "Will you handfast with me?"

"I am here, Boyden, am I not? Do you think I wear

sheer clothes such as these every day?"

"I need to hear your words, Scota."

She stared at their hands. "I agree to handfast with you for a year and a day, a trial-marriage."

"Forever, Scota," he corrected, placing his thumb under her chin and forcing her to look up at him. He was unaccustomed to her shyness. " 'Tis not a trial-marriage. Our handfasting ceremonies are to ensure couples be well matched and able to conceive a babe during a year and a day. I deem us well matched." He looked pointedly at her stomach and tried not to grin smugly. "And able to conceive a babe or two."

She smiled.

"Do you accept me, Scota?"

She considered, her hesitation unnerving him. "Yes," she said and his heart eased. He cupped the back of her head and kissed her lightly on the lips. "I willna give you up, Scota."

"Even if I wish it?" she said quietly, thinking back upon Derina's words. *If you are banned from the fey realm, you must leave him.*

He pulled back, searching her face, staring deep into her eyes. "Do you?"

"No, Boyden." She laughed tensely. "Do not mark my nervousness."

"All will be well," he reassured, taking her hand and putting it in the crook of his arm. "Come." He guided her forward. "Join me in the handfasting circle. Twilight descends, and I doona wish to keep an ornery druidess waiting."

They walked quietly together to the east side of Tara. Near a giant pillar stone and tranquil oak, Derina, and what remained of the tribe of the *Tuatha Dé Danann*, waited around the large circle of stones. They came out in support, showing their disagreement with the High King.

The children, Nora and Cavan, stood with their family, looking taller than when last they saw them. Nora waved, and Cavan gave a simple nod.

Young maidens, dressed in white robes of wool, tossed red flower petals along the perimeter of the stone circle.

Candles flickered, marking the four cardinal directions of the land and winds.

Boyden led his mate once around the gray circle of stones. With her on his arm, he entered from the east.

Derina insisted on performing the ceremony in place of one of the elders to show her strong disagreement with the king.

"You need to guide me, Boyden," Scota murmured. "Your ways are different from mine."

"Stand by my side, Scota and answer all truthfully." He led her to the center of the circle.

Upon the ground in front of them, in tufts of grass, waited a tiny, dark, wooden altar. Resting on its surface was a jeweled dagger, red cord, a small silver box, and a trowel.

Scota looked at the dagger and murmured, "This is very different."

Outside the circle, a chime rang three times to mark the beginning of the ceremony.

Derina entered the circle and faced them.

The druidess wore a red cloak formed of veils over her white robe. Dried rosemary, woven into her white plaits, made her look almost youthful.

"We begin the handfasting blessing. Are you ready, Boyden?" the ancient asked.

"Aye," he replied.

"Princess Scota? Are you ready?" the druidess prompted.

Scota nodded. "Yes," she answered, her heart pounding.

❧❧

"Let us begin in the east. Here we ask for the blessings of the element of Air, which brings truth, wisdom, and vision. May East and Air bless Boyden and Scota throughout their lives."

❧❧

"Now we turn to the south. Here we ask for the blessings of the element of Fire, home of passion, pleasure, joy, and happiness. May South and Fire bless Boyden and Scota throughout their lives."

❧❧

"Now let us turn to the west. Here we ask for the blessings of the element of Water, bringing tranquility, peace, emotion, and serenity. May West and Water bless Boyden and Scota throughout their lives."

❧❧

"Now we turn to the north, where the element of Earth resides, deeply grounded in strength, comfort, and support. May North and Earth bless Boyden and Scota throughout their lives."

❧❧

"And in the Center and all around us, above and below, resides the Spirit who brings blessings of love, magic, friendship, and community. May the Spirit of all things divine join us and bless Boyden and Scota on this sacred day."

❧❧

Scota faced Boyden, slipping her hands in his.

"Do any here seek to challenge this joining?" Derina asked, looking around and wrinkling her empty eye sockets. Several maidens giggled, but Scota tensed, straining in wait for a faery king's strong objection.

"Relax, Scota." Boyden's thumb glided over her flesh.

The druidess turned back to them. "Then, 'tis time to begin the joining. Twilight returns once more to us."

Scota glanced up at the tinting of a purpling sky, wondering how the ancient woman recognized the between-time.

"Do not ponder it, Scota. She is fey born."

"Quiet, Boyden," Derina snapped. "I am ready to begin."

He nodded to her, amusement tugging at the corners of his mouth.

"Boyden, do you come here of your own free will?"

the druidess asked with the authority of the highly re-
spected.

"I do."

"Scota, do you come here of your own free will?"

"I do," she replied softly.

"State your vows."

Boyden squeezed her hands. "Repeat these vows
after me, Scota."

She nodded.

"We commit ourselves to be with each other in joy
and in adversity."

Scota echoed the words.

"In wholeness and brokenness."

"In wholeness and brokenness," she repeated, her
stomach cramping slightly as if the babe or babes in her
womb were kicking out with joy.

"In peace and turmoil."

"In peace and turmoil," she repeated, a sense of permanence washing over her.

"Living together faithfully all our days," Boyden
said firmly.

"May the gods and goddesses give us the strength to
keep these vows. So be it."

She repeated the final phrase just as resolutely.

Derina placed a red cord over and around their right
hands, binding them together.

"Red symbolizes life and a handfasting commitment
for one year and a day." She began to knot the cord more
tightly. "This blessing be not of a trial-marriage, but one

of permanence and forevermore. Boyden has claimed the seed rooting in the bride's womb and in doing so, claims her, as well."

Offering up a simple blessing, the druidess bowed over the red cord. Returning to the altar, she picked up the jeweled dagger and handed it to Boyden.

"Do we cut the cord, Boyden?" Scota asked.

"Nay." He held the small dagger in his right hand. "Help me."

She lifted her bound wrist with his and watched as he cut a lock of her hair and placed it in the silver box Derina held open.

"Do the same to my hair, Scota, and doona cut too much." He held the hilt out to her, a teasing glint in his eye.

Scota reached for the ceremonial dagger. Seizing a tawny wave between two fingers, she sliced it free and held it up so he could see how much she took.

He grinned, and she placed the sun-kissed silk in the silver box over her own nightshade offering.

Derina closed the silver box and returned it to the altar. "For the future of the winds," she murmured. "Be understanding and be patient with each other," Derina said, backing away. "Be free in the giving of affection and warmth. Have no fear and let not the ways of the unenlightened give you unease, for the gods and goddesses be with you always in blessing." She stepped out of the circle.

Boyden picked up the silver box with his left hand.

"Do we bury it?" she inquired, looking at the trowel.

"Aye, in a moment. Open the lid with your left hand."

She opened it.

"Now we must hold our bound hands over the opening."

They did.

The air glittered above their wrists in a feeling of icy warmth. The red cord disappeared before their eyes and settled in the box, the knots intact.

Scota blinked.

"Close the lid, Scota."

The lid slipped shut from her fingers in silence.

"We bury the silver box in the center of the circle to safeguard our future. Place your right hand over mine." He picked up the trowel.

Scota placed her hand over his and leaned forward with him as he dug the hole in a patch of dirt framed by tiny white flowers.

Kneeling together, they lowered the silver box in the hole and covered it beneath a black mound of grassy dirt.

From outside the circle, Derina called out, "The circle be open and unbroken. May the peace of the Old Ones go in our hearts. Boyden and Scota be handfasted."

Somewhere close, a bell rang three times, a twinkling of sound in the air.

"We are one."

"Yes," Scota agreed, *at least for this day*.

"Come, Scota." He guided her out and around the circle before introducing her to his tribe and receiving a hug from Nora.

The celebration lasted into a night crowded with stars and a waning moon. Torches were lit, and a great feast offered. Children fell asleep in their mothers' arms. Boyden sat next to her on a grouping of white sheepskins. Platters of freshwater eel and fish were brought to them, and she valiantly sampled each, trying hard not to wrinkle her nose.

"You doona like eel, Scota?"

"I am not used to it."

He motioned to another girl. She brought over a platter of pink salmon, which had been cooked over flames and drizzled with honey.

"Try this." He took a small portion and placed it on her clay plate. She sampled it. In her mind she knew it tasted well enough, but her stomach decided, at this most inopportune time, not to accept any food without giving her much grievance.

"You are not eating, Scota?"

Her fingers moved restlessly in her lap. "It is only the merriment of the day."

He nodded, though she thought him not fully convinced in her answer.

Next came an offering of tripe, sheep's stomach cooked for several hours in goat's milk and herbs. She did not think her queasy stomach could tolerate this dish, either, and held up her hand to stop him.

"Boyden, no more."

He waved the girl carrying the tripe platter away.

"You have no appetite this eve?"

"My appetite left me at the sight of the tripe." She smiled weakly. She had eaten enough food over these last few days to last her a lifetime.

"Wait here." He climbed to his feet and disappeared into the crowd of revelers. A few moments later he returned, carrying a large silver goblet.

"Boyden, I do not want any mead."

" 'Tis not mead. I went to Derina and she gave me goat's milk laced with honey. She said it will calm your stomach." He offered it to her. "Try it."

Taking the goblet, she brought it to her lips and sipped. Soon, her queasy stomach rolled into quiet.

"Better?" He gave her a crooked grin.

She nodded. "Yes, my thanks."

"Doona suffer in silence around me. I promise, I am here for you, Scota."

She was not used to someone caring for her needs without being ordered to, as a slave was. Boyden stayed by her side because he wished it, but a powerful fey king could change all that.

He gave her a level look as if reading her thoughts. "The king willna separate us."

"He can spell cast you to forget me."

"I willna allow it, Scota." He captured her hand and kissed her fingers. "Finish your sweet milk. I wish to show you something."

Raising the goblet to her lips, Scota drank what remained and set the goblet aside.

"Done, my warrior?"

She nodded.

He climbed to his feet. Grasping both her hands, he pulled her to her feet and wrapped an arm around her waist.

"Come."

CHAPTER 23

AFTER A BLESSING FROM NORA and Cavan's family, Boyden guided his bride through the darkness of the trees. They walked around a thorn bush and paused on the slope of a rolling pasture lit with white flowers and the moon's embrace.

"What is this place, Boyden?"

"A place of new beginnings. Like you, a select few of my tribe doona like the below. They have decided to build their homes near the streams of Tara. I thought we would, too. Amergin did not attack this place, and so it remains belonging to us."

"The moon's light sheds her brightness, yet her light appears different here, more white than amber. It is as if I can see in the dark." She stepped away from him.

"This land is of Tara, Scota. It is enchanted, and those of the fey may always see in it."

"I am not enchanted."

"No matter how much I dislike it, the *Gaoth Shee* chose to link with you, and that makes you enchanted.

You also happen to carry a wind babe . . ." he paused and grinned, "or babes in your womb. Methinks you are more enchanted than me, my warrior."

She turned away, but not before he saw the saddened look on her face.

"You doona like the land, Scota?"

She shook her head. "The land is beautiful, Boyden," she agreed quietly. "I am honored to be here."

"What is it, then?" he asked, not understanding her sadness. He thought this place perfect for them. He could see a round cottage rising under the gentle shade of an oak or yew with a green meadow out back for their horses and goats. He could envision children running and playing among the wildflowers, the wind tangling their curls.

"Boyden, how can you plan for a future when the High King of the Faeries refuses to accept me?"

"He will accept you," he replied steadfastly. Any other future was absurd to him. He was willing to fight the king to keep her in his life, and would hold nothing back.

"Scota, look at me."

"Have you felt the wind?" she interrupted, lifting her face to the starlit night sky. There was an undertone of longing in her voice.

"Aye, she remains near me always, whether I will it or not." There was just enough glow to see the smooth paleness of his bride's cheek.

"I feel her presence, but she keeps her distance from me."

In the crimson veils of her nearly translucent gown,

she looked like a faery queen standing in sunset hues. "Do you miss her touch?" he asked, his voice joining the silence of the night.

"I do not know." She looked at him from over her shoulder. "When she joined with me, colors looked brighter, sounds were more melodic, the fragrance of the land drifted in the air so I knew each scent from blade of grass to the tallest tree. Your touch . . ." she paused, her features softening in remembrance, ". . . your touch sent shivers to the innermost core of me, heightening all my senses, heightening everything. I must confess to missing that part. Do you not?"

"I know not of what you speak," he replied dryly. "Never have I joined with her."

"Never?"

He could hear the astonishment in her voice and scowled. "She willna approach you again, Scota, unless I wish it. The Elemental understands my will now."

"Do you wish it, Boyden?"

His hands tightened by his sides and he looked away.

Scota studied him, feeling uneasy yet determined to find out the whole truth of the long-ago times. She had changed much since coming to this land of enchantment and mystery. She was no longer naïve in believing only one side of a tale. "Why do you deny your heritage?"

"By the winds," he muttered under his breath. "My heritage is one of death. How can you ask this of me?"

"Your heritage is older than the faeries, belonging to the before-time. With an ancestry to the ancient guardians and the blood threads from a Servant King of the wind, you are very special."

He did not reply.

"Was the Servant King just, Boyden?"

He looked at her, not appreciative. "What do you mean?"

"I ask a simple question. Was this king a just and fair king?" She met his gaze intently, dark to dark in the magical glimmer of land and night. "Did he kill and maim for his own pleasure and wealth? Did he rule in tyranny?"

"He was a just ruler of his realm."

She looked at him sideways. "How can you be so sure, Boyden?"

"I feel it within me."

She clasped her hands in front of her. "If this Wind King was a just ruler of his realm, then why do you deny his heritage?"

"I doona deny him."

"By denying *her*, you deny him."

Scota saw how her words hit their target.

"This *her* whom you speak of, is a magical, self-indulgent creature whose wish for freedom killed a fair king."

"Maybe he did not understand her needs," she suggested calmly in the face of his anger. "Perhaps you will be more perceptive." She smiled and added, "You are with me."

He gazed at her silently.

"You must try, Boyden." The moment of tact and delicacy evaporated, and she spoke her thoughts directly.

"You are the only one who can. The *Gaoth Shee* linked with me to get closer to you." She needed to reach him. "You said her wish for freedom killed the king."

"Aye, the king's brother acted upon her wish, and with his lover, they killed the king."

"Are you sure that is what truly happened?" she asked.

His lips tightened. "I have the blood memories of the Wind King, Scota. Do you question my memories?"

She answered slowly. "No, Boyden." She knew it would not be easy.

"What then?" he demanded, low and hostile.

"I question your interpretation of the events." She held up her hand to stay his retort. "Your linking with the Wind King gives you only his view. When the lethal wind linked with me, Boyden, she left behind impressions, faded images of the past, a residual wave of longings."

"What are you trying to tell me, Scota?"

"I do not sense evil in her or a lust for power or wealth. She simply exists. All I sense is a terrible loneliness. She is alone, Boyden, experiencing a loneliness you and I can never hope to comprehend, and if we ever did, I suspect it would drive us to madness."

"You speak of her with feelings in your heart," he uttered in low defiance.

"Boyden, no creature should be alone."

He frowned.

"Have you remembered the blood vow of the Servant King?" she asked, trying a different approach.

"I have not thought much upon it." He rubbed his ear.

"Why do you not ask her?"

"Ask her?" he echoed in surprise. "Summon *her*?" He let out an explosive snort. "Do you know of whom you speak, Scota? She is death."

"Is she, Boyden? Is she really?"

He stared at her, obviously incensed by her words, but that did not stop her.

"She killed only at the bidding of another, the bidding of the Wind Servant King. You have been so busy rejecting her and your heritage, perhaps the answers you seek lay with embracing her. Summon her, Boyden."

"I willna risk it." He gave an angry snarl and turned away.

Scota stood still, trying to understand his vehemence. His rigid figure appeared in the darkest of silhouettes against the field of white and yellow flowers. Why would he not try? She studied him and came to a slow understanding. "The wind will not harm me, Boyden."

"Can you promise me this, Scota?" He glanced at her.

"Search inside yourself, Boyden. She will not harm anyone or anything you hold dear."

"Why now?" he asked with a hollow and weary voice, the telling of his battle with the High King of the Faeries finally showing. "Why do you speak of this to me now?"

She stared past him to the field of soft glowing. "I am a princess, Boyden. Among my people, strength means peace. You go to face the High King of the Faeries from a weaker position because of our handfasting. If you meet him instead from a position of strength, with the wind beside you, will he not turn a more understanding ear to your words?"

He faced her. "Do you ask me to threaten the High King of the Faeries?" he asked angrily.

"Boyden, I do not ask you to threaten your king." She moistened her lips. "You do not have to say a word. The High King, sensing your renewed allegiance to the wind, will take control of his temper and prejudice, and I hope, judge me fairly. That is all I ask."

Hands on his hips, he tilted his face to the sky and exhaled loudly. Shaking his head, he snorted, then chuckled. "It would not surprise me if you could talk a king into giving up his throne."

"At the moment, I am trying to talk a stubborn and brooding king into claiming his heritage." She picked up a small rock and threw it aside.

He sighed and looked at her, a smile faint on his lips. "I willna kill the innocent for the sake of us, Scota."

"I would not ask you to. I ask only for fair judgment."

He nodded. "So be it. Stand away from me."

Boyden thought it would be the hardest thing he ever did, this summoning of an olden death goddess.

It was not.

It was infinitely and horribly easy.

Closing his eyes, he extended his arms from his

sides, palms upturned.

He willed the ancient wind near. "Come to me," he murmured.

All those life-long days of denial, when at least he knew what and who he was, withered away in a strange wave of welcomed relief.

He could not see her, but felt the cold pitch and breath of the air pick up.

Blades of grass rustled.

Flower stalks and petals trembled.

Tree branches swayed their leaves, murmuring of an ancient's presence.

"I BE HERE."

Boyden opened his eyes.

The Elemental stood before him in the likeness of his new bride. A crimson gown of crystals floated in the air about a slender body with gossamer wings. Shiny black hair drifted down her shoulders and arms, moving in an unseen breeze. Her face appeared snow white and was smooth and oval in the ways of the fey. Black brows arched on a sleek line like his beloved, but that was where the similarity of the reflection ended. Hard, jeweled eyes, laced with long silver-tipped lashes, moved slowly over him as if willing answers to all questions.

The whisper of her breathing resonated inside him.

He set his jaw and took hold of his emotions. "Show me your true form."

The borrowed image of his bride faded to swirls of black mist, darker than shade, darker than night. She became a living and glittering essence, and when he inhaled, he gave her permission to enter him.

Air and frost rushed into his lungs, snatching his breath, and his insides twisted in rebellion.

A wailing of memories . . .

A terrible loneliness . . .

"Show me the last memory of your Servant King," he commanded silently.

From the perspective of the ancient being, shades of the nightmare took form in his mind; swirls of black mist split and coalesced into shimmering tints and colors.

He saw a likeness of himself staked to the ground.

A gallant wheezing.

Red, black, wetness.

Dying . . .

"Daughter," the king called gently, his head falling low between his shoulders, a bowing in death's coming.

The child scrambled to her dying father, hugging him close with skinny white arms.

"Listen to me, daughter. With my death, the lethal wind goes free and our realm enters into chaos. Doona ever think of her or summon her. You have not the strength to control her, and she kills all she touches. Live your life away from here. When a male child returns to our line, the blood vow will stream in the reclaiming. Now go . . ."

Weeping, the grief-stricken child grasped the folds of her soiled gown and climbed to unsteady legs. In strangled gulps, she lurched to the two feathered mounts, falling down to her knees only once. Pulling herself up, she was careful to avoid the hooked white horns of the well-trained beasts. Grasping the golden reins of the closest one, she slid a small hand around the seat strap and hauled herself up into the light brown leather saddle, her legs disappearing among brown feathers. Taking the reins of her mount in a practiced hand, she glanced at the second bird. Riderless, the second animal would no doubt follow her lead. With a final anguished look toward her dying father, she commanded her mount into the air. The second bird followed.

Expansive wings extended, and with a few hops, they took to the air. The king watched his only child rise into the night sky and disappear among the most brilliant of star-filled nights.

His head dipped between his shoulders, and he wheezed, "Come to me, my White Wind."

The sound of the winds beat at the land giving way to a storm rising.

"I be here."

"Blood to Blooded, a taken oath. Breath to Vow, a forevermore. Honor to Obedience, a defended promise," the king rasped. "I restate my blood vow to you."

The air vibrated in an acknowledgment.

"You want your freedom?" he demanded in wrath with his last waning strength. "Seduced by treachery, gone behind my back instead of asking, so I gift it to you." He lifted his head, glaring at the swirls of black mist. "Forevermore are you free," he snarled in fury. "Forevermore are you alone."

A keening cry skirted the land and lochs, sending flocks of birds into the night.

"With this last breath, I give to you what you would not ask of me. He who comes after, blood of the blood-ed, blood of my blood, willna ever know you." Breath rattled in his pierced lung and side where his life's essence spilled, soiling the ground.

The king's eyelashes lowered, splayed against cheeks leeched of all color. With his dying breath, he whispered his will. "You are free."

Boyden stiffened. Within him, tumultuous memories swirled and faded to pitch and grief.

Betrayal.

Sorrow.

Rage.

All feelings belonging to a dead king.

Comprehension came slowly, a dimming now brightened, a denial once strewn in past and obscurity, now acknowledged, now whole.

In the deep shadowy reaches within himself, he finally understood the silent and unwritten blood vow of his kin. Not the tribe of the *Tuatha Dé Danann*, not the faeries, not the primordial guardians, but the other kin, the ones olden and lost to the before-time, the ones known as the Tribe of the Winds.

He was like none other ever born.

Through the generations, through the long passage of seasons, his royal bloodline became diluted with the magical, yet remained strong with blood remembrance.

In his mind, he saw the Servant King, tawny and proud, not listening to any of his advisers. It had been a fatal mistake of arrogance and youth, which led a realm teetering on rebellion to fall.

Boyden's fists clenched. Through hurt and betrayal, he had lashed out and banished the very thing he should have kept close. He should have understood.

As he understood now.

The Elemental was of the natural, a dark innocent. She was misdirected by a brother's treachery, a brother's lust for power and wealth.

The Wind King should have granted the Elemental freedom to roam the lands as she wished. Not to do harm, but to experience. And by so doing, she would have willingly come back to him. He should not have damned her to a forever aloneness, not cursed her from her bloodline.

Flinging back his head, Boyden opened his eyes. In the dark night above, stars twinkled overhead, sharing the sky with a crescent moon goddess.

He inhaled deeply.

Blood memories were intact. The olden past revealed

within him.

He remained the only son born to the bloodline of the Wind Servant King.

He was the Wind Servant King, reborn.

The scent of life and wildflowers filled his lungs.

"Boyden . . ." his warrior bride broke off, concern in her voice.

His being ached for her.

He turned to her, his beloved queen. Searching her face, he hardly recognized her with tears streaming down flushed cheeks. "Stand still, Scota."

She nodded.

Opening his mouth, he exhaled the ancient dark goddess from his body.

She came out of him in a rush of black mist and surrounded them, blocking out the land and stars. Out of the corner of his eye, his bride's crimson veils blew hard in the gusts of air, her body straight and true.

"Blood to Blooded, a taken oath," he spoke the ancient vow of his royal ancestor loud and clear. "Breath to Vow, a forevermore. Honor to Obedience, a defended promise." He paused, spreading his arms wider. "I restate my blood vow to you."

Black winds centered on him with a clinging chill of joy and acceptance.

"Never will you be alone again," he told her.

The winds eased to a gentle blowing.

"Come to me with all you question, all you need. Doona go to another." He pointed to Scota. "Never hurt her or my bloodline."

The moon and stars blinked bright in answer.

The green lands and tall trees materialized from gray vapors.

Boyden looked into his bride's eyes. They glittered with golden shards and tears of pride.

"I give you freedom," he spoke dispassionately to the *Gaoth Shee*. "Come to me when I call and do only what I bid, for we are of the belonging now."

The air quieted.

The land quieted.

Moon shadows returned.

Exhaustion clung to his bones.

A distant owl hooted, piercing the night with his predatory song.

" 'Tis done, Scota. The wind and I are one."

"Yes," she whispered.

He extended his hand to her.

With a harsh laugh of relief, Scota ran into his arms and held him. A deep tremor passed from his body into hers.

"Boyden, all will be well."

His head dipped to her shoulder with a grateful and tired sigh. Their legs giving out, they sunk to their knees into the cushioned grass, clinging to each other.

Warm breath caressed her neck.

"I am the Wind Servant King, Scota."

She pressed her cheek to his. "I know."

He lifted his head, and she stared into his amethyst

eyes, the gray hue rarely returning.

"Do you remember all of it, Boyden?"

"Aye, the blood memories flow clear in me now. It is as you said. I had to see both views, the king's and the wind's. Do you remember I told you the king's brother betrayed him?"

"Yes."

He sat back, resting a forearm on a propped knee.

She sat back, too. Easing on her hip and folding her hands in her lap, she waited for him to gather his thoughts.

"The brother was able to gain support because the king lost touch with his realm. In his overconfidence, the king dinna hear the needs of his people even though his advisers sought to counsel him. When the heavy rains did not relent, crops failed and people went hungry. When the king did nothing to help, the people turned to the brother." He smiled sadly. "In the same way as the *Gaoth Shee* turned to the brother when her wishes for freedom went unheard."

"Why did the king not listen?"

He shook his head. "I wish I knew. It was a time of anguish for him, a beloved mate recently lost. Methinks grief blocked out all else."

"Grief will do that."

He nodded.

"What happened to the lethal wind, Boyden?"

"As he lay dying, betrayed by his brother, the king granted the lethal wind her freedom but with a curse to remain alone forevermore. The darkest sister of the four winds was never meant to be alone, Scota. She needs belonging to do no harm. If I die without leaving an heir to the bloodline, there is no telling the havoc she would rain upon the lands and creatures."

"We must make sure to give her many heirs then," Scota said firmly.

"Aye, we must," he grinned through his weariness.

Tenderly, she pushed several strands of hair away from his eyes. "You must rest, Boyden."

He ran a hand down his face. "I feel as if a horse has galloped over me."

"You do not look it."

He pulled her gently into his lap. "Ah, what do I look like, my feisty and dominant wind bride?"

Scota wrapped her arms around his neck and snuggled, pressing her face into the warmth of his shoulder. *You look like a king.*

The sound of a bee came near her ear, and she swatted absently at it.

He stiffened beneath her. " 'Tis no bee, Scota."

She raised her head at the loud drone of bees suddenly surrounding them.

Before her eyes, tiny glints of amber splayed the land.

"The tiny lights you see are the piskies," he explained. "They call me to the High King."

"Not now," she protested.

"He knows I am weary and seeks advantage to bend my will to his."

Scota pushed off his lap in a rustle of red veils. "Give

me a blasted sword, and I will show him who has the advantage."

"Nay, Scota, you must remain here." He hiked himself up and kissed her lightly on the mouth. "I will return when I can."

With fists clenched at her sides, she watched him go.

CHAPTER 24

IN THE FEY REALM KNOWN to some tribes as the Otherworld, Boyden walked alone toward the throne hall of Tara. His boots sounded silent on the flat stone pavers and tiny fissures of green moss.

He wore his handfasting clothes, a sleeveless tunic cast in the colors of ending twilight, a shade preference dyed from the bilberry plant. His woolen breeches, dyed a darker purple, appeared nearly black to the eye. He had pulled his hair back and tied it with a strip of leather Derina provided. He knew the clothes fit him well by the look of admiration on his bride's face. It pleased him to see her thus. Without her by his side, he felt lost in the currents of the wind. He would never give her up.

She waited among his people in the above, a battle she stubbornly fought and reluctantly conceded to him. He knew her dread of interior places from their passage through the spriggan's cave and wished to protect her from the strain of it, especially now. He would protect his bride and unborns at whatever sacrifice to himself. Scota's passion and anger gave him the strength for his next confrontation with the king. He knew the tolerance of the leader of the fey was near ending. He must take care not to let his own fierce emotions override good judgment.

He entered the shafts of pink light marking the way to the throne hall. Embedded in the craggy stone walls on either side of him shone faceted gems and shiny crystals. Clear water trickled from cracks in the walls, a natural residence for the *undines,* or water faeries, when called before the High King.

In front of him, a massive archway of stone and moss rose above his head, signaling the entranceway to the great throne hall of Tara. He paused beneath it to gather his resolve and patience. On either side of his shoulders, brown vines climbed ever upward, intertwining with radiant and everlasting blooms of tiny white roses. He inhaled and exhaled, pushing aside the weariness threatening to weaken him. The roses' light fragrance reeked with presentiment.

"ENTER, WIND HERALD," the voice of the High King of the Faeries commanded from deep in the throne hall.

Boyden rolled his head on his shoulders to relieve tension and walked beneath the stone archway of blooms into a hall lit with shafts of pink light. The air felt ominous in his lungs, a marking of the suspension of seasons passing. He strode around a small grove of stunted white trees with branches thin as a child's finger and leaves no bigger than his thumb.

In front of him, several horse lengths away, stood

the infamous glacier white dais where the rock-crystal throne of the High King of the Faeries resided.

That was where the king waited for him.

"BOYDEN," the king greeted with the inflection of his brethren. "YOU HAVE CAUSED ME MUCH GRIEVANCE BETWEEN ME AND MY QUEEN."

"It was never my intention," Boyden knelt before the white dais, his knee sinking into soft, green-gray moss. He bowed his head respectfully.

"STAND AND FACE ME."

He stood, legs spread, hands locked behind his back, presenting no threat.

They always greeted this way before their argument, a ritual of blame and response. The king held him responsible for problems with the fey queen and he quietly remarked that it was not his intention to do so. The queen, although he had never met her, sided with him, as did the druidess.

"MY QUEEN GROWS ANNOYED WITH THE QUARRELING BETWEEN US. SHE RETREATED TO ONE OF HER SANCTUARIES NEAR THE ROWAN."

Boyden met the steady gaze of his royal adversary.

"SHE WILLNA RETURN UNTIL THIS CONFLICT BETWEEN US BE OVER."

He refused to be baited. "It is not my intent to cause discord between you and your queen."

"STILL, YOU HAVE DONE SO. IT ANGERS ME."

Boyden dipped his head in acknowledgement of the anger, refusing to be drawn into the argument with a denial, a weaker stance for him. It angered him just as greatly to battle for the acceptance of his valiant bride.

He knew this king to be a great warrior from the incursion times of Lord Bress, knew this king to be stubborn and powerful. It would take all his concentration and strength to have his will be done.

The High King sat on a throne chair crafted of olden rock crystals, gems of onyx, amethysts, and metalworked bronze. It was a symbol of the magical and the threat of the fey born. The king's tunic and breeches glittered with golden threads finely sewn in white fey weaves. His brows were thin and arched about eyes of icy jewels. Gold crystals glittered in long, brown plaits, framing an angular face both harsh and eerily fragile.

They were alone.

"I GROW WEARY OF OUR BATTLE, WIND HERALD."

"So do I."

"THE ONE YOU CLAIM AS BRIDE INVADED OUR LANDS WITH INTENT TO DO HARM."

Boyden told himself not to snarl his retort. " 'Tis true what you say. However, Scota also aided me in reaching the Milesian leader, Lord Amergin. She helped me convince the druidic bard of our innocence in the death of the traveler Íth, which has led to the ending of the invasion. You spoke to my chieftain and to the tribal elders. They spoke as I do about her efforts. We would still be in battle if not for her."

"UNIMPORTANT." The king gestured with a wave of his hand.

"How can it be unimportant?" he replied gruffly, struggling to keep his tone consistent and nonthreatening.

"WE SPEAK OF NOW-TIMES."

A muscle jumped in his jaw. "There would be no now-times," he ground out, "if not for her."

"SHE BE UNEQUAL TO YOU, WIND HERALD," the king said low with intolerance. He sat forward on the edge of his throne. "SHE BE NOTHING, A MORTAL BORN FROM AN-OTHER LAND ACROSS THE SEA, NO MATCH FOR YOU."

"She proved her worth to me and gained my respect and heart," Boyden countered. "She is my queen."

"WIND HERALD," the High King warned with an-noyance. "I AM THE HIGH KING OF THE FAERIES AND RECOGNIZE NO QUEEN OTHER THAN MY OWN."

He held the icy glare of the king and realized the time of dispute was coming to a close. A newer battle was about to rage.

"I remember my wind past, High King."

The king sat back on his throne with obvious dis-pleasure and contemplation, regarding him coolly with an unblinking gaze. "MEMORIES BE MOST DANGEROUS."

"To whom?" Boyden demanded, nostrils flaring.

"DANGEROUS TO FOOLISHNESS."

The air in the hall felt decidedly chillier, and an eerie breeze swept the perimeter of the room. It was not from the faery king.

"Do you threaten me, High King?" Boyden asked low, pushing down his fury. He knew the shadowy tales of this king's power, but refused to cower.

"Threaten? Aye. I willna have a treacherous Wind Queen tainting my realm."

Everything stilled inside Boyden. "You named her queen."

The king's gaze narrowed at his unintended slip. It was knowledge he had kept hidden for so long, but now it was revealed. "Aye, Wind Servant King. I know of you," he said sharply. "Better I should not."

Peril loomed in the air.

"Better you should have been honest with me," Boyden countered.

"I felt the taint of your heritage and acceptance of the Elemental the moment you entered my hall. Do you think to intimidate me with your lethal wind?"

"I doona threaten you or the fey realm, High King. I seek only who I am."

"You have discovered the clinging blood taint of the *Gaoth Shee*."

"Aye," Boyden answered. "I know what I am."

"So do I."

He dipped his head. "Given this, I ask you to accept Scota."

"Never."

He nodded wearily. "If you can not accept her, I ask you to allow us to leave your realm. Scota and I will settle north, far from Tara."

"You will remain where I can watch you. I command her away."

Boyden's eyes narrowed, patience evaporating. "I willna send my bride and unborn away. Would you give up your queen?"

"THEN NO CHOICE YOU GIVE ME BUT TO SPELL CAST YOU INTO FORGETFULNESS."

"You spell cast me and I will steal the very breath from your lungs," he warned with a voice brewing with growing rage.

The king was surprised. "DARE YOU THREATEN ME, WIND HERALD?"

"I willna attack, but I will defend me and mine."

The king rose gracefully from his throne, eyes glittering, face smooth and unreadable in the ways of the fey.

"SO BE IT." He flicked his hand.

In the next moment, Boyden's mind fractured. He grasped pounding temples and stumbled back from the unexpected attack. Never before had the king acted upon his threats.

"BORN OF THE WIND, MY PATIENCE WITH YOU BE OVER."

Boyden clenched his teeth with pain, fighting the dark spell seeping into his mind.

"By the winds, you willna steal my memories," he snarled.

"I TAKE WHAT I WISH TO TAKE."

He dropped to his knees in the soft mold, ears bleeding, mind splintering.

"DOONA FIGHT ME, WIND HERALD. YOU MAKE IT WORSE."

Boyden roared, giving voice to his agony.

The enchanted blood threads in his mortal blood were not strong enough to stay the willfulness of a powerful fey king.

His only choice. . .

Scota learned more about Boyden's tribe in the two days passing since he left her than in all the days she had spent with him.

She sat cross-legged in the grass while Nora stood behind, plaiting her hair into some semblance of order. The druidess stood off to the right, making a circle of stones upon the gentle slope of ground near the holly bush.

"Did you drink the goat's milk I brought, Princess?" the ancient asked.

Scota set the empty goblet aside. "Yes, I finished it."

"Good. Do you want more? I will send Nora."

"I need to finish her hair first," the child complained.

"No. I have had enough milk and honey for today." Scota patted Nora's hand soothingly. "I look forward to seeing how Nora does my hair."

"You need to drink more water and eat more fruit," the ancient mumbled, and another stone was added to the circle.

Scota returned her attention to the meadow. For the moment, everything seemed calm and purposeful. Children played in the sloping fields of wildflowers and trees, while families worked side by side to erect homes and futures in the bright warmth of afternoon light.

Her fingers tore at the broken flower petals in her lap, giving way to her continuing unease. Nora stood behind her, sure fingers plaiting her hair in a similar fashion to the druidess's white hair. The child was adding sparkling crystal beads instead of dried twigs of rosemary and Scota was thankful for it. She did not want decaying herbs in her hair, no matter how fragrant.

"Do you like plaits?" Nora asked. "All the females in my tribe wear them in this manner during the day, away from the face. I chose the clear beads to reflect the blue in your black hair."

Scota reached behind her and gave the girl's small hand a firm squeeze. "I like your choice of beads very much, Nora."

Gone was the bride in a fragile gown of crimson veils, replaced by a steady warrior woman in a sleeveless brown tunic and breeches . . . with a rounding belly.

"There." The girl patted her shoulder. "I am done."

Tossing the mangled flower, she touched her hair. "My thanks, Nora."

The girl child grinned, and in the next moment thunder cracked above their heads. Nora's eyes widened with fright.

Scota climbed to her feet, searching a blue, cloudless sky.

Like the druidess, the rest of the tribe straightened at the unexpected sound of storm.

All looked to the sky, searching.

Nora moved closer to the ancient, her face a mask of uncertainty.

"There are no clouds, ancient," the child whispered.

Scota exhaled loudly with understanding. "They battle."

"Aye," Derina agreed with extreme disgust. "It has come to that."

"I must go to him." Scota reached for the leather scabbard and bronze-hilted sword she propped against the trunk of a yew.

"To what end?" the ancient prompted. She dropped her latest rock and stepped over it.

Scota secured the scabbard to her back and handed the druidess her hazel walking stick.

"Princess, this battle must be between them, king to king."

She turned on the druidess. "Over me, Derina! They battle over me."

"Lower your voice; you frighten Nora."

Scota gazed down into the girl's pale face. "You understand why I am upset, Nora?" she asked gently.

Nora blinked and nodded.

"You can do nothing to help him," the druidess argued with sullen insistence.

Stepping away from both of them, Scota reached over her shoulder for the sword's hilt and pulled the sleek weapon free. With a few thrusts, she tested the balance. "I will not know what I can do until I get there."

The ancient's mouth flattened. "How do you think to travel to the below of Tara? You are unwelcome there."

"You will take me, Derina," Scota replied resolutely.

The ancient snorted with disagreement.

"Snorting will not change my mind, Derina. I wish to leave now, if you please." With an expert flip of hand, she thrust the sword back into the leather scabbard and went to kneel in front of Nora. "My thanks for the hair beads, Nora. They are lovely."

The child smiled, but her eyes remained fearful.

"I need you to return to your family now. Will you do that for me?" Scota asked.

"Are you going to help the Wind Herald?"

"Yes."

Nora nodded and wrapped her arms around Scota's neck. "When I am older, I will be strong and tall, like you."

Scota hugged the girl child back. "Stronger, I think. Now go."

She climbed to her feet and watched the girl scamper across the fields to where her family had returned to the labors of erecting their new home.

"What of your unborns, Princess?" the druidess asked, coming to stand beside her.

"I will protect them. For now, my interest is in saving their father," she replied without turning to the druidess.

The ancient sighed heavily. "I canna change your mind?"

"Why would you want to, Derina?"

"Stubborn, willful . . ." she muttered under her breath

and turned to her right. "May the gods and goddesses aid you. Now follow me and hurry up." The druidess walked briskly with her walking stick, around the holly, to a grouping of leafy green yews a few horse lengths away.

"Derina, do we not need to find a prism shield or trickle of water in order to enter the below?" She ducked under a low hanging branch and nearly toppled over the wise woman.

The ancient had stopped abruptly and was pointing at a gray-dappled, lichen-covered, phantom tree, in a small clearing. "This be named the Best of Creatures, Princess."

"The Best of Creatures looks like a large tree stump to me." It rose to the height of a man.

Derina placed both hands on the knob of her walking stick and released an impatient sigh. "They be calling me the blind one. Climb up and see."

Scota stepped closer to the green moss and gold lichen growth and wrinkled her nose. The stump smelled of decay and measured at least two horse lengths in diameter.

"Climb up." The druidess gestured with her stick. "This be once a magical rowan tree, cursed and withered to stone from the before-time. Her roots sit above a fey-path leading to the throne hall of Tara."

Scota looked at Derina. "I heard rowans provide sacred ways to the Otherworld."

"Aye, you heard well. They are trees precious to us."

Scota sunk her hands into green and brown rot and hiked herself up.

"Be careful, we doona wish to upset the living force of the tree trunk. Do you see a half-moon prism rock?"

"Yes, Derina." Scota pushed the moss aside, and a gust of air hit her face, sending a chill into her blood.

"That be your way to the great throne hall."

"How do I . . ." she sought to ask direction, but her hand passed through the prism as if reaching through water.

"You carry the babes of the wind in your womb," the ancient explained. "The olden entranceway recognizes you and allows passage. Remember, Princess. Doona challenge the High King of the Faeries. You canna win through force."

"It be far wiser if the High King of the Faeries *doona* challenge me," she remarked, using the druidess's word, and leaned down into the prism. In the next breath, she felt a sense of dislocation . . .

. . . and landed on her rump in a tunnel of purple smear.

Scota gripped her belly protectively and released a harsh breath. The feypath stunk of rotting crops, the residual scent of fey spitefulness.

Beaded plaits whipped about her face and into her mouth.

Through a teary gaze, she surveyed her surroundings.

A single brown vine, splayed with white blooms, crawled along the stone wall as if pointing the way.

She climbed to her feet and followed it.

Around a small bend, she came to a crossway of multiple tunnels.

Scota chose the one where the vine shot into shafts of pink light. As she trotted on, the stink of the feypath began to fade. Up ahead, the single brown vine joined a multitude of others above a stone archway riddled with white blooms in fey splendor. It was an entranceway to a great hall being blasted by winds.

She reached over her shoulder and wrapped her fingers around the smooth hilt of her sword . . . and entered the turbulent wind gusts.

Waves of dizziness drove him to his knees once again.

"STOP FIGHTING ME," the High King said tightly.

Boyden snarled an oath and fought to retain all he was. The *Gaoth Shee* was turning the throne hall into a place of glacial winds. It had already toppled the crystal throne chair from the dais.

He pushed to his feet. His mind was consumed with pain, a refusal to succumb to a stronger power. Icy water pierced his skin, driven from the cracks in the stones. Behind him, the white tops of the stunted trees were bowed nearly to the ground. He could feel the strength of the king increasing, battering at his will and spirit, and the *Gaoth Shee* waiting for his summons to kill.

He lifted his head defiantly, blood streaming from his ears and down his neck. "I will never succumb to you."

A sudden movement caught his eyes.

Crystal beads.

He blinked.

Out of a wall of swirling winds, a flash of brown charged forward, knocking the High King from the dais.

Immediately, the boiling pain in his mind ebbed.

When he blinked again, his warrior bride had planted one foot on the king's chest and threatened the neck of the fey royalty with the tip of her sword.

By the winds. They were in trouble now.

"I should kill you for trying to hurt mine," his bride spat in fury at the fey king.

"Scota," Boyden said, stumbling forward, "release him."

"I refuse to release this selfish bastard!" she snapped, full of righteous fire and brimstone.

In the next instant, the king winked out from under her foot, nearly toppling her over in surprise. Shards of silvery light flashed in her face and she pivoted, instinctively, ready to meet the threat.

But it was not in time.

In a burst of white light, the king rematerialized with a sword in hand and swatted hers away with a single blow of incredible strength.

Boyden bolted between them with a snarl of warning and retribution on his lips.

The king's eyes hardened.

The velocity of the winds in the hall increased with a biting chill.

Their breaths frosted fury and temper.

Neither king gave way.

Scota squeezed Boyden's arm, his body a shield of

tension in front of her. They were going to kill each other over her. She could not allow it.

"Do not do this, my love," she whispered into his bloody ear.

"He refuses to accept what is, Scota."

The hurtful words echoed inside her, creating a well of sadness. "Boyden, he has the right to ask me to leave his realm. All he says is true. I did invade the land. Please, my love, we will find another way."

Her mate did not respond, caught in a male's primitive insistence on protection.

"Please, Boyden, I am cold."

Immediately, the winds calmed in the throne hall, the chill leaving the air.

"Dim-witted and foolish!" the druidess called out with a shrill voice of bad temper from behind them. The ancient stomped into the hall, her walking stick leading the way. Face flushed, white hair disheveled, twigs poked out about her head. She looked decidedly wind-blown and mad.

The High King's jeweled gaze moved to the small, white-robed interruption.

"DERINA. I DINNA CALL YOU."

"I come anyway!" she snapped and pointed her walking stick in their direction. "Either release him or accept her."

" 'TIS NONE OF YOUR AFFAIR, OLD ONE, BE GONE."

She walked between the two tall and feuding kings and climbed atop the dais for added height.

With a quick turn, she poked the High King in the chest with her walking stick. "I may be old, but I am far wiser than you, dim-witted one."

The king rubbed the spot, a brow lifting. "You dare to call the High King of the Faeries dim-witted?"

"Derina," Boyden warned and received a jab in the ribs for his trouble.

"Be quiet, you." She turned back to the High King. "I call you dim-witted, and I call the tawny-maned one stubborn. Neither of you be thinking clearly."

"Then I suggest you enlighten us, Wise One."

"Do you wish to make the winds your enemy? Better to have an ally in the northern lands than both of you be dead. Release Boyden and let him return to the white fells of his ancestors."

Boyden stared into the king's contemplative and faceted eyes while keeping Scota protectively behind him.

"You show great restraint, Wind Herald, but never could you have won."

"Mayhap," Boyden answered, poised for battle, yet hopeful for freedom.

"Still you remain defiant."

"Always," Boyden replied.

The king nodded, and the druidess gave a single snort of displeasure.

"Be quiet, Derina." The High King held up his hand. "Your words speak a truth I did not consider. 'Tis wiser to have a powerful ally in the north."

Boyden waited for the king's decision, the nails of

his warrior bride digging into his arms.

"WILL THE WIND SERVANT KING AGREE TO SERVE THE HIGH KING OF THE FAERIES?"

"Nay," Boyden answered, restricting his annoyance. "The Wind Servant King agrees to offer friendship and strength to the High King of the Faeries whenever he needs it and expects an equal commitment in return."

"THE FAERIES DOONA COMMIT."

Boyden smiled scornfully. "Neither does the wind."

"Stop this, both of you!" Scota stepped out from behind Boyden just as Derina jabbed the two willful kings in the ribs.

Poke.

Poke.

"Ouch!" Boyden covered the tender spot and glared his displeasure at the white-haired attacker.

Holding his side in turn, the king muttered under his breath. "I DOONA LIKE BEING POKED."

"Then listen!" Derina commanded, and the High King nodded.

The hazel walking stick was a convincing weapon, Scota decided, much better than a sword.

Scota looked between the two kings. "Friendship and agreement serves well both the High King of the Faeries and the Wind Servant King. It is a power no enemy can tear asunder. Do you not agree?" she asked innocently, silently thanking Derina and biting back a smile.

The two kings wisely looked once more upon the druidess before both nodded.

"I RETURN FREEDOM ONCE MORE TO THE WIND HERALD."

Scota stepped back, fighting tears of joy.

"MAY HE BE A WISE SERVANT KING AND FOREVER FRIEND TO THE FAERIES."

Boyden nodded. "Forevermore do I offer friendship."

The High King echoed the commitment. "FOREVERMORE."

In the next instant, he winked out, leaving behind shards of silver light where once he stood.

Derina whooped, tossing her walking stick into the air.

With a joyous cry, Scota wrapped her arms around Boyden and fiercely kissed her Wind King until he fell over the toppled crystal throne chair.

They had won their right to a future.

CHAPTER 25

LIGHT DWINDLED IN THE BLUE sky, and the warm breezes gave a restful day. They sat at the edge of a fire circle's glimmer, the druidess strangely pensive. Boyden held Scota close to his side, the scent of his mating claim on her forever strong in his lungs. The glow and warmth of the orange and blue flames offered a peaceful respite, easing the lingering tension from his body.

"Do you wish for more water, my warrior?" he inquired.

She shook her head and patted her stomach. "I am full for the moment."

They planned to leave in the morn and travel north by feypath to White Fells, the ruined castle fortress of the Wind Kings. In his mind, he saw misty images of the fells, upland pastures. They were faded and dull near a ridge of clouds.

"Derina, you doona need to journey with us," Boyden said quietly, putting his bronze goblet down. He was concerned about the stamina and well-being of the wise woman.

"I must guide you to White Fells, Boyden. 'Tis not an easy place to find."

"We will find it."

"No doubt you would eventually find it," she agreed. "Your blood directs you, but it be hidden well in a far-away land you doona know." She pointed at Scota's stomach. "You doona have the time to search for it, if you wish your sons born in the northern lands. Besides, I must attend the birthing."

"I am many months away from giving birth, Derina," Scota added, her voice husky with restfulness. "We can send for you when my time draws near."

A short silence passed, and the druidess shook her head. "Your time will come earlier than a single babe birthing, Princess. Many moonrises earlier." She held up a hand to stay the questions. "I will explain."

When she did not, Boyden arched a brow in inquiry. "Derina?"

"I am gathering my thoughts."

"A long or short gathering?" he asked politely.

"Long to some, short to others." She patted his knee in a motherly fashion. "Time moves differently in the fey realm and in all feypaths. This particular feypath I must take you through be verra old." She shifted on her hip, relieving a dull ache down her leg.

"How old?" he inquired.

"It be from the beginning-time of the guardians. Few know of it, still fewer have ever traveled it."

"You have traveled it?" he asked.

She nodded, giving no further explanation.

"This feypath be the only way to reach the northern lands?" Scota asked, feeling a slight trepidation.

"Aye, it be the easiest and best way to go if you wish to reach it before the babes be born. It exists deep, winding beneath land and water." The ancient rubbed her temple.

"Go on, Derina. I would hear all of it," Boyden said.

"When you and the princess returned to the above from the hall of the High King, a sennight went before, yet you felt only a few hours had passed."

"What are you trying to tell us, Derina?" Boyden frowned, his voice low.

"This feypath be of living shadows, a journey long and hard. I must guide you, Boyden. Seasons pass in the above while you travel for what feels to you only days. When you leave the darkness of the feypath to return to the above light and air, the birthing time of your sons arrives."

"How can this be?" Scota looked to him for explanation and he could only shake his head.

"It be, Princess," Derina said. "Doona ever question the magical, never would you find answers. I canna give you an exact time of the birthing. Methinks sometime in the whirling month, *Feabhra*."

"*Mi Na Ngaoth*," Boyden murmured thoughtfully, scratching his chin.

"What is *Mi Na Ngaoth*?" Scota asked, looking

between them.

" 'Tis the month of the winds, Princess," the druidess answered. "The month of the winds, a magical time." She finished her mead, set the goblet on the ground near her right knee, and pushed to her feet using her walking stick for balance. "Doona worry, I willna slow you down. I move quicker in the fey realm."

Boyden reached over to assist the ancient and found his hand grasped firmly. "Derina, my thanks for everything," he said, unable to find the right words to express how he truly felt.

She smiled in understanding, giving his hand a quick squeeze before releasing him. "My thanks for the food, Boyden. I dinna like the mead, too sweet, but the mutton tasted well enough. Mayhap a wee bit more time cooking over the fire, and I would have enjoyed pudding with my meal."

He grinned at her criticism, and she arched a brow at him. "I be old and tired."

"Not so old," he said fondly, "not so tired."

She huffed with feigned displeasure. "Good eve to you."

He nodded. "Good eve."

"Good eve, Derina," Scota offered beside him.

In silence, they watched the fey born wise female disappear into the growing night.

"She is not what she seems."

Boyden thought his warrior bride extremely perceptive. "I suspect so, but Derina willna ever reveal what she keeps hidden. She is fey born, Scota. Their ways are different, and I learned long ago not to question, but to accept." He took her hand and kissed the tips of her fingers. "I am merely grateful to be considered among her friends."

She smiled. "So am I, Boyden."

Her gaze slid away from him. "The month of gray blasts seems so far away, Boyden. Yet, Derina says when I leave the feypath . . ." she shook her head, hesitating, looking back at him with concern. "Can we not remain here until after the birthing?"

He knew it not possible for them to stay and wiggled his brows to ease her disquiet. "And test the terrible temper of the High King?"

A smile spread across her face. "I suppose not," she said and added, with a touch of devilment, "I would not want you to hurt him. He is the High King of the Faeries, after all."

He could not restrain himself and looked at her sideways. "Aye, that be the way of it. Me hurt him."

Her eyes sparkled, an intense shimmering making him grin. She looked a highborn queen, her black hair pulled away from her face in shiny plaits woven with crystal beads. He would do anything for her.

Behind them, a dog barked and a child called out to his father, a reminder of life and simplicity. They both looked over their shoulders.

Fires lit up the warm night, families gathering in rest from a hard day of work.

"My tribe will find peace here," he murmured, "both in the rolling hills of the above and the magical of the below. They will become whole and part of the faeries, a final changing and acceptance of destiny."

A hand rested lightly on his thigh. "We will find peace in the land of your ancestors, Boyden."

"Aye." He covered her smaller hand with his and asked, "How are you feeling?"

"Hungry," she replied gravely.

He lifted a brow. "You ate but moments before."

She touched her stomach. "Tell them."

He chuckled and she gave him a weak scowl, her eyes dancing with truth and mirth. He looked up at the purpling sky, a lingering weariness still plaguing him. "Twilight leaves us for night. Come, let us seek an early rest."

He climbed to his feet and took her hand, helping her stand.

"Our bed awaits, my Wind Queen." He led her to the holly bush where he spread out blankets and white goatskins in preparation.

"Derina told me the holly guards the inner realms of the fey."

He nodded, yawning. "The fey willna bother us tonight." He took her hand, guiding her down onto the bed he had made.

"Are you sure, Boyden?"

"Aye."

He lay on his back. She settled down and snuggled close, her finger lightly tracing his jaw. "Derina said the qualities of the holly bush support courage and maleness."

"Why do you think I chose this bush? I want my sons to be strong."

"What of your bride?" She lifted her head to look at him with those glorious eyes.

He grinned and gently pushed her back down to his shoulder. "Strength and courage abound in her already. I wish only for us males to keep up."

"Honey talker, they could be daughters."

"Nay, methinks not this time. Sleep, Scota, the days ahead will be long."

They were in the feypath.

"By the winds, I canna tolerate this stink much longer," Boyden complained under his breath and Scota bit back a smile.

"It is not so bad if you do not dwell on it," she offered calmly, standing in murky shadows. After all she had lived in this magical land, she no longer feared closed-in places.

He looked at her menacingly. "I doona dwell on it, I breathe it." He eyed her up and down, his hands shifting to the straps on his chest that anchored the sword scabbard and leather bags to his back. "How do you feel?"

"The same as when you asked me but moments before."

He hiked the provisions on his back higher and scowled.

"I am well, Boyden," she answered.

He studied her quietly and possessively. Leaning forward, he caught her chin and kissed her gently. "I love you, my warrior."

Unaccustomed to such open affection, she held still.

He stroked her hair, a glide of soothing fingers. "I have always loved you," he said huskily, his mouth brushing hers. Her lips met his, and she grew lost in the taste of him, a momentary reprieve from the discomfort growing in her body.

Up ahead the druidess called shrilly, "Boyden!"

He stepped back and winked, a hot glance simmering. "I am chastised." Bowing, he swept his arm wide. "After you, my rounded warrior."

She glared at his seductive smile. Cupping her stomach, she walked around him.

The druidess frowned deeply at her, displeasure clearly outlined in the set of her mouth before she turned and walked away into shadows.

Above their heads, moisture no longer dotted stone crevices and dripped chill upon them.

With each new step into the moving drafts of heat and cold, Scota felt her body changing. She felt pressure and heaviness and stretching, even though her stomach appeared no bigger than when they first entered the feypath.

They were nearing the end of their journey, the druidess leading the way in the purple smear. Vines, dark and black, climbed out of stone cracks on one side, while spirals, triskeles, and etchings of the wind decorated the flat stones on the other.

All sounds belonged to them, echoing into hollow nothingness. As she walked around a bend and entered another draft of warm air, Scota felt movement within her womb. She reached out a hand to steady herself. A sudden fatigue came into her, a difficulty in balance and in walking. She held her rounded stomach. Feeling discomfiture, she expected it to expand suddenly in a magical weight gain at any moment. She wore a baggy woolen shirt Boyden had given her. It belonged to him, a lavender shade many sizes too large for her. The loose brown breeches fared no better, barely staying above her hips even with the laces tied tight. The only things fitting true were the black boots on her feet.

She took a deep breath to regain her equilibrium and felt an ache grow in her lower back. To her way of thinking only a fortnight had passed. The fourteen days were not many, but Derina warned her to expect quick changes in her body.

"Scota?"

A large hand pressed into the small of her back, offering comfort.

"Is it your back?" Concern tightened his features.

She dragged air into her lungs, battling a momentary shortness of breath. "I am well, Boyden," she reassured.

"You look white as snow."

"I do not doubt it." She gave him a weak smile.

"Her time nears," the druidess said.

Scota looked up.

With an expressionless face, the ancient stood in a

shaft of fake moon shadow. She pointed to a half-moon rock embedded in stone. "We have walked under land and sea to land again. Magic and passings have come as in the before-time. Once we be granted passage through the half-moon rock, time resumes in the mortal ways and the birthing begins. Be you ready, Princess?"

Scota nodded and went to join Derina.

She gasped in surprise as a painful cramp rippled through her womb. In disbelief, she looked down at a slightly larger stomach.

"Loosen those breeches and carry her, Boyden," the druidess commanded. "She enters labors. It be as I expected with multiple babes; the four winds be rebirthing."

"Four?" He sounded disconcerted, but not nearly as much as she felt.

"Aye, we have been too long in the feypath."

He removed the smaller dagger from her waistband.

"Boyden, what are you doing?"

"Loosening." He pulled the waistband of her breeches away from her flesh, an easy task given their enormous size, and with a single swipe, sliced through the laces.

She made a grab to hold them up. "Was that necessary?"

"Aye." He jammed her dagger next to the larger one in his waistband and yanked her breeches farther open.

"Boyden! Enough."

He stepped closer. "You are beautiful when angry."

"Do not attempt to honey talk me."

"What better time to honey talk my mate than when

she is about to give birth to my sons?" Boyden moved quickly and lifted her into his arms. "I willna have our sons born in the stench of a feypath."

"They may be daughters, Boyden," she disputed with a mild tone.

He guided her arms around his neck. "Next time, my warrior."

"Hurry, Boyden," the druidess urged. The half-moon rock slid open beside her.

Boyden followed Derina into the purple light, a sense of dislocation washing over him. Heat turned into cold drafts of air as he walked through. Bright lights flashed before his eyes. Scota strained against him, her body returning to the ways of the mortal time.

In his arms, she became suddenly . . . very rounded and gasped loudly in his ear. Alarm bolted through him and he stumbled on a rock, landing hard on his knees in cold virgin snow. Breath frosted in front of him, and he blinked to clear his vision.

They were in the side garden of a castle's ruin, lit by cold sunset shades.

White Fells.

"Bring her over here, Boyden."

Looking over his shoulder, he hauled himself up, holding tight to his squirming burden. "Hang on, Scota."

"Hurry," she rasped. "They are coming."

Stepping around a collapsed garden wall of stones, he sprinted into a sprawling courtyard covered in freshly fallen snow.

Before their eyes, an ancient fortress of gray stone and mud rose in silent menace, surrounded by barren trees.

"Derina?" he called out.

"Inside, Boyden."

"Almost there, Scota." He darted toward the entry-way.

"So are they," she hissed.

Climbing the five stone steps quickly, he squeezed around a dead tree and ducked under the fallen archway, coming to an abrupt halt in a vine-covered foyer.

"Derina!"

"Down the passage, Boyden."

He dashed down the hall and entered a room of gray. Orange shafts of light streamed through openings in a ceiling. On the west side, the druidess waited near a large column of stones climbing high and disappearing into the ceiling. At the base of the stones was a black-ened opening in which a magical fire lived.

" 'Tis called a hearth, Boyden. Bring Scota here."

He did not question the ancient, but stepped around patches of snow and headed for the roaring blaze.

In the blink of an eye, the fey born ancient prepared a clean place for birthing. In front of the hearth lay a bed of white linen, woven blankets, strips of cloth, pots of boiling water, and bunches of women's herbs. He did not ask how she managed to prepare all so quickly or where she retrieved the pots and water as the tips of his mate's slender fingers were digging holes into his nape.

A groan burst under his chin, and he swiftly placed

Scota on the white linen and knelt beside her.

"Easy, Scota." With a quick shrug, he removed the leather packs of provisions he carried on his back. They landed on the stone floor behind him with a loud thud. He kept the scabbard and sword on his back and the daggers at his waist, in case they were not alone.

A hand shot out and grabbed a handful of hair, tugging him forward.

"Where are we?" his mate demanded, her voice breaking, eyes shiny with pain.

He met her concentrated stare. She was breathing in gulps, his nose touching the tip of hers.

"White Fells, I suspect."

She released him abruptly, grimacing. "Good, I wish my sons to be born in the land of the winds."

"I thought they were going to be daughters."

"Shut up!" Her lips worked, panting with exertion. "This is all your fault."

"Aye." He could not deny it.

She started swearing at him, and he sat there, dumbfounded.

"Wash your hands and arms, Boyden."

He rose and did as the druidess bid using one of the pots of water. Sweat dotted his brow. This was worse than he ever imagined.

"Spread the blanket out, Boyden. She gives birth fast and quick."

"How do you—" A scream rent the air followed by a babe's piercing cry and then another.

He watched with awe, feeling a surge of dizziness, while the druidess assisted his mate in bringing his four tiny sons into the world.

Two days had past. Her body sore, Scota lay on a make-shift bed of hay and warm blankets, watching the Wind Servant King quietly. Fire roared in the stone hearth behind her, adding warmth to the chilly air in the hall. Another morning had come to the late days of *Feabhra*, February.

Her king stood at the foot of her bed, looking down at their sleeping sons, the glow of the fire adding shimmer to his mane of hair, the front of him contoured in dark shadow.

Wrapped in swaddling cloths, the babes slept soundly on blankets near her hip. One of them sprouted a thatch of black hair on his pate; the other three appeared bald.

Her king looked up slowly and grinned. "Unreasonable, my Wind Queen. Four additional mouths to feed instead of one. How will I ever manage it?"

"Well enough, I suspect. Where is Derina?"

"Gone down to the village."

"What village?" She arched a brow and tried to sit up.

He was beside her in a moment, sitting on the edge of the blankets and pushing her down gently. "If you agree to remain still, accept bed rest, and not wake our sons, I will tell you all that happened while you slept."

"You should not let her go alone, Boyden. She is old and blind."

"Scota, one does not tell a fey born druidess what to do and survive unscathed. Doona worry, I watched from the ridge gate. The villagers greeted her with food, having seen smoke rise from the fortress's hearth."

"Why did she go?"

"To seek out the simpler and women of the village to help us with our sons."

Tilting her head, she looked around him to the four sleeping babes. *Yes*, she thought, *we need help,* and settled back down. "We are not alone in this place?"

Fingers caressed her cheek, gentling her. "Below this ruined fortress of distant views lies a sprawling village and surrounding farmlands. Does it make you feel better to know we are not?"

"Yes." She stared up into his gray eyes, the hint of twilight and gold barely contained. She was hopelessly smitten with him, overwhelmed with unruly emotions of love, pride, hope, and wanting. Without him in her life, she would have died young, on the sharp end of a sword or arrow, on some unknown field, forgotten and uncared for. Instead, she found a home within his heart.

His lips curved in a tender smile, a golden Wind King of brilliance and strength. After a small falter, she whispered, "I love you, Boyden." It came out clumsily, the words barely audible.

"I love you, too." A thumb traced her brow. "Did

you know I fell in love with you the first day I saw you?"

She grimaced. "I staked you to the ground, demanding submission."

"Ah, did I give it to you?"

"No, you fought me," she admitted.

"Then I will allow you to teach me how to submit . . . after you have rested long and well."

His warm tone made her smile. "It may take the rest of my lifetime to teach you."

"Aye, I look forward to it," he parried with a glint in his eyes and she laughed softly.

"Now rest before the druidess returns and yells at me." He brushed his lips against her temple. "You and our sons are safe."

Scota closed her eyes in contentment and weariness. "Stay close, Boyden."

"Always, my warrior." Boyden took her smaller hand in his.

EPILOGUE

Boyden stood on the ridge overlooking the sloping meadows below him, a ruling king of justice. At dawn, he donned a worn tunic and breeches with a pair of comfortable scuffed boots. He had been intent upon working the fields alongside the farmers, but a small dispute over a pig took up most of the early morn.

He rested his hand on the dagger sheathed at his waist. Farmers and their sons were haymaking in the bright sunlight of mid-morn, an important crop for livestock during the winter months to come. Two wolfhounds bounded after a group of young girls in a fun chase.

Behind him, a gate hung open on well-made hinges. The main entrance to the ruins of an ancient fortress, it led into an inner courtyard of flat gray stones, long ago etched with spirals and symbols of the wind. Crowning towers and walls protected the inner walkway where sentries stood guard among ancient oaks while village craftsmen rebuilt the breached living quarters. A terrible battle raged here long ago, one of fire and death, destroying much of what was. He experienced no blood memory of it, so it must have happened after the death of the Servant King.

He nodded to one of the sentries. He did not command the warriors or the craftsmen to come to him. Word had spread of his arrival, and they simply showed up in the courtyard one morn, vowing allegiance to the reign of the new Wind Servant King.

And so he was, he mused, settling his hands on his hips. All he endured before meeting Scota dulled with the happiness he felt being with her and his sons. He preferred being a father and a mate than a king, but accepted what he was, a restoration of an ancient power forever contained. He would teach his sons to accept their heritage, as well, he thought. All of them were blooded to the *Gaoth Shee.* The lethal wind lingered near, watchful of her bloodline.

The scent of lavender touched the air, and he felt a tug on his leg. He looked down at the cherubic face of his dark-haired son.

"Conall, where did you come from?" Lifting the child, he settled the boy in one arm and turned to greet his beloved.

Scota smiled warmly. "Good morn, Boyden."

"Good morn, my queen."

He took her chin and kissed her lightly on the lips. Behind them, one of the helpful village women stood watch over their three other sons, as yellow-haired as their sire. The children tumbled playfully in the tall stalks of grass and wildflowers, their chubby arms batting at each other in glee.

Scota thought it a fine summer day to share her news with him, but the telling became difficult the more she tried to approach it. "I heard this morn some of the craftsmen found strange bones in the back courtyard."

Her son took hold of his father's long plait and yanked. "I know," Boyden replied, making a face and freeing his hair. "I commanded the bones not be disturbed."

"What are they, Boyden?" When she went to the grave earlier, she felt a strange sensation, a movement of air and wing.

" 'Tis hard to explain." He shifted his son and gestured to the south meadow where a herd of pale horses grazed, their long white tails swishing.

"The way we ride our horses, my ancestors mounted large birds."

"They flew the air?" she asked incredulous.

"Aye."

She gave a little laugh, finding it hard to imagine. "This place be more enchanted than the faeries."

"Aye." He chuckled and flipped Conall on his back. Holding him close, he tickled the child on his belly.

Their son squealed in delight, and Scota smiled at the antics of father and son. She glanced over her shoulder. Her other three sons were still tumbling, still laughing. She nodded to the village woman, grateful for her help, and put her hands behind her. Turning back, she looked out upon the working farmers in the lower meadows. Like her handsome Wind King, she had donned a comfortable purple tunic and breeches for rolling in the grass with her precocious sons. She adored them. As soon as they could hold a bow or sword, she would teach them the ways of defense.

"You will need to build more rooms in the fortress," she said simply.

"Scota, there are ten rooms." He brought Conall back to his brothers.

Her fingers tightened behind her. "I know it well."

"We will make due with what we have for now."

He returned to her side and she nodded, evading his gaze. "It may become crowded in a few months."

Silence.

She cast him a sideways glance to see if he understood.

He was staring at her. "By the winds."

"Aye," she said.

"Aye?"

"Oh yes, AYE!"

He grinned. "When?"

"Next spring."

He reached for her, his hands burying in her hair. "Unreasonable, my Wind Queen. More mouths to feed? How will I ever manage it?"

She kissed him and murmured against his seeking lips, "Well enough, my love."

He laughed proudly. "Aye, we will."

With expert grace, he lifted her in his arms and

spun about.

"Boyden!" Scota wrapped her arms around his neck, sputtering on a golden plait. "P-put me down. Are you maddened?"

"For you I am." He set her on her feet and stepped boldly back, sweeping his arms wide as if to encompass all the rugged land, all the crystal lochs, and all of the cerulean skies.

"I give you Scotland, my love. Forevermore."

And he did.

NOTES ON TEXT

(Where I could, I listed pronunciations in parentheses.)

Amergin— According to some histories, Amergin was a son of the king of Spain, who led the Milesian warriors in an invasion of Eire (Ancient Ireland). He was said to be a druidic bard, able to combat the magic of the *Tuatha Dé Danann*.

Brú na Boinne— An olden description of the passage tomb, Newgrange, which sits five miles west of the town of Drogheda near a large bend in the Boyne River.

Daoine Sidhe— (pronounced "deena shee") Faery folk.

Drogheda— (pronounced "draw-da") "Bridge of the Ford"; a port town in the county of Louth (on the border of the county of Meath) near the Boyne River.

Fortnight— Fourteen days.

Gaoth (pronounced "gwee")— Wind.

Íth — Íth was said to be an uncle or great-uncle of the king of Spain, who sailed to Eire (Ireland) and was killed in a misunderstanding by three Irish kings. When his body was brought home, the sons of the king of Spain sought to avenge his death.

Idir— Between.

La buidhe Bealtuinn— The yellow day of *Beltane*, May.

Months— *Aibrean* (April); *Bealtuinn* or *Beltane* (May); *Lughnasa* (August); *Feabhra* (February); *Iúl* (July).

Mi Na Ngaoth— Month of the winds (February).

Rígdamnai— Persons eligible to be king, set apart from remoter relatives.

Samhioldanach— Equally-skilled-in-all-arts.

Sennight— Seven days or one week.

Shee, Sidhe, **or** *Sí*— These are a few of the various names for the faeries of Irish and Scottish Gaelic.

Stray sod— Enchanted faery ground, where people wander lost.

Tá tú go h-álainn— (pronounced "taw two guh haul-inn"): "You are beautiful."

Titim gan éirí ort— (pronounced "chitim gon eye/ree urt"): "May you fall without rising."

Teamhair na Rí— The Hill of the Kings.

Tuatha Dé Danann— Collective term coined in the Middle Ages for the people of the Goddess Dana.

Undines— Water faeries.

AUTHOR NOTES

THE MORE I RESEARCH AND delve into the many realities of ancient Ireland, the more I realize I have a lifetime of learning ahead of me. The history of Ireland can be described as a crooked road of which darkness, legend, and the real weave into storytelling.

Long ago, it was a land of winds and of oak-woods except for the bog and mountain areas. Intensive farming overtook the yews, oaks, and hollies, giving way to a sense of the land we have today. Ireland is still one of the windiest places in the world due to the influence of frontal depressions caused by the earth's movement, and as I wrote this book over five blistery months in 2006, I gained a deeper respect for the gusting currents that toppled a dead tree branch (the size of a small oak) onto my house.

In *White Fells*, I revisit the ancient Irish text known as the *Lebor Gabála*, Book of Invasions. The Milesians, known also as Hiberi, Iberi, Gaedhal, Gaeli, and Scotti, were the final invaders of Ireland.

On one Sunday afternoon, the tale of Íth caught my attention. He was a traveler who sailed to Hibernia (Ireland) and met the country's three kings. In a tragic misunderstanding, he was killed and his body sent home. In vengeance for their uncle, the sons of King Mil Espáine took to their ships and conquered Hibernia (Ireland). The *Tuatha Dé Danann* were defeated at the battle of Tailtiu (pronounced "telltown") and after a short resistance a truce was reached. The Milesians retained the above ground, and the *Tuatha Dé Danann* went below, becoming the faeries . . .

However, a few researchers maintain . . . that the Milesians never existed.

An interesting side note: Some ancient texts mention a mysterious woman named Scota, who accompanied the sons of King Mil across the sea. Very little is known about her.

A special presentation of R. Garland Gray's

FEY BORN

CHAPTER 1

Drumanagh, Eire
Spring

HE STOOD AT THE EDGE of the high ranging meadows where the horses of the tribe grazed. Darkly lashed eyelids closed in exquisite pleasure. Slowly, his head tilted back, long brown hair flowing down his bare back in dampening glints of red and gold. It began to rain, a gathering of gray clouds muting the light of the late afternoon. He sighed deeply, tasting the sweet air of *Meitheamh*, June, in his lungs and savoring the touch of cool raindrops upon his naked and responsive flesh.

He was fey born, a purebred creature of sensations and selfishness. A legendary guardian of the waters, he was crafted of cruelty and enchantment, a being to be feared; a being whose true form must remain secret. He knew he should not be here and thought of the olden ways with a sharp surge of resentment. There was no sense in being bored, he thought rebelliously.

Wearing his mortal appearance, he lived among the tribe of the *Tuatha Dé Danann* now. A fierce, loyal, and constant warrior — he slowly grinned — answering to the given name of Keegan. The name meant "highly spirited." An admirable name, he chuckled darkly. *If only they knew . . .*

Lana, a farm girl of unimpressive worth, at least that is how she thought of herself, stumbled back behind the ancient oaks and nearly dropped the druidess's basket of herbs. She had been making her customary visit to see Lightning, the aged sorrel stallion, when fat raindrops plopped and splashed upon the land. Dashing into the tall oaks for cover, a shortcut back to the village, she had never thought to see *him*.

Like that!

Lana set the basket down on a dry spot beneath a thick canopy of branches and took a moment to catch her breath. Swiping a drenched blond curl out of her eyes, she peered around the thick tree trunk, unable to help herself. The fading light caught the silver glint from the cuff he always wore on his right wrist.

She looked at the lines of his body and blinked to clear her vision. Lightning and three black mares calmly grazed around the naked warrior in acceptance of the afternoon rain showers. From what she could see, Keegan's silvery gray eyes were closed, his angular face tilted upward as if listening to the rain's chant of faery whispers. The corners of his lips slowly curved and Lana had the impression the raindrops sang to him of their joyous journey from the stormy clouds to the green land below.

She watched him in silent fascination as any female would. His lean, well-built body was turned slightly away from her, offering a splendid view of long limbs and curved buttocks. If she leaned right, she might get a glimpse of that very impressive male part of him. Good sense took hold, however, and she decided to stay under the protection of the trees. Besides, she could see him well enough from here, she reasoned. He looked taller without clothes. All that smooth skin she could just imagine running the tips of her fingers over the ripple of muscle and strength.

Lana drew back. She must learn to curtail her over-active imagination. She might be impulsive, but she was not stupid. The gentle sound of the rain pattered consistently in her ears, and she tugged the laces of her damp tunic closer with cold fingers. Never could she hope to know the remote Keegan in that way, or any warrior, given her frail condition.

He stood not ten horse lengths from her, his dark hair falling in wet plaits down his broad back. He was not born of her tribe. However, he had earned the right to belong to the warrior class of the *Tuatha Dé Danann*. He came during the time of shadows only two summers before. A freeman, he worked hard and trained hard with sword, spear, and shield. Last year he fought bravely in the battle of Kindred, the recapturing of their ancestral home from the invaders, yet still he was considered an outsider by many.

He did not partake of their ways, and did not seek payment for his fine skills. Instead, he offered to help her father in the fields. A warrior on a farm? She shook her head in bewilderment and rubbed her wet nose. If she remained much longer, she might catch a chill, but feminine curiosity took hold of her and she could do nothing else but look.

"Caught in the spring showers, too, Lana?"

Lana straightened abruptly in surprise, her hand clenched across her chest. With flushed cheeks, she stared guiltily at the white-haired druidess, Derina.

"Your heart bothers you?" the druidess asked in concern.

"Nay," Lana choked, embarrassed at being found gaping at the naked warrior. She took a recovering breath, feeling the familiar twinges inside her chest. Everyone in the village knew of her weak heart, lack of stamina, and occasional fainting spells. However, unlike some others, the ancient was always helpful and sympathetic, which was odd since most members of the druid class were callous. She heard so, anyway.

"Come to visit that mean-tempered stallion again?" the druidess prompted, moving under the protection of the canopy. "What be his name?" Her white brows drew together and then she answered her own question, a common occurrence. "Lightning, methinks."

"Aye." Lana bristled slightly at the description of her friend. "Lightning is not mean-tempered, at least not to me," she whispered, hoping the naked warrior could not hear them. "He has mellowed much over the years."

The druidess was not listening to her.

She shifted right and appeared to be looking, if looking could be used to describe one who had no eyes and yet could see.

"Ah," the ancient said in a hushed tone, understanding immediately. She pointed her walking stick. "You be visiting another kind of stallion today."

Lana turned apple red. "I am not visiting," she said firmly in a hushed tone.

"Watching then."

"I am not watching," she protested.

The ancient smiled. "I would."

Lana looked away, wondering how the blind druidess could possibly know.

"He fascinates you, Lana?"

"Please lower your voice. I doona wish him to hear us."

The druidess nodded and hunched her shoulders, leaning forward. "He fascinates you?" she repeated her question with less volume and more emphasis.

"Aye, he does." Lana admitted grudgingly. Keegan captivated her interest since he first came to the tribe two seasons before. He always smelled clean and fresh like the rain even when soiled with toil and sweat.

"I know," the ancient replied as if reading her mind. She tapped a bent finger on a wrinkled cheek. "I may be one hundred and . . ."

". . . three," Lana offered.

"What?"

"You are one hundred and three summers."

"I know how old I am," the ancient grumbled. "Now, what did I want to say? Ah, I may be one hundred and three summers, but my fey sight remains strong. This gift be from our fey brethren."

"I know."

"It allows me to see shapes and movement; otherwise I would be walking into trees and tumbling into lochs."

"I know," Lana repeated patiently.

Empty eye sockets crinkled in merriment. "Now tell me, why does he interest you?"

Lana shrugged. "He is different, ancient."

"Different how?"

She wished the druidess would keep her voice down. Taking a moment to stem the flow of her tumultuous thoughts, Lana found she could not describe what she felt and instead blurted, "He looks perfect."

"You think so, do you?" The druidess laughed and Lana quickly motioned her to lower her tone.

The druidess nodded and then whispered, "I would not call him perfect, young Lana. His voice is too deep."

"Nay, 'tis not."

"His hands and feet look a wee bit large, methinks."

She shrugged. *Mayhap.* "His eyes are the pale gray color . . .

". . . of rainstorms," the ancient continued with hushed gaiety.

"Aye," Lana answered in all seriousness. "And his ways are different than ours, too."

"This be true, yet has he not earned honor among us?"

"Aye," Lana acknowledged easily, having seen the quickness and strength of his battle skills.

"What else be bothering you about him, young Lana?"

She took a breath. "Derina, a warrior does not work on a farm."

"That one does."

The druidess made her answer sound so simple. Lana pointed over her shoulder. "He stands in the rain un-clothed."

"Mayhap he needs a bath." Leaning heavily on the walking stick, the ancient looked around her, lips curving in what seemed to Lana a bold appreciation indeed.

"I have decided the shape of those hands and feet be perfect. Our fey brethren could not have crafted a finer male form." The ancient laughed softly at a secret known only to her. "Do you wish to discuss another part of him then?"

Lana shook her head self-consciously. Thank the goddess the warrior could not hear their conversation.

"Then I be curious and ask, did you find my linseed, Lana?"

"Aye, I have it here in my basket." Lana walked back to where she left the basket. "It is still early yet, but I have found a good patch." The blue flowering herb soothed the coughs and problems of the chest several members of her tribe occasionally suffered.

"Good," the ancient remarked, and followed. She tapped her walking stick against the tree trunk. "The spring shower has paused for us so you may walk back with me. Come, my robes be damp, my bones be aching, and my stomach pains me again."

Lana could not help but smile. "Your stomach grumbles, does it now?" All in her tribe knew of the ancient's complaints. She picked up the basket and settled it on her hip.

"Lana, has your father made more of his sweet mead?" the druidess asked nonchalantly.

"Aye," she said and laughed softly, "I will bring some to you this eve."

✳ ✳ ✳

Keegan let a smile curve his lips as he listened to the ancient one's inner thoughts.

"I have fetched her away," Derina remarked in her mind so that he heard.

"I am in your debt, ancient."

"You should be." She gave her thought to him in a huff.

The druidess kept his secrets, an olden pledge always to serve the fey. She came as he bade. Being fey blooded herself, she responded to his mind call and claimed his inquisitive onlooker from the small grouping of trees beside the meadow. Lana was a lovely, sickly female of little worth. He valued strength and had little tolerance for fragility and weakness. Still, she was pleasant to look upon and he enjoyed the way her nose wrinkled when she smiled.

He turned away, his nostrils flaring in recognition of a familiar scent.

He did not want Lana to see the golden territorial goddess who also came to the rain drenched meadow and now stood in silent splendor, watching, waiting, her sweet fey scent filling the air.

Lana and Blodenwedd, though mortal and faery goddess respectively, were crafted of the same sunlit hues. Lana's mortal shades were softer than Blodenwedd's and he found her black eyes strangely alluring, certainly more so than the goddess's piercing amber.

Keegan felt wisps of gold in the air touching his skin and heard the horses move away.

"RAIN," the golden perfect one said.

He did not answer, did not move.

"RAIN," she hissed at him in exasperation, using his faery name.

Keegan lowered his head and stared down into flashing amber eyes with silver tipped lashes.

"Blodenwedd," he replied, bowing his head respectfully to the territorial goddess.

She pulled back the white webs of her robe's hood and Keegan once more looked upon the excellence of her features.

"WHY DO YOU STAY AMONGST MORTALS AND NOT YOUR OWN KIN?"

Boredom, he thought and arched a brown brow at her reproachful tone. The fey born always believed themselves superior to mortals, though they themselves were not immortal, only extremely long lived.

"FOOLISH," she spat when he did not answer.

"Not foolish," he said very slowly. The tedium of life had led him to their mortal brethren, an inner curiosity, an interest to be part of their responsiveness to the land.

"I SAY FOOLISH."

She was in a foul temper, he mused, nothing new. He adjusted the cuff on his wrist. "Foolish is the territorial goddess who continues to desire the Dark Chieftain of the *Tuatha Dé Danann* for her own when the Faery King has pledged her to another."

Her gaze slid away and he felt a twinge of regret for his harshness.

"I NO LONGER DESIRE HIM," she murmured.

"Good."

"I DOONA LIKE THE NEW ONE EITHER."

"If you doona like the king's choice for your mate, Blodenwedd, then you should tell him."

"TELL? HE DOONA LISTEN TO ME," she said with an impatient turn of her hand.

"Who did he choose for you?"

She looked back at him, a dark light in her eyes. "YOU."

He smiled only slightly at her mischief. "Why are you really here, great goddess?"

"YOU DOONA BELIEVE ME, RAIN?" There was an open challenge in her voice, a menacing quality to her tone.

"Careful, Blodenwedd," he warned silkily, his resentment aroused. He could detect the fragrance of her, the changing scent meant to dull his senses. "I am not like mortal men who bow to your every wish."

"YOU ARE MALE BRED," she said, her eyelids lowered, and he felt the inspection of his man-parts.

A flicker of annoyance gleamed in his eyes when he saw appreciation light her face. He waited for what he knew was coming.

"RAIN, I WISH YOU TO BE MY CONSORT."

He placed a finger under her chin and lifted her gaze to his. "The king dinna pick me, did he, Blodenwedd?"

"Nay," she grumbled, admitting to the devious lie, and whirled away.

"Blodenwedd."

"I want you instead." She tossed her silken mane.

"You doona want me."

She turned back, her gaze hot and expectant, roaming boldly up and down his naked body.

"I can make you want me, *Báisteach*."

He did not like it when she used his olden fey name. *Báisteach* meant Rain. Keegan locked his hands behind his back in rebuff and looked up at the clouds. He could feel her anger and resentment brewing just below the surface. "Goddess," he said with extreme patience, "you canna make me want or do anything I doona want to do."

"Be you sure of that?" she murmured coyly.

He looked into her cold, lovely face. The game she played no longer amused him. "Be you sure, Blodenwedd?"

At his returned challenge, she pulled back in stunned silence. He guessed his defiance rankled her a wee bit. The look she bestowed on him was filled with such hatred he felt his only recourse was to . . . chuckle.

"How dare you!" she spat in a full temper, the urge to kill shining in her eyes.

He peered at her with a strong conviction. "Why did you come here?"

She made a distasteful sound in her throat. "Wants you now to Come."

"Who wants me?"

"The high King. Come now." She turned away, expecting him to follow like an obedient slave.

He did not move.

She stopped and looked over her shoulder, golden tresses glimmering with raindrops. "Rain," she said in irritation.

"Blodenwedd," he cajoled.

He saw she struggled with his sweet and patient tone. "COME NOW!" She actually stomped her foot at him.

"I will come after the storm abates and twilight passes into night."

"NOW, I SAY."

"After."

Her wraithlike body stiffened, her face turning cruel. "YOU NOT BE SPECIAL, NOT EVER, GUARDIAN OF THE WATERS. I DOONA KNOW WHY I WANT YOU."

A passing fancy, he mused. Whenever Blodenwedd did not get her way, he knew from experience she could become malicious.

"After," he said calmly, which only infuriated her more.

"YOU SHOULD HAVE DIED AT BIRTH."

"Then who, lovely goddess, would you dream about?"

Her slender chin jutted out and she hissed at him.

He arched a brow.

She shimmered then, dissolving into threads of golden light and nothingness, or as the piskies would say, winked out.

Spoiled, self-indulgent goddess used to having her own way. He knew her infatuation with him would pass in time, as it had passed when all she could talk about was the Dark Chieftain of the *Tuatha Dé Danann*.

Taking a deep, calming breath, he closed his eyes and threw back his head.

"Drench me," he called out to the clouds. Heavy rain fell from the sky. He could not command rainfall. Only when the clouds were full with moisture could he beseech them. Being a full guardian of the waters, he sensed all things having to do with water and always knew when rain was about to fall.

"More," he whispered and fell to his knees, arms outstretched in entreaty, hands open. He glimmered in the way of his faery brethren, his body changing, eyes tilting at the ends, ears pointing. Gossamer wings unfolded from his back, forming into a webwork of shimmering silver, gray, and black filaments.

He stretched out his magnificent wings fully, relishing in the freedom of his true fey form.

ISBN#9781932815825
US $6.99 / CDN $9.99
Mass Market Paperback / Fantasy
Available Now
www.rgarlandgray.com

For more information
about other great titles from
Medallion Press, visit

www.medallionpress.com